JANUARY CHRONICLES
ISAAC'S LEGACY

Stu Schreiber

27TH STREET PUBLISHING

Copyright © 2017 by JanMar, LLC

Excerpt from *JANUARY CHRONICLES: COOP and the COW-BOY* © 2017 by JanMar, LLC

Published by: 27th Street Publishing, California

www.27thstreetpublishing.com

ISBN 978-0-9965493-3-2

1) Thriller 2) Sci-fi 3) Fiction 4) Mystery

First Edition

Book design by 27th Street Publishing

Special Thanks

This book is dedicated to my wonderful friends who have all contributed in their unique way. Thank you, Maureen & Rock Dime, Stan Silbert, Kim Fishman, Connie Shaner, Marvin & Maureen Brown and Ed Chow.

1

"MOMMY, MOMMY, screamed the young girl. "Papa Lenny won't wake up!"

Sirens soon filled the air of the normally quiet park in this small Illinois town on what was anything but a typical September Saturday morning. As the EMT's loaded the dead body of the frail grey haired man into the ambulance, the local sheriff drove into the adjacent parking lot.

Jan Cooper hugged her crying eleven-year-old daughter, Isabella, as they sat motionless on the grass twenty yards from the park bench where Isabella discovered the hunched over body of her Papa Lenny. Ernie, the Cooper's white lab, sat directly in front of his two stunned masters instinctually guarding their privacy.

As Sheriff Mills approached, Ernie wagged his tail, recognizing the familiar scent. Kneeling on one knee the Sheriff whispered in Jan's ear, "So sorry, he's gone. Now's not the time but I'd like to stop by later to fill in details for my report—just routine stuff."

With both arms still wrapped around her daughter, Jan looked up and nodded, "I can't believe it Sheriff! I just can't believe it! We'll be home."

Jan wasn't prepared for the finality of this unexpected loss. As tears painstakingly rolled down her face she tightly held Isabella, only to be met by a blank stare from her beautiful daughter who faintly uttered the same word over and over and over, "Why, why, why, why?"

The chaos quickly evaporated into the warming air as Jan, Isabella and Ernie sadly lumbered the three blocks to their apartment. As they walked up the stairs Isabella clutched her mother's arm as they passed #11, Leonard Rosen's apartment. Once inside, #12, their apartment, Jan, Isabella and Ernie sat together on the floor, resting their backs against the couch as they gazed into space. When Isabella finally spoke, it's in the French her Papa Lenny had been teaching her. "Pourquoi est-il mort?"

Roughly able to translate, Jan attempted to console her sobbing daughter. "I'm not sure, Bella. Sometimes it's just time. Maybe he was sick and didn't tell us. Now he's at peace."

She knew Leonard wasn't the picture of health but didn't think he was dying—either. The suddenness of losing their neighbor left unanswered questions. Leonard wasn't just a neighbor, especially to Isabella. He was a Grandfather, friend, babysitter and teacher. They spent hours and hours playing on the computer often speaking only the French he so loved.

Stretching as she stood, Jan attempted to alter the mood. "Bella, I'm going to make us some tea. Ernie, Ernie, here's a biscuit. You're such a good boy. Bella, please, please talk to me."

With the support of Ernie's back Isabella stood and in a barely audible voice whispered, "What happened to Papa Lenny? Why did he die? Pourquoi?"

Hugging her daughter, Jan tried to offer perspective, "Sweetie, I'm not sure. Maybe he was sick and didn't tell us because he didn't want us to worry. I do know how much he cared for you and how he loved to spend time with you. He said you gave him life. He enjoyed watching over you when I was out. He loved telling you stories, teaching you French and playing on the computer with you. Those are memories you'll always have. Papa Lenny will always be part of your life." Her explanation did nothing but unleash more tears.

"But I miss Papa Lenny already. Why did he die? Pourquoi?"

"Sweetie, I don't know why—only God knows why. Here's some tea. Do you want something to eat?"

Not even looking at the mug of tea, Isabella turned

and walked towards her bedroom mumbling, "Not hungry. Going to lie down. Ernie, Ernie!"

With Isabella and Ernie resting in bed Jan sat at her kitchen table, sipped tea and reflected on what she knew about Leonard Rosen. Although he moved next door six years ago, she knew little about this grey haired, sweet old man's past. He had no visitors, never mentioned any relatives, children or an ex-wife. His reference to growing up in Ohio came only when she asked him about the tattered Cleveland Indians baseball cap he wore all the time.

On the way to the bathroom to wash her tear swollen face Jan checked on Isabella to find her snuggled next to Ernie on the bed, both asleep. Emotionally exhausted, Jan walked back to the living room and collapsed on the couch, only to be awakened by the doorbell. Peering through the peep hole she immediately recognized the name badge of the 6'6" Sheriff. "Gosh, I must have dozed off. Please, come in. Isabella's resting but we can talk. How about a cup of coffee or tea or maybe a glass of water?"

Before the Sheriff sat down at the kitchen table he acknowledged Ernie with a vigorous side rub. "Thanks, a cup of Joe—black, please. This is routine stuff, you know, usual paperwork. Who discovered Mr. Rosen?

Time? Witnesses? Anything unusual?"

Placing the steaming cup of coffee on the table in front of Sheriff Mills, Jan answered his questions in rapid succession. "Isabella discovered Leonard hunched over on the same park bench he sat on every Saturday morning. It was about 9:30 and nobody was in the immediate area. The two tennis courts had doubles matches, there was a kid's soccer game on the field at the other end of the park and there were a few dogs chasing tennis balls. The usual Saturday morning activity."

Unable to write as fast as she spoke, the Sheriff took a big gulp of coffee and paused before asking a few more questions. "Did Isabella say anything? Do you remember?"

The volume in Jan's voice rose an octave. "I'll never forget, Sheriff, I'll never forget the way she screamed MOMMY, MOMMY! I ran over—fast as I could to see what was wrong, but it was too late, I'm afraid we were too late. Isabella hasn't called me mommy since she was five. Now she's almost twelve."

"Jan, did you know if Mr. Rosen had heart problems or any other major health issues?"

Shaking her head, her voice lowered, "No, he never complained about anything. I wouldn't say he looked like the picture of health but I'm shocked he passed so abruptly—just shocked. Was it a heart attack?"

Taking another swig of coffee, the Sheriff raised one bushy eyebrow, "Maybe, but can't be sure—yet. Oh, do you have any idea who to contact?"

"Sorry Sheriff. I've been thinking and don't know of any relatives or even close friends. I can't think of any visitors—either. Who should we call? What about arrangements and his things?"

Finishing his coffee and closing his note pad the Sheriff stood and answered as he started walking towards the door, "I'll wait till Monday then have your landlord let me into Rosen's apartment and see if I can find a will or the name of someone to contact. Thanks, Jan. I know this has to be very difficult. Hope Isabella's okay? Know more on Monday. Bye Ernie."

Relieved their meeting took less than twenty minutes, and she didn't have to wake Isabella, Jan said goodbye to Sheriff Mills. Ten minutes later, she was startled by her daughter's scream, "MOMMY, MOMMY!" Rushing to Isabella's side she wrapped her arms around her shaking daughter. Overcome with emotion a trembling Isabella was barely able to speak, "I saw Papa on the park bench—I saw him again!"

"It's okay Bella. It's okay." Jan hugged her daughter until Isabella felt up to a walk with Ernie. As they left their apartment and passed #11, they paused and stared at what was now a depressingly cold closed door. Ernie, sensing their emotion, pawed at the door of his old friend.

Tears again streamed down Isabella's face, "It's not fair, it's just not right. Pourquoi, pourquoi?" Their walk was slow and silent. There were no answers, only sadness and questions.

Food seemed superfluous but Jan asked anyway, "How about a sandwich? Ernie, I know you're hungry."

A still lethargic Isabella shook her head, "I'm not very hungry. Maybe half a sandwich au beurre de cachuete et gelee."

Jan immediately knew what her daughter wanted because Isabella often asked for her favorite sandwich—in French. Leonard took joy in teaching his young neighbor a language he loved. Ironically, he didn't seem at all interested in France, just enjoyed speaking it. Isabella, on the other hand, couldn't wait to visit Paris. As Ernie cleared his bowl, Jan and Isabella nibbled on their peanut butter and jelly sandwiches. Leaving half her sandwich for Ernie, Isabella softly raised a question bothering her, "What will they do with Papa Lenny?"

"I don't know, sweetie. Sheriff Mills is coming back Monday to check on things."

Trying to shift attention away from Leonard Rosen, Jan turned on the TV—settling on a reality cooking show with chefs scurrying around a stainless-steel kitchen. Totally oblivious to the TV, Isabella reflected on a favorite memory. "I'll always remember Papa Lenny's story of Camelot. I was much younger when he first told me about Prince John and Princess Jackie but I still love that story."

Jan remembered how fascinated Leonard was with President Kennedy, even having a framed portrait of him on the wall behind his computer screen. She often heard Isabella repeat Leonard's story about Prince John and Princess Jackie and how they loved and were beloved by all they served. "Papa Lenny's story is true, Isabella. President Kennedy and Jackie, the First Lady, were the closest America's ever had to royalty."

2

Tossing and turning through a restless night, Jan's mind jumped between how Isabella will handle her first experience with death and her own questions about Leonard Rosen.

Sunday morning, normally meant the church around the corner, but not today. Isabella was still sound asleep and even though prayer seemed appropriate now—more than ever, God would have to wait. Ignoring her preference for tea, Jan instead started a pot of coffee. Opening the curtains above her kitchen sink brought in a bright sunny morning and the start of a beautiful late summer day.

Following her normal morning routine Jan logged onto her computer and quickly scanned the online versions of the NY Times, Chicago Tribune, Washington Post, Wall Street Journal and TMZ. Washington gridlock, global terrorist attacks and the latest realty star in rehab firmly met the delete key. Without missing a beat, she clicked onto the Raleigh Star-News, the local paper's website. A journalism degree from Northwestern over qualified Jan for her title, Chief Reporter, among a staff of only a dozen employees. Since the paper only published M-W-F, she checked Monday's paper before she logged onto her Gmail. Her lone message was from Howard Nafzinger, her boss and owner of the paper.

Heard about Rosen's death. Know how close you and Isabella were to him. He seemed like such a good man. Call me if I can help with anything. H

She knew Howie would hear about Leonard's death since nothing in Raleigh got past him. Outwardly hard-nosed he was much more than just a boss. He was also a best friend and mentor. As she often did, and in a reflective mood, she thought back to their first meeting seven years ago.

It certainly didn't look or feel like a newspaper. Remnants of the insurance brokerage that previously occupied the office were still plainly visible: the wall clock, a half dozen State Farm banners and a white board listing potential clients. She didn't expect the Chicago Tribune but she was a little disappointed. Then a gravelly man's voice greeted her. "Assume you're Cooper. I'm Nafzinger."

Turning to face him all she saw was a short, overweight, balding man with black horn-rimmed glasses, a paint splattered flannel shirt and jeans with the cuffs rolled up. She shook his extended hand. "Hi, I'm Jan Cooper, glad to meet you. Hate to state the obvious but you sure look like that guy on TV my mom watched years ago. Lou what's-his name."

Nodding, as if he had heard the comment a hundred times before, their now routine banter began immediately, "Oh, you must be referring to the handsome Ed Asner who played the brilliant Lou Grant on TV. You know if you cut your hair you could pass for Mary Tyler Moore, his co-star. Enjoyed your resume but are you sure you're ready for a small-town paper?"

Quickly sensing some type of repartee, she was game, "Are you? This certainly isn't the AP."

He obviously enjoyed the verbal volley, "I like to think I can mentally out maneuver my employees but you're going to be a challenge I think I'll enjoy."

"But I've never even worked for a paper before."

"My dear January, you were #2 in your class at Northwestern."

She pretended to be perturbed, "Do you perform background checks on all your prospective employees? How did you dig up my name was January?"

Shaking his head, then smiling, his retort was on point, "I'm a reporter. I dig for the truth then write about it. Does that work for you?"

Two minutes later Jan was hired as the only reporter for the Raleigh Star News, circulation 9,463, and Howard Nafzinger became her boss and just Howie. Although she'd never win a Pulitzer at the Star News there were other benefits. Her hours were flexible, pay was enough to live on, and she loved being able to take Ernie to the office.

Finishing her daydream, loud screeching brakes interrupted her second cup of coffee. As Ernie came running into the kitchen she peered out the window to see a large moving van in the middle of the street with a black SUV parked directly in front of it. Two burly men, obviously movers in matching short sleeved maroon shirts, were talking to a tall, dark haired guy in a light blue oxford shirt and khaki pants. Who could be moving from her building and—come on—this was early Sunday morning.

This strange scene piqued her investigative nature and she walked back to wake her daughter, "Good morning Bella. Throw on some sweats, grab Ernie's leash and let's see what's going on downstairs."

As they collectively stood by Ernie's favorite tree the tall guy in the preppy clothes approached. His big smile seemed genuine and very appealing, "Beautiful morning! I sure hope we didn't wake you. I know I like to sleep in on Sunday mornings. Excuse me, I'm Charles Montgomery, from Veterans Affairs."

Jan looked at the business card handed to her by one Charles Winston Montgomery, Special Assistant, Department of Veteran Affairs, Washington, DC. While she tried to figure out what the hell this fit, tanned, very good looking middle 30ish civil servant was doing in front of her apartment building with a moving van early on Sunday morning, he bent down to say hello to Ernie.

"I just love labs. Had one when I was growing up. Sophie was my best friend. What's your dog's name?"

"This is Ernie, Mr. Montgomery. He'll love you forever if you keep rubbing his belly."

"Please call me Charlie. Guess you live in this building."

Welcoming possible flirtation, Jan made a suggestive comment to her daughter, "Bella, why don't you take Ernie upstairs and have some breakfast? I'll be right up."

Now, one on one, she felt free to playfully respond, "We do live here, Mr. Montgomery, what gave us away?"

"Just a wild guess. Did you know Leonard Rosen?"

Shocked by the question, her voice shot up several octaves, "Leonard, Leonard Rosen. Are you moving his stuff? It just happened yesterday? How in hell…?"

Sensing her alarm, Charlie cut her off in mid-sentence, "I got the assignment last night and drove down from Chicago this morning. Instructions were to move out the contents of his apartment, I think it's #11. That's all I know."

In disbelief, Jan took a step back and asked the obvious, "I didn't know the VA picked up the possessions of the just departed?"

"We do all sorts of things for Vets—most you never

hear of."

"Leonard lived next door to us. I didn't think he had any family."

Trying to turn the conversation away from Leonard Rosen and towards the beautiful woman standing in front of him Charlie deflected, "Don't know about family. Us meaning you, your daughter, husband and Ernie?"

"Oh, sorry, I'm Jan Cooper. We live in Apt. #12. Isabella and Ernie discovered Leonard hunched over on the park bench yesterday."

When one of the movers approached, Charlie knew it meant getting back to work, "I'm so sorry you and your daughter had to discover Mr. Rosen. I didn't know. Excuse me, Miss Cooper but I've got to let the movers in."

"How did you get a key?"

Charlie nonchalantly replied, "Picked it up at the office before I drove down."

Really, that's interesting! Jan headed upstairs as Charles Montgomery conferred with the two movers. She couldn't help but check-out the lock on Leonard's door. Once inside her apartment she stared at the deadbolt on her door before she locked it.

Isabella and Ernie were sitting on the living room floor amongst the contents of a large legal box. Without having to ask, Jan recognized all the gifts Leonard had given Isabella over the years. "Bella, did you eat?"

"Ernie and I had Fruit Loops. Qui est cet homme ?"

"Mr. Montgomery. He works for the government. He's moving Papa Lenny's things."

"Where's he taking them?"

"I don't know. We'll have to ask him."

After Jan heard the door to Leonard Rosen's apartment open, the mover's heavy footsteps could be felt in her apartment. Ever inquisitive, she peered outside her kitchen window to see Charlie Montgomery roll up his shirt sleeves showcasing his triceps. Obviously, he knew his way around the gym. Armed with a clipboard loaded with invoice looking papers, he headed back upstairs. Then Jan realized in the haste of the morning events she was a disaster—hair-a-mess, no make-up, frumpy sweat pants—yuck.

Thirty minutes and a remarkable makeover later she looked like a different woman. Freshly washed, her wavy shoulder length auburn hair perfectly framed her classically beautiful profile without need of makeup. Tight jean shorts wrapped around fit hips and her white halter top revealed a flat tummy and the outline of perky breasts. After trying on five pairs of shoes she decided on plain white Ked sneakers.

"Playfully, Isabella asked, "Hey Mom, where you going?"

Even though escaping her precocious daughter's scrutiny was near impossible she tried anyway, "Oh, I just felt like freshening up."

"Well, I'm sure he'll think you're hot."

Blushing, Jan tried to act indifferent, "Hot, who—what are you talking about?"

Isabella was amused at her mom's embarrassment, "Mr. Mont—what's his name."

Not wanting to get any deeper into this conversation she playfully replied, "Oh, thanks for reminding me Bella, I'd better check on the movers."

"Sure, Mom!"

Walking down the hall she tried to discreetly peak into #11 almost colliding with one of the movers backing out a well worn leather chair.

"Excuse me, Miss."

"Sorry, I didn't mean to get in your way."

"He's inside."

"He who?"

"Charlie."

Jan could hear him talking to the other mover in the bedroom. Large boxes were stacked halfway to the ceiling of the dining room and the just removed chair left the living room somewhat bare. As Charlie walked into the living room their meeting eyes brought smiles.

Charlie couldn't fake what he saw, "Whoa, I mean—holy—I mean I'm glad you stopped by Ms. Cooper. It is Ms.?"

Pleasantly surprised by his comment Jan countered, "Please call me Jan, Charlie. I thought you might like to join us for lunch?"

"That would be great! I have some questions I need to ask you, anyway. Will noon work?"

"Sure, see you then. Oh, by the way, I'm divorced, Cowboy."

Raleigh, IL was a small town, not quite 50,000 and a world away from Chicago. Attractive single men were rare, at least those who caught Jan's attention. Back in her apartment she found Isabella and Ernie still on the cluttered living room floor amongst all of Papa Lenny's gifts.

"Bella, we'd better clean up. Mr. Montgomery is joining us for lunch. Put everything back in the box and we'll go through it later. Better get dressed, too."

"I am dressed. When's he coming?"

"In an hour."

"He's hot!"

"Bella, please…"

Isabella seemed more herself. Only eleven, but often

acting well beyond her years, her daughter seemed very aware of the challenges facing single moms. Though Jan's ex, Isabella's father Rick, an attorney in Chicago had remarried, she hasn't had a serious relationship since they divorced. They tried for years to make their relationship work but ultimately agreed they were never meant to be married. Both acknowledged the priority of maintaining a civil relationship for Isabella's sake and their friendship was genuine.

3

Soup and salad was easy, also saving a trip to the market. Answering the door, she tried but couldn't muffle the metal clicking sound from unlocking her deadbolt. Charlie smiled broadly as he entered the apartment and seemed to take in the entire room, in just a few seconds, moving nothing but his eyes. Still holding onto the door knob Jan's sexy pose was intentional as she softly asked, "Are you finished at Leonard's?"

"Almost, he didn't have much furniture, just lots of papers, boxes and tons of computer gear. He seemed to keep all sorts of odd things. How long did you say you knew Mr. Rosen?"

"He moved in about six years ago. For the first six-months we didn't talk much except to say hello, but we gradually became very good friends. He adored and had a very special relationship with my daughter, Isabella. Where is my daughter? Bella, are you hungry, do you want something to eat?"

From her bedroom Isabella yelled, "Not hungry, you two enjoy lunch!"

Jan was amused at her daughter's response. She must approve of Charlie. Not by accident, Jan noticed Charlie wasn't wearing a wedding band, but he was wearing the two cutest dimples and a wonderfully infectious smile.

"Jan, this is a real treat. Thanks for inviting me. I'll bet you spin?"

"Now there's an interesting juxtaposition. What gave you that idea?"

With a big smile showcasing those dimples, Charlie sheepishly responded, "Just a wild guess reinforced by your toned legs and the bike shoe sticking out of your gym bag in the living room. I spin, too, when it's too cold to ride outside. You know Chicago. Getting back to Mr. Rosen's belongings, the VA will try and find an heir. They'll go through all his paperwork back at headquarters in Chicago. One of the movers is going to drive his car back to Chicago. I can't believe the low mileage on a car twenty years old."

"Is this what you do?"

"I do a variety of things. I'm afraid none very exciting. What about you?"

Her response came in a split second, "What about me? What would you like to know?"

"Lots of things but first let me finish the questions about Leonard Rosen. Do you mind if I take notes?"

"Fire away, Cowboy. Notes are fine for Leonard's questions but I don't think you'll need them for me. Let me get our soup."

Their obvious chemistry overcame the awkward circumstances of their meeting. Jan was still confused over exactly what Charlie did for the VA but surprisingly felt very comfortable around this tall, handsome stranger.

Soup spoon in one hand, pen in the other Charlie continued, "Did Mr. Rosen ever mention any family or friends?"

"No, never. No visitors—either."

"What kind of mail or packages did Mr. Rosen get?"

"Very little. I never saw him get much except for Fe-dEx boxes with gear for his computer. Think he paid his bills by computer, too. Oh, almost forgot all the Grateful Dead stuff. Hard to believe but Leonard was a Deadhead.

He got all sorts of Dead paraphernalia in the mail. You know, posters, T-shirts, CD's. Go figure."

Charlie nodded as he wrote, "You're right, never would have guessed a Deadhead? Explains some of the things in the boxes. Did Mr. Rosen ever discuss his profession or who he worked for?"

Amazed he was able to eat, write and talk simultaneously, Jan quickly swallowed a mouthful of salad before responding, "No, except I think he did something with computers for the government. You saw his simple furniture, but he always had the latest computer equipment. He spent most of his time on his computer."

"I don't know what he did and when I asked him questions about what he did for a living he deftly change subjects. I'm normally very good at getting answers but not with Leonard. He was adept at responding without answering. He'd say his work was boring, tedious computer work which seemed reasonable since he'd play the Grateful Dead and sit at his computer for hours and hours. Thank God, he wore headphones. Those songs go on forever. I pray my daughter hasn't become a Deadhead."

As they both laughed over Deadheads, Charlie continued, "He had three photos on the wall above his desk. President Kennedy was obvious. Jerry Garcia now makes sense and there was a third photo of a teenager standing next to an older man. The inscription on the photo was blurred but it looked like; *Share your wonderful mind ...* I think it's signed by *Richard Schneid*...something. Do you know who's in the photo?"

"The teenager was Leonard standing with a man I think he referred to as a teacher or professor."

"Interesting. Did Mr. Rosen ever leave things with you or have you keep anything for him?"

"No, like what?"

"Nothing in particular. These are just routine questions. Did Mr. Rosen have a storage unit outside his apartment?"

"Don't think so, never mentioned one."

"Did Mr. Rosen talk about his health or have any health issues?"

"Don't think so."

"Did he get many phone calls?"

"Practically none and he put an end to all the solicitation calls soon after he moved in. I remember because he showed me how to stop the calls by going to a website."

Anything else you can think of that might be helpful?"

"Not really, except he was a Cleveland Indians fan, always wore this old Indians ball cap and loved to speak

French. He was teaching French to my daughter."

"He seems to have been quite a character."

Finished with their chicken noodle soup and most of their salad Jan had more questions. "Where did you say you live, Charlie?"

"Chicago's home. I need to be close to my boys."

Relieved and hopeful, Jan asked redundantly, "Oh, you have kids?"

Charlie started to play with his phone as he answered, "Max is 12; Harry's 9. I think I've only got a few hundred photos of them. Here's the most recent."

"They're adorable. They look like their dad. I always wanted a son, and Mrs. Montgomery?"

Anticipating the question, Charlie was ready with his reply, "We divorced a few years ago. Thankfully, we're still friends. She's remarried and very happy. We share custody of the boys."

Sensing commonality, Jan eagerly dug a little deeper, "Did you grow up in Chicago?"

"No, Pennsylvania, went to Annapolis, served in the Navy, and then law school. Hey, I thought I was asking the questions."

"It's sort of my job; can't help myself."

"What is your job?"

"I'm a reporter for the local paper. My background's

journalism. Nowadays I seem to spend most of my time copying and pasting."

"So you're a single mom?"

"Yep, my ex and I were college sweethearts but our American dream didn't last very long. He's an attorney in Chicago but he keeps an apartment here in Raleigh so he can also be close to his daughter. He's a wonderful dad. It's a shame our marriage didn't work. He's remarried like your ex."

Now even more interested Charlie continued, "How did you end up in Raleigh?"

"When we lived in Chicago I was a stay at home Mom attempting to write a great novel. After we divorced, I needed to get away and Raleigh seemed far enough yet still close enough—if you know what I mean."

"And what about your novel?"

"Maybe one day. I think I still have one in me."

Charlie glanced down at his watch and shook his head, "Where did the time go? I'm afraid I've got to get going. Thanks for lunch and answering my questions about Mr. Rosen although I enjoyed our personal conversation much more. Please call me if you think of anything else about Mr. Rosen. More importantly, the next time you come to Chicago please give me a call. I'd love to have dinner with you and discover what else you do to stay in such fantastic shape besides spin."

"Why Charlie, are you asking me out?"

"Well, I don't meet many very fit, very attractive, very intelligent women. I'm usually a little shy with someone I've just met. I'd like to see you again when it's not business related."

"I like your style—Cowboy. I hope it's not just those dimples. Hold on a sec. Bella, come say goodbye to Mr. Montgomery."

Almost instantly Isabella came running into the dining room as if she had heard their entire conversation. Ernie followed and, as if on cue, sat down in front of Charlie with his right paw extended onto Charlie's knee.

Kneeling, Charlie petted Ernie as he spoke, "Isabella, I'm sorry we didn't get a chance to talk but I hope we do—soon."

"What will they do with Papa Lenny's stuff?"

"I'm afraid I don't know Isabella but if I find out I promise to let you know."

"Au revoir, Monsieur Charlie."

"Au revoir, Isabella."

Isabella retreated to her room as Jan walked Charlie to the door. She was already thinking of excuses to visit Chicago. Something about him both attracted and fascinated her. Then crowded by the ever-jealous Ernie, their bodies pushed together and paused for a good ten seconds until Ernie began to whine.

Charlie thanked Jan—again for lunch, said goodbye, smiled, tilted his head, gently squeezed both her hands and uncharacteristically planted the softest kiss on her lips. It was a good-bye right out of a Harlequin novel and a bold chance taken by a man who appeared anything but shy. It was also the most romantic meeting of Jan's life.

The door no sooner closed when Isabella reappeared. She didn't need to say anything. She just looked at her mom, smiled and put her hand in the air for a high five. Jan tried to give her daughter a stern look but instead grabbed her hand turning the high five into a big hug. Emotionally exhausted a quiet Sunday afternoon and evening was just what the Cooper's needed.

4

Howard Nafzinger bought the Raleigh Star-News after a total burn-out as the Chicago Bureau Chief for the AP. Jan, one of his first hires, claims she's learned more about journalism during her first two weeks at the paper than she did in four years at Northwestern. Howie was a living library. He was a search engine long before Google, housed in two bulging rolodex files on his desk. If Howie didn't know the answer to a question he usually knew someone who did.

"Howie, I'm totally bewildered."

"Bewildered? That's a new word out-of-your mouth. What's up?"

"It's Leonard Rosen. Something's not right."

"Sorry, but what's so strange about an old man dying, happens every day."

"Don't be so damn cold. What's strange is bright and early yesterday morning a moving van pulls up to our apartment building supervised by a VA agent to collect Leonard's stuff. How could that be? He died less than 24 hours earlier. How did they know? And on Sunday?"

Taking off his glasses Howie's voice conveyed confusion, "What the hell? Assume Rosen was retired military?"

"Not from what I know. He always seemed antiwar and against our ongoing military build-up. How did the VA know?"

"What was the VA's guy's name? Remember?"

"Actually, I do. Here's his card."

As Howie read the card his other hand started to spin a rolodex, "Let me make a few calls."

Too anxious to sit around and wait for Howie, Jan went back to her office and Googled every relevant key phrase about the VA she could think of. The results were mostly useless statistics: 171 medical centers, 350 outpatient clinics, 126 nursing homes, assumed command of National Cemetery's from the Army in 1973. Then one phrase gave her a sliver of hope, "Every veteran deserves a proper burial." Unfortunately, when Jan Googled VA Death Services she found 48,500,000 entries. Like most, Jan scanned the first page skipping the other 48,499,990 entries. She found nothing close to what she was looking for. Frustrated, she dialed Charlie's number.

"This is Charles Montgomery. Please leave a message."

"Hi Charlie, this is Jan Cooper, in Raleigh. You do remember me? I thought of something about Leonard Rosen. Please call me when you get a chance."

Howie's fingers stopped at "Mc" where he found the card he was looking for: William McGregor, Executive Director, Midwestern Region, Department of Veterans Affairs. Although he hadn't spoken with Bill in almost ten years, golf buddies forge timeless friendships.

"Bill, Howie Nafzinger. I was hoping you'd still be at this number. How the hell are you?"

"Shit, Naf, you bastard. I heard you were killed in Afghanistan years ago. Are you calling to pay me the $100 you've owed me for ten years?"

"You'll get the $50 when I die, fuck face. I want you to smile at my funeral. I'm down here in Raleigh busting my ass doing real journalism. Haven't they retired your God damn number at the VA by now? You must be pulling down more tax dollars than the President."

"Thanks for your kind words, Naf. I retire next year. I'll make a note for my assistant to invite you to the retirement dinner even though you won't come. Just send a check. How's your golf game, Mr. Four Putt?"

"The same it's always been, terrible, but I can still beat your sorry ass. What about you? Still losing a dozen balls every nine holes?"

"I only lose a stroke a year. I'll still be shooting below 100 when I'm 80. Howie, I love you, but why are you calling me? What do you want?"

"We had an unusual situation come up over the weekend and I hope you'll have some answers. Jan Cooper, my reporter, and her eleven-year-old daughter discovered a 70ish neighbor, Leonard Rosen, hunched over dead on a park bench near their apartment last Saturday morning. He lived alone and never mentioned any relatives or friends during the six plus years he lived next door to Jan. Then early yesterday morning, a moving van pulls up to their building supervised by a suit who hands her a card that says he works for the VA. He's there to pick up the dead guy's possessions. I didn't know the VA provided this type of instant service?"

"We don't! Naf, lay off the devil weed. What's the VA guy's name?"

"Charles Winston Montgomery, Special Assistant."

"Hold on! Name doesn't come up on my computer. Let me check further and I'll give you a call back. Hey Howie, I miss your sorry ass."

The Star-News offices were sparse. Jan's small office was adjacent to Howie's and the thin walls only slightly muffled conversations. She walked into Howie's office seconds after his phone call with Bill McGregor ended. His hand motioned her to sit in one of the two mismatched wooden office chairs in front of his oversized mahogany desk. As if shuffling a deck of cards Howie found what he was he was looking for in his other rolodex, Louis W. Barker, Assistant Director, Federal Bureau of Investigation.

"Lou, Howie Nafzinger, how the hell are you?"

"Will wonders never cease. I heard you died in a train crash in Istanbul. I can't get you Redskin tickets."

"That's the second crazy story of my death I've heard in the last 15 minutes. Hope I don't disappoint people by merely dying from cancer or a heart attack. Lou, give me your take on something. Since you thought I was dead you obviously don't know I'm living in Raleigh, about a hundred miles south of Chicago. Have a little paper here. An odd situation came up over the weekend and I thought you might be able to shed some light on it."

"Shoot!"

"Jan, my star reporter had a neighbor she and her daughter discovered hunched over dead on a park bench Saturday morning. He was 70ish and had no relatives or heirs as far as they know. No visitors either. All she knows is he was a computer nerd. Anyway, the local sheriff was going to rummage through his apartment today but now he's not going to find anything. Early yesterday morning a big moving van with two movers pulls up to the apartment building supervised by another guy claiming to be from the VA, and loads up everything. His card said he was a VA Special Assistant. What do you think?"

"Sounds like bullshit—cover for something. Doesn't figure to be us—either. How much do you know about the dead guy?"

"Almost nothing except he spent most of his time on the computer. And, he was a Deadhead, a Cleveland Indians fan and spoke French. His name was Leonard Rosen."

"Snoop around and get me more relevant info on Rosen. Then call me back. Obviously, somebody cared about him. Oh, my family's fine. Thanks for asking, you bastard!"

It took them less than fifteen minutes to discover Charles Winston Montgomery probably didn't work for the VA and the VA wasn't in the practice of picking up the possessions of the recently departed.

Who was Charles Winston Montgomery and why were Leonard's possessions picked up in such a bizarre way? Unfortunately, Sheriff Mills knew less than they did. His voicemail to Jan stated he knew nothing about Leonard's cleaned out apartment until the apartment manager unlocked the door. When her phone rang, she decided to take the call in her office.

"Hi Jan, this is Charlie."

Belligerently, she answered, "Who the hell are you and who do you really work for?"

Caught totally off guard Charlie tried to regroup, "Whoa! You've been busy. I shouldn't have underestimated your investigative skills. I'll be back in Raleigh tonight and I'd like to explain."

Still fuming she snapped, "Is lying part of your job? How does anyone ever trust you?"

Charlie tried to explain as he pleaded for forgiveness,

"Jan, I'm truly sorry. I apologize. Just give me a chance to explain. Sometimes my job gets in the way. I'll be down around 5:30. I need to check something out in Rosen's apartment. I'll stop by if it's okay?"

"Do I have a choice? By the way, have you spoken with Sheriff Mills today?"

"No, he's next on my list. I'll see you tonight and explain things."

5

Wisely, Charlie arrived bearing gifts: a rawhide bone for Ernie, an artsy book on Paris for Isabella and a bottle of the perfume Jan had on Sunday. Ernie was all over Charlie long before he could get the rawhide bone out of the plastic wrapper and Isabella thanked Charlie as she quickly started looking at the Champs Elysee and Eiffel Tower. Jan found it both clever and very attentive Charlie identified her perfume and very sweet he brought her a bottle. It's become even more obvious awareness must be part of whatever he does.

Still standing in the living room, Charlie began his excuse, "I'd really…"

"Hold on a sec, Bella, will you take Ernie for his walk—thanks Sweetie."

"Oui, oui! Merci beaucoup, Monsieur Charlie."

She waited until Isabella and Ernie left, "Thanks for the gifts Charlie. Very sweet, but now why don't you tell me your real name and who you really work for?"

"Can we sit down," suggested Charlie as he moved towards the kitchen table. "I apologize, I'm sorry. I do owe you an explanation. I'm a Special Agent for the National Security Agency, better known as the NSA."

Rarely surprised, his answer wasn't what she expected, "You're a spy, like 007? Do you know Snowden?"

"I wouldn't call my work anything that glamorous, I don't know Snowden and my name is Charles, only that's my last name. My first name is Clifton, Clifton Montgomery Charles. Most of my friends call me Cliff."

"Good, I'll call you Charlie. What about the story of your, hmmm, ex-wife and the photos of your two sons? Is that bullshit, too?"

"That's all true. Please understand the sensitive nature of my job sometimes requires I reframe the truth. But, it doesn't mean everything I say is a lie. I've thought about you a lot since yesterday."

"And, are you misrepresenting the truth now, Charlie? Is that part of the job?"

"I guess I've got that coming. I hope I can earn back your trust."

"Time will tell—Charlie—time will tell. What about Leonard Rosen?"

"I really shouldn't say anything about Mr. Rosen. It's for your own good."

"Bullshit, Charlie, we're done here."

"God Jan, we can use you as a negotiator. Alright, you win, but please don't write a story about what I'm going to tell you. This is confidential—off the record. Okay?"

"You have my word, which I always keep."

Charlie took a deep breath looked straight into her eyes and started to explain, "Leonard Rosen was a very special government intelligence officer. When he retired from the NSA they insisted he change his identity and re-locate to a location of his choice. However, with that demand came government oversight. Translation: the NSA wanted to keep tabs on Leonard Rosen. I still don't know his real name. Believe me, this is all pretty extraordinary. I've seen this treatment for special operatives but never for someone on the information side. And you were right, we can't find any close relatives or friends."

Surprised, Jan still had questions, "But how did you know he died?"

"We monitored him electronically and when he didn't

log in Saturday night we knew something was wrong. Before you ask let me tell you I have no idea exactly what he did for the Agency. I do know it must have been top secret and highly sensitive to get this type of treatment. My understanding is his personnel file has been sealed under the National Security Act, which means it's only to be opened by Congressional or Presidential authority. Obviously, that's not normal procedure."

"What do I tell my daughter? She wants to know what's going to happen?"

"I'm sure you'll come up with something. Maybe give her some closure with a little memorial service? Invite a few people, pay your respects and let your daughter celebrate her friend's life. I'm sorry I don't have a better suggestion, but it helped my sons when an Uncle died suddenly."

Surprised and pleased at his sympathetic idea her demeanor softened—slightly, "Very thoughtful and I really appreciate your sensitivity. She also wants to know what's going to happen to all his stuff. I think you promised her an answer."

"I did and I'll talk to her."

Jan's questions were short and to the point probably because her head was spinning rapidly trying to digest Charlie's story. Everything seemed plausible and it didn't take much to give this cute guy from Chicago a second chance.

The footsteps running up the stairs and down the hall were unmistakable,

"Bella, Charlie has some news on Papa Lenny he wants to share with you."

"Isabella, we can't find any relatives of Mr. Rosen. We'll keep searching and store his possessions in a special locker for at least a year. We're also going to keep trying to find an heir or a will Mr. Rosen may have left. Your mom thinks perhaps a little memorial for Mr. Rosen might be appropriate."

"Bella, what do you think?"

"You mean like a funeral?"

"No, more a time to remember Papa Lenny and a way to say good bye—just a few of us. We can even play Grateful Dead music."

"Papa Lenny would like the Dead to play. Oops, sorry, didn't mean to say it like that."

Before the conversation wandered Charlie licked his lips, "Well I'm starved. Can I take you two ladies to dinner?"

Jan welcomed the invite but wasn't sure about the logistics, "Bella, do you have any homework?"

"No, did it."

"Okay, Charlie, why don't you relax with Ernie, your new best friend, while I freshen-up? Bella, you need to change, too."

The decision of what to wear quickly rearranged her focus from Leonard Rosen to Charlie. Her favorite, size 2 jeans were an obvious choice as was the tight-fitting jersey top. Isabella joining them on an almost first date did feel a little weird—like putting the cart before the horse, but she wanted to know more about her "Cowboy".

6

Mario's, the downtown Italian restaurant, was both a compromise and a wise choice. Isabella could still get her pizza or spaghetti while the atmosphere was infinitely more adult and quieter than her favorite—Pizza Katie's.

Even though Jan felt reasonably comfortable with Charlie, she wanted a second opinion before she went any further with her romantic fantasy. She texted Howie, "Having dinner with VA guy @ Mario's. Like u 2 meet him. Stop by, please."

They drove in Charlie's black Suburban. The SUV seemed normal except for the extra-large black screen in the middle of the dashboard, the visor over Charlie's head with two black and one red button, and the special lock on a very large center console. Of course, Isabella had questions about the screen, the red button and the big lock. Charlie danced around the questions with vague answers Isabella wasn't buying but accepted for the moment out of courtesy. Jan enjoyed sitting back and listening to their interaction, a pleasant departure from being the target of her inquisitive daughter's never ending questions.

Mario's, the best of four Italian restaurant in town, as usual, was busy. Charlie asked for a booth in a quiet area towards the rear of the restaurant. Isabella sat between Jan and Charlie and her steady stream of questions didn't stop, jumping back and forth between her Papa Lenny and Charlie. Even at eleven she was adept at screening potential suitors for her mom. Then a familiar voice interrupted the conversation, "Well, well, what a pleasant surprise to see you two here!"

Jan faked her surprised look, "Howie, this is a coincidence. Who are you here with? Why don't you join us? Oh, sorry, Howard Nafzinger, this is Char..., I mean Cliff Montgomery, I mean, he's the VA gentleman I may have mentioned to you who picked up Leonard's things."

"Oh, right, I remember. I've got some guests joining me in a few minutes but I guess I've got time for a quick drink."

Howie's timing was perfect. He shook hands with Charlie and then gently nudged Jan to scoot over so he could sit down. Howie's conversation hovered between generalities, small talk about Chicago and what it must be like working for a government agency. Their man-to-man conversation was the perfect opportunity for Jan and Isabella to excuse themselves and head for the women's restroom.

Howie didn't waste any time, "So, I know you don't work for the VA. Who do you really work for and why all the attention on Rosen?"

Charlie wasn't really surprised at Howie's directness but still stated the obvious, "Boy, you cut right to the chase. I trust you'll respect the sensitivity of our conversation. Has to be off the record."

"Sure, Charlie, nothing leaves this table."

"I work for the NSA and I can tell you Leonard Rosen wasn't his real name. We can't find any heirs; he was re-located to Raleigh after his retirement and he held a very sensitive intelligence position leading me to believe he was very special."

"The NSA must have a very important reason to be interested in Rosen or whoever he is." Then changing his enunciation without raising his voice, Howie stared directly at Charlie, "Look, Jan's like a daughter to me. Don't play her or hurt her. Understood?"

"I appreciate your candor and, by the way, my real name is Clifton Montgomery Charles."

Howie was facing outward and saw them first, "And here are the two most beautiful gals in the restaurant. We must be two lucky guys."

"Howie, you're going to make me blush. Bella, perhaps we should leave again just to see what these two can dream up to say next time?"

"Uncle Howie, are you older than Papa Lenny?"

The question abruptly brought the three adults back to Leonard Rosen. Howie's answer was muddled in the innuendo he's so expert at as he said his goodbyes. Dinner finally arrived but became an afterthought as Isabella yawned. It was past 8:00 and the only sign Charlie needed to get a few doggie bags and ask for the check.

The short drive home didn't stop Isabella from quickly falling asleep. Then, as Charlie carried Isabella upstairs, Jan felt something else she hadn't experienced in a long time—safety. As he gently placed the groggy Isabella on her bed, Ernie licked both their faces. Before she asked, Charlie found Ernie's leash and the two, now good buddies went for a walk. Jan still wanted a second opinion. She grabbed her phone and texted Howie. "What do u think?"

His response came in seconds, "ok but be careful."

Relieved, she couldn't disguise her feelings as the boys returned. She praised both, simultaneously, petting Ernie and gently placing her hand on Charlie's shoulder. Then somehow all three ended up on the floor. Charlie reached for her hand, but not by accident, caught her hip. When she didn't flinch except to move closer he pulled her in until their bodies met. Then nudging the small of her back with his other hand he conveniently pressed his body into hers. Their second kiss was romantically perfect. Trembling lips gently paused a half-inch apart for several seconds before touching, then pulled slightly away, then openly locked together.

When she instinctively started to follow her normal reaction, and pull away something magically pushed her back for more and they playfully rolled on top of one another until rudely interrupted by Ernie's jealous whines. Bodies entwined, they couldn't stop laughing.

7

Jan's attempt to sleep was disrupted by thoughts of Charlie. What was the life of a spy? Was lying, deceit and ulterior motives part of his job? Was it a 24/7, military chain of command—anytime, anywhere scenario? It seemed like an impossible life. No wonder his marriage failed. Was she jumping to conclusions? Of course, there was another side: their chemistry, their connection, and those dimples. How different would it be if he was a professor, a businessman or practiced law? Was intrigue part of the attraction? She continued to ponder when her alarm brought her back to reality.

"Bella, time to get up. I'm going to take Ernie out. Please take your shower and get ready for school."

"Oui, Oui."

Her thoughts switched from Charlie to Leonard as Ernie pulled her past #11. She was still curious about Leonard Rosen and what was so important about what he did and was determined to find answers.

One of the advantages of living in a small town is almost everything's just around a couple of corners and the Star-News was a five-minute drive from their apartment and Isabella's school. Ernie accompanied Jan to the office most mornings. His presence had a soothing effect on everyone, and of course Ernie loved all the attention and affection. Using intuition beyond canine instinct, he gravitated to the person at the Star-News who seemed to need unconditional love the most each day.

Arriving before Howie, Jan went directly to her office, logged onto her computer and immediately entered www.nsa.gov. Interestingly, the homepage had the look and feel of a large software company full of slogans like "Where Intelligence Goes to Work" and "Defending Our Nation—Securing Our Future." The Agency was created November 4, 1952 by order of President Harry Truman. Much of the text on the website was clearly ambiguous including their Mission Statement.

"The National Security Agency/Central Security Service (NSA/CSS) leads the U.S. Government in cryptology that encompasses both Signals Intelligence (SIGINT) and Information Assurance (IA) products and services, and enables Computer Network Operations (CNO) gain a decision advantage for our allies under all circumstances."

After reading the Statement for the third-time she still had no clue what the NSA did and wondered how Snowden's version might differ. Perusing other areas of the website did nothing to clarify anything except prove everything appears to have been written by a team of attorney's intent on writing the most convoluted meaningless verbiage possible. Frustrated, she turned to another source: Wikipedia.

"The National Security Agency (NSA) is an intelligence organization of the United States government, responsible for global monitoring, collection, and processing of information and data for foreign intelligence and counter-intelligence purposes – a discipline known as signals intelligence (SIGINT). NSA is concurrently charged with protection of U.S. government communications and information systems against penetration and network warfare.

Although many of NSA's programs rely on 'passive' electronic collection, the agency is authorized to accomplish its mission through active clandestine means, among which are physically bugging electronic systems and allegedly engaging in sabotage through subversive software. Moreover, the NSA maintains physical presence in a large number of countries across the globe, where its Special Collection Service (SCS) inserts eavesdropping devices in difficult-to-reach places. SCS collection tactics allegedly encompass close surveillance, burglary, wiretapping, breaking and entering. Originating as a unit to decipher coded communications in World War II, it was officially formed as the NSA by Harry S. Truman in 1952. Since then, it has become one of the largest U.S. intelligence organizations in terms of personnel and budget, operating as part of the Department of Defense and simultaneously reporting to the Director of National Intelligence."

The cloud of secrecy surrounding an agency of the United States government was troubling. What happened to transparency? Thankfully, Howie interrupted her research, "How did it go with James Bond?"

"Very funny! Howie, what do you know about the NSA?"

"I know enough to know I really don't know much except for the Snowden file dump."

"You're a big help."

"If you're trying to find out something about Charlie or Rosen—good luck. You're going to need a lot more than Google and Wikipedia."

"Help me Howie, please." Jan discovered long ago

how to get Howie's help. He almost always fell for the 'damsel in distress' plea, even though she hardly fit that description.

Since Howie understood the fierce, often disruptive nature of the intelligence community, his finger stopped on "C". Rival agencies were much more likely to reveal info on another agency than their own. All three of Howie's contacts within the CIA were either now retired or employed on an as needed basis. Coincidence or not, all had written or were writing their memoirs. Dale Pftizer was one of the three.

"Hey Pftz, Howie Nafzinger. It's been a long time, how are you?"

A raspy voice seemed surprised, "Sweet Jesus, I heard you died in Katrina. Must have gotten you confused with somebody else. If you're not dead what the hell are you doing?"

"I retired years ago and bought a small-town paper in Raleigh, IL. Some of us, without best sellers, need to keep working. I enjoyed the last one. It'll make a good movie although I couldn't tell who the hero was?"

"Obviously, I was the hero but I know you're not calling me for a plot clarification or an autographed copy. What do you want?"

"Tell me about the NSA."

"Tell you what. Never liked them and still don't. The guys who run the joint always overplay the smarter card even though their Intel guys are the best. They just don't like to share information. We'd be a lot safer if they did. Snowden sure shook them up."

"I'm trying to find out what I can about a former Intel guy of theirs who recently died. He was important enough for the NSA to give him a new identity, relocate and monitor daily. Is that the norm?"

"No, it's not the norm. He must have known a lot. Let me guess, you don't have much to go on?"

"Well, he was a Deadhead, a Cleveland Indians fan and liked to speak French. That must help?"

"Quit smoking that shit. That's it, that's all you got?"

"Unfortunately, yes."

"Call me back when you at least have something I can work with."

"Thanks for nothing, Pftz. Good luck with the movie. George Clooney's perfect as you!"

Howie wasn't surprised at Pftizer's response. The battles between intelligence agencies have been well documented for more than a half century. Leonard Rosen would be a tough cookie to crack.

Once again, Jan pleaded for help, "Howie, I'm lost. I don't know where to turn for answers. Leonard's a total mystery and now I'm wondering if Charlie's going to be the same?"

"Look, this whole thing might be beyond us. Let me try some other contacts, call in some favors. In the meantime, get tomorrow's paper ready for print."

"Okay, let me proof a few stories and I'll have it ready in twenty minutes. Oh, Howie, I was thinking of having a little memorial for Leonard on Friday afternoon. It will help Bella. I think I'll call Charlie and ask a few neighbors and maybe Sheriff Mills. What do you think?"

"Count me in. Now finish tomorrow's paper."

Weeknights, normally routine at the Cooper's, was different this Tuesday. Jan promised Isabella they'd go through Leonard's gifts. The four piles on the living room floor were split into Cleveland Indians souvenirs, Grateful Dead memorabilia, articles and books on John Kennedy, and an assortment of French menus, magazines, newspapers and movie DVD's.

"Mom, what's your favorite movie?"

"Hmmmm, lots of favorites. Forrest Gump, Shawshank Redemption, Meet the Parents, Titanic. Where did that question come from?"

"Close Encounters was Papa Lenny's favorite. I watched it with him when you were out one night. Papa Lenny gave me the DVD. He said the scene where they play the music notes was his fav."

"I liked Close Encounters, too. Spielberg is my favorite director. Loved ET, scared silly by Jaws, Schindler's List was powerful. By the way, I'm thinking of having a little memorial service here on Friday afternoon for Papa Lenny. Pick out some things you know he was fond of and we can hang them on the wall or place them around. Okay?"

"Oui, peut-on jouer de la musique Grateful Dead?"

"Of course! Play whatever songs you want and put what you want to share of Papa Lenny's on the couch, okay?"

"I want to play *Truckin' and Ripple*. They were his favorites."

8

Jan loved a good mystery but the Life of Leonard Rosen wasn't a board game, a movie or a novel. Wednesday, a slow day at the paper gave her time to snoop online for answers. A Google search of Leonard Rosen turned up a whopping 10.4 million entries and Jan realized she needed to be more creative and a lot more targeted. She tried combinations connecting Leonard Rosen with the NSA, the Grateful Dead, and France but found nothing relevant. Then she combined Leonard Rosen with Cleveland Indians and bingo!

Albert Leonard Rosen (born February 29, 1924), nicknamed 'Al', 'Flip', and the 'Hebrew Hammer', Member of the Cleveland Indians Hall of Fame.

That explained the name Leonard Rosen. He was a popular Cleveland Indians third baseman in the '50s. It made perfect sense but any relief of finally coming up with something tangible quickly evaporated. Charlie already told her Leonard Rosen wasn't his real name.

Despite her research that extended well into Thursday afternoon, the name Albert Leonard Rosen was the only bit of information Jan uncovered. Howie's many calls proved just as fruitless.

9

Friday quickly arrived, and with it the memorial service for Leonard Rosen. On the outside of Leonard's apartment door Isabella hung a Grateful Dead poster and a Cleveland Indians pennant. Grateful Dead music filled the air of the Cooper apartment as a few neighbors, Howie, Sheriff Mills, Isabella and Jan reminisced about Leonard. Isabella, Jan and Ernie all wore Grateful Dead tie dyed T-shirts and Cleveland Indian ball caps. Leonard's eclectic tastes created a scene some-where between "Woodstock" and "Little Miss Sunshine".

Unfortunately, Charlie was a conspicuous no-show—without even a call. Jan did her best to hide her disappointment but both Howie and Isabella could see she was very upset. The five-word text message she received in the middle of the memorial did little but upset her even more. "So sorry, can't make it."

10

Saturday marked a week since Leonard Rosen's death. Frustration and confusion continued to consume Jan as neither she or Howie had uncovered anything significant about Leonard. Making matters worse, there were still unanswered questions about Charlie.

Fixing tea, she couldn't help viewing a 7-day virtual

slide show featuring the untimely death of Leonard Rosen and the unexpected arrival of Clifton Montgomery Charles.

"I didn't sleep much."

"Good morning Bella, I didn't sleep well either. Will you take Ernie out? Can I fix you some breakfast?"

"Just a little juice and toast."

Not wanting to go back to the park, and attempting to get Isabella's mind off her Papa Lenny, Jan suggested Isabella get together with a couple of her girlfriends.

Hoping to find a sweet apologetic email from Charlie, Jan turned on her computer and found a very unexpected email. She CLICKED and—SCREAMED!

Jan, Mon ami
Camelot
Relier les points
LR

Her body shook from head to toe as she knocked her cup of tea to the floor. She read the four simple lines 20 times ignoring the hot tea and broken china at her feet. Still trembling, she heard Isabella and Ernie running up the stairs.

Trying to calm down, she took two deep breaths hoping not to alarm Isabella, "Bella, please don't let Ernie come into the kitchen until I clean up the mess I've made."

Curious as to what mess, Isabella held on to Ernie, "What happened? What mess?"

"I just spilt my tea. A little accident—that's all!"

The normally fastidious Jan grabbed two dish towels to soak up the tea as she picked up the bigger pieces of broken porcelain. Her mind elsewhere she threw both the wet towels and broken pieces in the trash.

Trying but unable to hide what she'd just read, she uncharacteristically yelled at her daughter, "You've got to eat something! What do you want?"

"I told you, some juice and toast, but I'm going to take a shower first."

"Oh, I almost forgot, they're picking you up at 9:00. Bella, what does 'relier les points' mean?"

"That's funny, Papa Lenny use to say it to me. It means connect the dots."

The bizarre email still left Jan shaking unable to think of anything else. Anxious to call Charlie and Howie she was relieved when Sandy's dad finally arrived.

Who sent the email? What did connect the dots mean? Was it from Leonard? She called Howie, then Charlie, neither answered. She left them the same voice mail.

"This is Jan. Call me ASAP, it's very important!"

She wasn't sure what to Google? Her limited tech knowledge left her bewildered over how Leonard could have sent her an email. Camelot had to be about President Kennedy, but then what? As she reflected on Leonard's photo of John Kennedy and the stories of Camelot her phone rang.

The man's voice was unmistakably Howie's, "What's up?"

Hysterically she tried to explain, "Oh my God—Howie! I can't believe it! I just got an email from Leonard!"

"Shut the fuck up! What!" incredulously shouted Howie!

"You heard me, I got an email from Leonard this morning!"

Howie realized he heard what she said the first time, "How the hell… Probably an old email lost in cyberspace. What's the date and time?"

Staring at the email Jan quickly responded, "It's dated today, about an hour ago, and it's from LR. It reads,"

Jan, Mon ami
Camelot
Relier les points
LR

Analytical Howie didn't surprise, "Has to be Kennedy—and French for connect the points or dots. Don't touch your computer. Stay calm, sit tight, I'll be right over."

Still in her pajamas, she was about to jump in the shower when her phone rang again. This had to be Charlie. "Jan, I'm so sorry about yesterday but I wasn't able to access any communications. I apologize."

"Charlie, save your apology for later. I got an email from Leonard this morning. It says:"

Jan, Mon ami
Camelot
Relier les points
LR

Charlie's voice was calm but direct, "I'm leaving right now. I'll be there as soon as I can. Have you told anyone else?"

"I just got off the phone with Howie, he's coming over."

"Oh! Of course, but please don't touch anything on the computer, Please!"

"That's what Howie told me."

"And call me if anything else happens, okay?"

"Hurry Charlie, please hurry."

The doorbell rang just as she finished her make-up. Howie carried his coffee in one hand and her soy latte in the other.

"Let me see it!"

"Here, sit down, look for yourself. Charlie, said not to touch anything, too."

"You called Charlie? Why? Is he coming?"

Trying not to assume a defensive position she answered matter-of-factly, "I just thought he should know. After I told him he said he was driving right down. I called you first Howie!"

"Well, my tech knowledge is a little better than yours and I do know it's possible to send emails that are almost impossible to trace and I think you can also delay delivery. Should be easy to check. I'm more interested in the why and what. We know Rosen was a computer geek who worked for arguably the top, most secretive intelligence agency in the world."

"Howie, he also loved John Kennedy. He had a photo of him on the wall above his computer and he loved telling Isabella his bedtime version of Camelot, but that still doesn't tell us why or what. Does it?"

"Connect the dots! The intel guys use the expression to explain disparate bits of information connected to present a theory. What dots are we supposed to connect?"

Jan had only one possible answer, "Kennedy and Camelot, I guess."

Howie took off his glasses signaling he was perplexed. "The big question is what the hell did Leonard Rosen have to do with Kennedy? When did he start working for the NSA?"

"I don't know but Charlie might."

Changing his tone to Fatherly, Howie cautioned, "I know you're hot for this guy but I still don't trust him. Be careful! Just show him the email and you ask the questions. I'm still not sure who he's working for. Now I'm going to the office to make some calls."

"Thanks for being so protective of me. I know—he's a spy! Call you later."

11

Jan was nervous, confused and uncharacteristically perspiring heavily. Luckily she had time to freshen up before Charlie arrived. At almost exactly two hours from their phone call the doorbell rang. There stood Charlie, in his workout clothes, holding a big, beautiful bouquet of flowers. Surprised, and forgetting how upset she was, the flowers were tossed onto the couch as she gave Charlie a big hug wrapping her legs around his waist.

Charlie's apology seemed genuine, "I'm really sorry about yesterday. There was absolutely no way I could reach you from where I was, absolutely no way to get in touch with you. Jeez, you feel great. I was on my way to the gym when you called, didn't even change."

"Cowboy, shut up and kiss me."

Chemistry's great when it's easy and natural and it was difficult for Jan to resist pulling Charlie down on top of her on the couch, but there was a specific reason Charlie had rushed down to Raleigh. Moving to her laptop they read the four lines aloud together. Then Charlie right clicked the mouse four or five times nodding his head. "I think we can assume he intended you to receive this email when you did. It's also safe to assume we're not going to be able to trace it and I'm not sure it matters— anyway. I'm more interested in the content or context. Did you email each other before?"

"Occasionally, when we were making plans involving Isabella and I needed to confirm the time."

"Where is your precious daughter?"

"She's at friends. Why do you think Leonard sent this? How did he know he was going to die? Why wait until he dies?

"Good questions. My guess is perhaps he knew he was dying and programmed the email to be sent predicated on his death or some other event. But, why not just tell you or someone else?"

"Do you think you can find out anything from the NSA?"

"I seriously doubt it. The Agency has layers of filters and protocols preventing anyone from snooping around and I mean anyone. Security was tight before Snowden, now everything is on continual lockdown. I'll try but don't get your expectations too high. I don't want to be implicated in anything and neither do you. Trust me! Until we know who and what we're dealing with we need to be very, very careful. This isn't a game!"

"I guess you know how they play, don't you Charlie?"

"I'm sorry to blow holes in the fantasy life I supposedly lead but I'm as confused as you are about this. You have to believe me!"

"God, I hope so, Charlie!"

Jan felt overwhelmed by this secret spy agency, the NSA. It was the thousand-pound gorilla in the room, difficult to ignore and impossible to understand regardless whether the subject was Kennedy, Leonard or Charlie.

"I'm sorry but I've got to get back to Chicago for

Max's 12th birthday party."

"Thanks for getting here so quickly. I appreciate it. The email's left me with nothing but questions. Charlie, I don't know what to do. I'm sorry to act childish but..."

"You're not acting childish. Not at all. We can't forget Leonard had to know what he was doing. Call me anytime, okay?"

"Thanks Charlie. Now you better say goodbye to your neglected buddy and get to your son's party."

Charlie rubbed Ernie's belly, gave Jan a big hug then rushed out the door and ran down the hall. Five seconds later he was back at her door. When the door opened, he passionately kissed her down onto the couch. Not soft and tenderly but firmly nibbling on her lower lip, his tongue fighting her for top or bottom. After three minutes of Jan rocking on top of him their eyes locked and knowingly nodded together. If he didn't leave now he'd never get to Max's birthday party.

She watched from her kitchen window as he got into the black SUV. Amazingly, just before he closed the door and without ever noticeably looking up towards her window he waved and smiled. It was impossible for her not to think, of course, he's a spy. A spy she had become more than just attracted to. Standing in the kitchen, her face flush from sexual arousal she pondered how her life had changed so radically in a week. Now the damn email, from a dead Leonard, was turning her curiosity into a frantic obsession and she was falling deeply for her spy.

12

At almost 5:00 Isabella could be heard running up the stairs. As always, Ernie was already waiting at the door.

"Bonjour!"

"Hi Bella, how was your day with the girls?"

"So fun, we played some games and Sandy's Mom took us to lunch and the mall."

"I thought maybe we could watch a movie tonight. What do you think? Maybe pizza, too?"

"Sounds good. I'm not very hungry, but I know the movie I want to see."

"What movie, sweetie?"

"JFK!"

"JFK, where did you hear about JFK?"

"Pappy Lenny and IMDb."

"What's IMDb?"

"It's the Internet Movie Database. I thought everyone

knew about IMDb. The movie was made in 1991, way before I was born. Kevin Costner's the star. I think he was in the Wolves movie. It's about this D.A. from New Orleans who investigates the President Kennedy assassination. Did you see it?"

"I did. You sure know lots about it. It caused quite a stir. The director's Oliver Stone who's made a bunch of controversial movies. I'm sure you can find out lots of information about Oliver Stone at your IMDb. Let's rent the DVD."

"We don't have to; I already have it."

"What—how did you get it?"

"Papa Lenny gave it to me."

"I should have guessed. Okay, I'll call and order pizza."

Isabella amazed her mom—constantly. Obviously, Leonard had influenced much more than her computer skills.

"Bella, will you take Ernie for a walk before the pizza gets here?"

"Oui. Viens ici Ernie!"

To refresh her memory of the movie Jan read a short review.

"Kevin Costner, as New Orleans District Attorney Jim

Garrison, analyzes the actions of the F.B.I. and others he suspects of covering up evidence of multiple shooters. Garrison thought their motive was to escalate the United States participation in the Vietnam War. The belief was President Kennedy was attempting to prevent any further U.S. action in the war."

She now remembered the controversy and the criticism of Stone, accused of taking all sorts of liberties to help prove his conspiracy theory. Of bigger immediate concern was her discovery the film was rated "R". As best she could tell, the "R" was for intense scenes and language. She'd watch it with her hand near the remote just in case.

Movie night was an almost regular Saturday event at the Cooper's and pizza complemented it perfectly. While they waited for their pie Jan explained Oliver Stone's reputation and specific point of view following up with a question. "Bella, did you ever talk about this movie with Papa Lenny?"

"Oui, Papa Lenny said it was one of his favorites. He said we should watch it sometime. Pourquoi?"

"Just curious."

The movie was more than three hours long. Isabella barely lasted through the first half but Jan watched the entire movie as her daughter and Ernie slept curled up under a blanket next to her on the couch. Her heightened interest of Kennedy kept her wide awake through the full "Director's Cut" DVD. The movie raised more questions than it answered, but it was late, and bedtime at the Cooper's.

13

What a difference a week makes, and Jan was glad some normalcy had returned to Isabella's life. Her own life was a different story. Church was around the corner and, not surprisingly, Ernie was the adopted star/mascot of the congregation. He'd sit or lay down next to Jan but not before he greeted everyone and received their affection. Sometimes she wondered if Ernie was a human social butterfly in another life.

Returning home Mom tried to interest her daughter in food, "How about pancakes?"

"I'm not real hungry, maybe just one."

"Are you ever hungry? I'm going to make some. Ernie will eat what you don't. Thanks for staying awake during Pastor Heath's sermon. Wish I could say the same for your dog."

"Why is he my dog when he snores in church?"

"Bella, how did you like the movie?"

"It was okay, I guess. I'm not sure I remember the ending. I didn't understand a lot of what was going on. Were the Kennedys like the Bushes?"

"Hmmm, I guess you could say so in a roundabout way. It was more than fifty years ago, a very different world. Don't forget, your mom wasn't born until 1981."

"I know, May 4th. You're a Taurus. The pancakes are good but I'm getting full."

"You barely ate one. Here Ernie, your favorite Sunday breakfast."

14

"Charles, we might need you on the West Coast this week. We'll know more later today. Just be packed and ready. One more thing, the Leonard Rosen case is officially closed. Understood!"

"Yes sir."

Shit, thought Charlie. The first part of the call from his boss was routine, it happened almost every morning.

It was the specific reference to Leonard Rosen that was unusual. A few seconds later Charlie realized what must have happened. All NSA's vehicles are equipped with GPS tracking. They knew he had gone back to Raleigh— twice. As Charlie played back the past week, he knew his infatuation for Jan clouded his judgment and caused a rookie mistake—never let your personal life interfere with work. The phone interrupted his train of thought.

"Cliff, are you picking the boys up from school today?"

"Yes, Kathy, just like every Monday. They'll stay with me tonight and I'll drop them off at school in the morning."

"Come on Cliff. Just like every Monday? I know your intentions are good but your follow-through sucks."

Having enough of the conversation, Charlie ended it. "Kathy, I've got to run. Talk to you later in the week."

Unfortunately, it was a conversation much like hundreds of conversations they had both in and out of their marriage. Kathy was a hundred percent correct. Unfortunately, Charlie's intentions and Charlie's reality were very different and Charlie knew it. He also knew his job either directly caused their divorce or at the very least contributed significantly to it. It was the price agents paid in service of their country or so Charlie rationalized. The tragedy was the two innocent victims, Max and Harry, and that caused Charlie to constantly question his career choice. He could be sitting in a law office somewhere with only an occasional drive to the courthouse interrupting a very lucrative, very routine, very safe lifestyle. The early morning call from his boss only drove everything home—yet again!

Leonard Rosen remained an enigma to Charlie further complicated by the Saturday email and reference to Camelot. What did Rosen know? What was his connection to Kennedy? Unfortunately, employed by a hierarchy fixated on the chain of command, his boss had given him a direct order. The Leonard Rosen case was closed!

A hundred miles to the south Jan and Ernie walked into the Star-News office. "Hey Ernie, how's my boy?"

"Good morning to you, too. Howie, what did you find out?"

"Nothing—absolutely nothing. The powers that be have apparently tied a knot around everything. Whatever happened, it's done and closed. Sorry Jan, but we're dealing with the real 'A' team here."

She was disheartened Howie seemed so resolved, "Don't you find all this strange? What about the email and moving out his things the next day? Or Kennedy? I know it's all so conspiratorial but there's got to be something. Howie, I know there's something."

"I know you well enough to know there's no way in hell you're going to let this go. And, I agree with you—there must be something. I just don't think we've got a chance in hell of finding out what it is. Let me know if you come up with anything, but now we've got real work to do. Finish the article on the doughnut shop robberies!"

Jan couldn't help but chuckle as she left Howie's office and thought of the relative news value of a couple small town doughnut shop robberies when so many questions remained unanswered about Leonard Rosen, Kennedy and the NSA.

15

It took her all of thirty minutes to finish the doughnut shop story and get to the thick paperback sitting on her desk. The JFK movie had stirred her interest so fervently she picked up the Warren Commission Report from the town's used bookstore. Intimidating, the 888-page report was presented to President Lyndon Johnson on September 24, 1964, and made public three days later. Its conclusion—Lee Harvey Oswald acted alone in the killing of President Kennedy and Jack Ruby acted alone in the murder of Oswald. These findings provoked controversy and were continually challenged.

Three hours later with blurred vision she questioned what the hell she was doing. Investigators and reporters spent years and even decades analyzing, re-creating and disputing the findings. She wasn't going to come up with anything new. Her approach was wrong. She needed to shift to Leonard Rosen and connect those dots.

Setting the Warren Report aside, she Googled the Kennedy Assassination and the NSA and discovered 1,184 pages of National Security Agency files related to the assassination of President John F. Kennedy. Then while surfing the web she discovered a fascinating notation.

In addition to the 1,184 pages of National Security Agency files there was a separate 227-page report containing information on the challenges officials had in working with the NSA, concerning releasing Kennedy assassination related documents.

Her search turned up other very interesting articles raising even more questions particularly about Castro.

Did factions of the U.S. national security participate in a plot to kill Kennedy? What about Castro and some reports that suggested he viewed the Kennedy assassination as a disaster, supposedly supported by the NSA.

In August 1997, almost 34 years after JFK's death, the Assassination Records Review Board, a special committee appointed by Congress to facilitate the release of records on the incident, released 84 NSA documents.

Based on the new documents—the first NSA records on the Kennedy assassination ever released to the public— Castro was convinced the forces that conspired against Kennedy were also gunning for Cuba. Castro supposedly took to the airwaves to warn the Cuban people.

When President Lyndon Johnson appointed the Warren Commission to investigate the Kennedy assassination, Castro and the Cuban media continued their charges of a sinister cover-up and suggested an investigation of the CIA was called for and the appointment of CIA director Allen Dulles to the Warren Commission was a sham and eliminated an objective view.

The more Jan searched the more she confirmed what

she already knew. The Kennedy assassination remains the ultimate mystery of the 20th century with many conspiracy theories. Clouding questions even more was the role the NSA played in this jigsaw puzzle. What did become obvious was the conflict between the NSA and the CIA. How did Leonard Rosen fit into this? What was he trying to tell her in his email?

Then she played the "what-if" game. What if Leonard somehow "connected the dots" of the Kennedy Assassination and solved the puzzle? Then again, what did it matter—now?

16

Since Howie wasn't on the phone she started talking as she entered his office, "Who do you think killed John Kennedy?"

"Definitely not just one person and definitely not just Lee Harvey Oswald. I was seventeen when it happened but I remember exactly what I was doing when I heard the news. Then Ruby kills Oswald. Unbelievable! The Warren Commission was a joke designed to look like an objective report when it's been proven to be a white washed politically biased contrived exercise. To answer your question, I don't know, Castro, the mob, the CIA, the Ruskies. Who knows? We'll never know for sure!"

"Whoa! That wound you up? Sounds like you've given that speech before."

"Remember kiddo, Kennedy not OJ, was The Crime of the Century. He was young, handsome and represented hope and a brighter future. Then in broad daylight, rifle shots in Dallas and Camelot is dead!"

"Howie, what's your best guess about Leonard Rosen's connection?"

"I'd guess Rosen had some type of information either before or after the assassination. I don't see much value in whatever Rosen's connection might be. Who cares? Nothing is going to rewrite history—not now—no matter how compelling!"

Sensing Howie was ready to let it go, she reloaded, "I agree, but don't you think Leonard knew that? If he had something that would rewrite history he could have gotten it to the NY Times or Washington Post or somebody in the media long ago. Or, why not just tell us? Why did he send the email and what's the connection to his death? What's he trying to tell us? It's driving me crazy!"

Howie pleaded his case, "Look, we don't know who or what we're dealing with here except it involves the most secretive intelligence organization in the world. Kennedy was shot more than fifty years ago. Come on, let it go—please."

"I guess you're right, but..."

Returning to her office, Jan couldn't let go of everything happening around her. Although she appreciated the routine and quiet sanity of her normal life she felt more alive than she had in years. There was the excitement, the mystery, and of course, Charlie. What about Charlie? She understood it was insane to have a relationship with a spy. Who wants that kind of life? Yet despite all logic, she didn't want to let Charlie go—not just yet. She dialed his number. As usual she got his voice mail. Seconds later her phone rang.

"Hi Coop, got your message, what's up?"

"Coop? I haven't been called that since high school. Sort of like it. I didn't recognize your number. Where are you?"

"I'm walking outside my apartment and this is another phone. I think it's best we use this number. If you call me, you won't get a voicemail but I'll see you called and I'll call you back."

"Is this part of the spy thing?"

"This is a secure line. Something happened this morning and I think it's prudent to take some precautions!"

"What happened? What kind of precautions?"

"I was told, in no uncertain terms, the Leonard Rosen case was closed. They know I went back to Raleigh several times. Our SUV's have GPS. They track everything. It was a careless mistake for me to take the SUV."

"They, them! It sounds so bizarre to hear you talk about they and them."

"I know. It's weird, but my job's not the norm. What else is going on?"

Showing her frustration, Jan tossed a hand in the air as she tried to explain, "It's this whole Leonard Rosen thing. I'm totally frustrated. I've done more research this morning and now I'm even more confused. I can't make heads or tails of anything. Howie, who can usually figure out almost everything, has given up and suggests I do the same. He says the reference to Kennedy doesn't matter anymore since it was fifty years ago and we're not going to rewrite history. What do you think?"

"I think he's probably right but my gut tells me there's more to this story than just Kennedy. It was very strange the way I was told the Rosen case was closed, but as much as I'd like to help you try and solve this, I'm afraid I can't."

"I understand, but does that mean I won't see you—again?"

"Coop, our relationship was never about Leonard Rosen. At least I hope not. Is it?"

"God, no! Guess I just needed to hear you say that."

"We do have one little problem we'll have to overcome."

"What?"

"Well, you'll either need to visit me or I'll need to drive a different car when I drive down to see you."

"When, Charlie? I want to see you. I'll drive to you."

"As soon as possible. I might have an assignment out-of-town but we can still plan. When can you come?"

"It'll have to be when Isabella's with her dad, Wednesday or else on the weekend."

"Well, I have my boys on Mondays, Thursdays and every other weekend."

"What if I drive up Wednesday afternoon? I'll confirm things with Rick but I think it'll work."

"Who's Rick?"

"Oh, didn't I mention Rick—my ex?"

"So his name is Rick. I didn't know his name. Just do me one favor."

"What?"

Charlie smiled as he suggested, "Bring your toothbrush!"

"Oh Charlie, that's the most romantic thing anyone's

said to me in a long time. I think I'm blushing. I can't wait to see you and hold you. Bye Cowboy."

17

At 2:45, Jan left work to pick the girls up from school. Ernie, as usual, spotted them first. "Hi Sandy, hi Bella, how was school?"

Sandy was the sweetest of Isabella's girlfriends and couldn't contain their news, "It was so fun, Ms. Cooper. We got an 'A' on our history project."

"Fantastic, girls! I'm proud of you. Sandy, I'm sure your parents will be very pleased. We need some ice cream to celebrate."

"Mom, I want a peppermint cone!"

"You girls can have whatever you want."

Ice cream devoured, they dropped Sandy off and headed home. Back at their apartment Isabella took Ernie for his late afternoon walk while Jan called Rick and left a voicemail confirming he was picking Isabella up from Sandy's at 5:00 on Wednesday. That meant he had to leave his office in Chicago by 3:00.

Sorting through junk mail she lit up with a big smile

as she thought about Charlie's three words. "Bring your toothbrush." How fun, how romantic! It had been a long time. She couldn't help but fantasize! She flashed back to all those James Bond movies she saw as a young girl. What to wear? What to pack—a sexy nightgown?

Then Isabella interrupted, "What are you doing? You know you're smiling."

"Oh, just thinking about work. Did you bring your history paper home? I'd love to see it."

"Don't you remember? It was your idea. Remember? It was about John Kennedy and what he meant to America."

"Of course I remember the Kennedy report. I'm proud of you, Bella."

After dinner Isabella and Ernie did homework while Mom indulged herself in the wonderful joy of a full-blown daydream.

Charlie's apartment was dark except for the glow of a dozen candles. The Bee Gees, How Deep Is Your Love filled the air and the champagne, strawberries and chocolate were the perfect aphrodisiac. Their first kiss lingered as the Brothers Gibb sang their classic hit for the third time and Charlie carried her to his bed.

"I'm done with my homework. Why do you still have that silly grin on your face?"

"Just thinking. Your dad's going to pick you up Wednesday from Sandy's and take you to school on Thursday. Ask him to stop by the apartment and pick up Ernie after he gets you. I've got to drive up to Chicago Wednesday afternoon and I'll probably stay the night."

"I'll bet you're going to see Charlie. That's so cool! Is he a spy?"

She couldn't believe her daughter's question! "What, where did you come up with that idea? Hate to disappoint you, but the spy talk is just fantasy stuff."

Placing a hand on her mom's shoulder Isabella played the big sister, "You like him—I can tell. He's really cute and you need some action."

"Oh my God. Thanks for your concern sweetie, but that's my job, to worry about you. I like him, but he lives in Chicago and works all around the country. Sort of makes it difficult, don't you think?"

"You need to have fun. Charlie's cool and hot!"

She was sure her face was red after the relationship advice from her seemingly twenty-year old, 11year-old, "Well, I'm glad you approve. Now get ready for bed. Come on Ernie, get your leash, let's go for your walk."

As she walked out the door she pondered what it was

going to be like when Isabella started dating?

18

Jan spent Tuesday morning getting her hair and nails done, and shopping for cute, sexy panties and matching bra. You only get one chance for a first impression and she was determined to be a WOW! She hadn't spent much time with Charlie and had lots to learn, but the chemistry, the attraction, the lust was there. Compatibility remained the challenge. There was potential but only time would tell. Getting ready for her field trip did take her mind off Leonard Rosen. Charlie was all she could think about.

She was even able to get back to the gym for an hour spin class, taught by Tony, one of her two favorites and some weights. It felt good to sweat. The rest of the day passed, uneventfully, thank God. No crazy emails, no cancellation call from Charlie, only the excitement of anticipation that carried over into her dreamy sleep.

Ernie always got anxious when he saw a suitcase. This Wednesday morning two suitcases were being packed for their overnights, but only one looked like it was for a week's trip. Jan packed for any contingency. Would they go out? Where? Casual or trendy? It was Chicago! Four pairs of shoes might seem like a lot but she followed the female code—better to over pack than want something you didn't bring. Isabella couldn't resist as she looked at all the clothes, "Are you taking everything in your closet?"

"Very funny! I'm not sure what we're going to do—best be prepared."

Of course, Isabella spotted the new bra and panties right away, "I'm sure he'll love your hair and sexy, new…"

"Bella, stop it— please! One day you'll know what it feels like to meet a guy you like."

"Sorry, I was just kidding. Charlie thinks you're hot. You must see that."

"I sure hope so. I'll drop Ernie off at our apartment before I leave. You and your dad can pick him up after you leave Sandy's. Your dad's got dog food at his apartment. Show him your history project, he'll love it."

She was anxious entering the Star-News office and Howie picked up on it right away. "So you're driving up to Chicago this afternoon?"

"How did you know? Guess there's no secrets around here."

Not letting go, Howie probed, "Are you staying with what's his name? The spy guy? Charlie…or Cliff, or whatever his name is? I don't want to play the Father but you do know what it will be like to have a relationship with James Bond— right?"

"Yes, Dad. Let's not call it a relationship just yet. Okay?"

"Whatever you say. When are you coming home?"

"I should be back by noon tomorrow. Then I need to pick up Ernie from Rick's apartment. I should be in the office by 1:00."

"All kidding aside, have fun, you deserve it."

"Thanks Howie!"

19

The drive to Chicago was perfectly uneventful. Charlie's apartment was in a hip neighborhood of Chicago, the West Loop. Jan wasn't familiar with the area but Google maps led her right to his Fulton St. address. Nervously excited, she decided to leave her suitcase in the car and walk up the stairs to his third-floor apartment holding only her purse and a toothbrush. She didn't have time to knock when the door opened. Nothing was said as they hugged and pushed and pulled each other into the apartment.

"God, I'm so glad you're here! I've missed you."

"I miss you, too, Cowboy!"

"Can I help you with your toothbrush?"

"I've got a little suitcase in the car—too."

"You look fantastic, and feel even better. Did you get your hair done? I like it."

She smiled, it was wonderful to meet a man who noticed, "As always, you're very observant. A girl does what she can. I like your place. The dark leather suits you and could you have gotten a bigger TV?"

"Don't forget, I've got two growing boys. Let me show you the rest of the place."

There was no questioning the masculinity of this apartment. The leather living room ensemble was complimented by a huge entertainment center with an X-box and all sorts of other video gaming paraphernalia. The walnut dining room set appeared ruggedly functional. The walls were filled with framed posters of Chicago sports greats: Michael Jordan, football's Walter Payton, Gayle Sayers and Dick Butkus, baseball legend Ernie Banks, hockey icon Bobby Hull, and the most recent, the Chicago Cubs 2016 World Series Champions. Photos of the boys were all over and there were the obligatory ruler height marks on the kitchen wall. A large microwave, a small table and four chairs completed the kitchen. The hallway led to the boy's bedroom, a bathroom and Charlie's bedroom and bathroom.

His room had a king size bed, dresser and a large desk with an oversized flat computer screen. Next to the desk was a rather ominous three drawer metal filing cabinet with a conspicuously large bizarre looking lock that was a reminder of who lives there.

"You're such a guy's guy Charlie. Where's all the spy stuff?"

Wrapping his arms around her waist Charlie whispered in her ear, "The James Bond gadgets are in the hidden room behind the bed. I'm afraid I don't do anything as exciting as you think. I hope it's not going to be a big disappointment. I don't even carry a gun, most of the time."

Playfully, she poked his belt buckle, "Are you packing now?"

To make an obvious point Charlie pressed his body against hers before he said, "I think you can figure that out."

The mood between them was playful and hot but still had the undertones of being a little awkward. They both sensed the passion but also knew they hadn't spent much time together and certainly very little time alone. They needed to get physically acquainted.

Charlie offered a solution, "What do you say we go for a little walk? I'll show you the neighborhood and we can grab a cup of coffee or tea?"

"Great idea, Cowboy! We've got a lot to talk about."

"I love it when you call me Cowboy. Are you from Texas?"

"You're funny. I was born and grew up in St. Louis. Is it possible for a girl to have a serious relationship with James Bond?"

"I'm not James Bond. That's fantasy, movie stuff. My job is much more mundane, like what you saw the day I met you, mostly routine, lots of paperwork and occasionally watching over people."

"Really, so you're not really a spy—spy?"

"I can assure you I have no rocket launchers in my brief case or watches that blow up a car."

Not satisfied with the answer she probed deeper, "What about your schedule? Do you have one?"

"Sure, but it's not 9 to 5 and I travel a lot—sometimes at the last minute. You're obviously concerned about my lifestyle. I understand."

"What do you think your ex would tell me?"

The question caught him off-guard, "Gee, you're pulling out the heavy artillery. Can I get a rain check on that one for a little while? I'm sure you'll meet Kathy."

Sensing she hit a nerve, Jan tried to lighten up—a little, "Sure Charlie. I'm just trying to figure out what I might be getting into. Be flattered, I like you and am very attracted to you but I like to know who I might be sleeping with."

"Now, you're getting me excited."

"Settle down. This could be your lucky day!"

20

The round of verbal foreplay did much to ease any awkwardness as they walked hand in hand. Then as if getting a director's cue, Charlie stopped in the middle of the sidewalk, wrapped his arms around her, pushed the small of her back into him and gave her a long soft kiss. As her knees buckled she grabbed onto his taut, strong shoulders. Their bodies fit together perfectly when she stood on her tip toes. She could feel his excitement. The instant chemistry they felt the first time they saw each other quickly reignited.

Although she was falling for her Cowboy, she needed more assurance, "I don't want a fling. I want more. I need more. Where are you? Are you there?"

Charlie looked her in the eyes, softened his voice and said what every woman wants to hear, " I'm so there. I want to be in love—with you!"

Again, they hugged and kissed, only this time the passion meter was even higher. Now it was powered by exploring hands. Oblivious to passerby's they stood slowly hugging, groping and kissing for several more minutes until a passenger in a car driving by yelled, "Get a room!"

Laughing together Charlie had to ask the obvious, "Coop, the coffee shop is around the corner. Do you still want tea now?"

"It's either tea or your bed, Cowboy."

"I do believe you enjoy teasing me, don't you?"

"Hey, give me credit for bringing my toothbrush. That was a leap of faith."

As they turned the corner the quaint local coffee shop did look inviting and Charlie surprised her, yet again, "You sure you don't want a soy latte?"

"Now how did you know that?"

"I spy!"

"Ok, I'll pass on a soy latte and go to our second option but can we talk about Leonard. Can we talk about him on the walk back to your place?"

"Sure, I don't think anyone's listening. I'm just not sure I know more than you do?"

"What's your take?"

"I can tell you it's not routine for the NSA to relocate and create new identities for every Tom, Dick or Harry. Rosen obviously knew lots of highly sensitive information. Snowden gave the Agency a big jolt. No telling what Leonard knew or for how long. Hell, the NSA kept relevant information on the Kennedy assassination under wraps for more than thirty years."

"What about the email? What was he trying to tell us? He knew what he was doing."

"You're going to drive yourself crazy trying to figure this out. I've had to deal with these intel guys before. They talk a different language, live in a different world. Let's get back to us. Can we walk a little faster?"

"Only if we stop again in the middle of the busy sidewalk for another five-minute kiss."

"That'll be easy!"

"Just one more thing. If Leonard wanted to leave us a message, why not just leave us a message instead of the cryptic few lines? He must have wanted to set things in motion. Is that possible? Does that make any sense?"

Charlie knew exactly how to respond. He put his

hand on her lower back and pushed her into him once again. Then he gave her exactly what she asked for—a five-minute kiss.

21

Like any mortal man, Charlie was in disbelief over the size and weight of her suitcase. He couldn't help but notice the sexy bra, panties and black nightgown that fell out as she opened the suitcase on his bed.

"I get it. You're going to try and seduce me. How clever, but totally unnecessary."

"In your dreams! Where we going for dinner so I know what to wear?"

"There's a great steakhouse called Carmichael's a half mile away. How does that sound?"

"Great! Now get out of here while I change and freshen up."

"There's no rush, is there?"

"Settle down, let's keep building the mood. I need the romance."

Carmichael's looked delicious. They gave the appearance of the perfect looking couple. She wore dressy jeans that accentuated her long fit legs, 3 ½ inch midnight blue heels, and a tight long sleeve low-cut top. Charlie wore his version of her jeans and a baby blue long sleeve shirt that matched his eyes. They walked into the restaurant holding hands and were still holding onto one another when the cheese cake they were sharing for dessert arrived.

Back at Charlie's, her romantic fantasy evening was revised to one large candle, John Legend and white wine. It was perfect! Charlie's gentle strength was irresistible. Her playfulness added fun to their passion which lasted the better part of an hour.

Once again, she surprised him with her directness, "Charlie, do you want more children?"

"Coop, we used a condom."

"Not this moment, silly, in the future."

"Gee, I don't know. Max and Harry keep me busy. Why, do you?"

"I always wanted a big family. It was only me and my brother. I'm not sure it's healthy for Isabella to be an only child."

Feeling comfortable, but not that comfortable, she pulled the sheet over her breasts, "I was just thinking out loud. I tend to do that—lots! By the way, how old are you?"

"I'm 38, be 39 in February. What about you?"

"Thirty-six, my birthday's May 4th. I'm sorry; did I spoil the mood?"

"You didn't. Roll over!"

As great as the sex was, she loved the feeling of just lying in his arms—even more. A bed can be a lonely place and for the first time in years she felt totally secure and at peace. It was a level of intimacy impossible to match and they fell asleep wrapped together.

Turning over to snuggle, all she got was an arm full of pillow. The digital clock read 4:30. Where was he? She tossed on his blue shirt and walked into the living room. He was on his computer. Placing her hands on his shoulders she planted a kiss on the back of his neck, "Good morning Cowboy. You're sure up early."

By habit, Charlie closed the top of his laptop as he responded, "Good morning sunshine, I hope I didn't wake you. I tend to get up early. I'm catching up on some email. Coffee?"

"Coffee would be great, but first how about a big hug?"

"How about why didn't I say that. What a great night. You're amazing and wore me out. I slept like a baby."

"A baby who snores."

"Are you sure? I didn't think I snored. I know I don't

snore when I'm alone."

"Very cute. It wasn't loud or annoying. It was a little shhhhhhhhhh sound. I liked it."

Deftly changing the subject, Charlie stated the obvious, "Nice shirt. How do you like your coffee?"

"Just a little cream, please." Who gets up at 4:30? Her challenge would be to keep him occupied and in bed longer.

"So January Cooper, what do you think?"

Jan smiled, "I wondered how long it would be till you called me that? Listen, I like you a lot, but it would be naive of me to say I'm not worried about your job. It's very intimidating and I'm afraid of what it will do to our relationship."

"Point well taken."

"Now you sound like an attorney."

"I am an attorney, remember? Are you seeing anybody else?"

"Hell no! Are you?"

"No, and I certainly don't want to—now! We need to spend more time together. We'll have to get the scheduling thing down but we'll be able to work it out."

"I feel the same way. I'd like to meet your boys, too."

"You will."

"Good coffee, Charlie. I'm going to jump in the

shower."

"Not if I get there first."

"We can share. We've got time, don't we?"

"I don't need much time!"

"I get that impression, Cowboy!"

22

The drive home passed quickly as she relived every moment of her overnight. They got to know each other, laughed, played and became exclusive. The sex was great but it was the romance Jan savored. If only the damn "spy cloud" didn't hang over them. Only time would tell.

After picking Ernie up, she headed to the paper to finish a few stories and get Friday's paper ready for print. Ernie greeted the staff as she headed straight to Howie's office. "You know I miss Chicago. It was good to feel the city vibe—again."

Without looking up from his computer screen Howie fittingly responded, "Did someone say something? Oh, it's you, my missing reporter, Jan Cooper. I guess we've eliminated hello."

"Of all the people to give me a load of crap."

Howie raised his eyes over his reading glasses that were halfway down his nose and asked the obvious, "How was the spy who loves you?"

"Very funny. Did I miss anything here?"

Not wanting to pin her down on Charlie—just yet, Howie proceeded to the more mundane task at hand, "As a matter of fact you missed a lot. Another robbery but this time it was the Dunkin' Donuts. You need to get right on it. Maybe you can interview the guy behind the counter who apparently offered the robber coffee and a jelly doughnut after handing over the cash."

"Howie, seriously, do you have anything new on Leonard Rosen?"

As if on stage, Howie barked out a simple one word answer framed as a question, "Who?"

"So you've given up?"

"The man's dead. Let him rest in peace. Now go finish tomorrow's paper, and on your way out send Ernie in. I need to see him."

The doughnut robbery was full of humor regardless of which version you believed. The first had the robber asking for a doughnut and coffee before he asked for the cash. The second version had the employee, a 19-yr. old named Bert, hand the robber money and then ask if he wanted to buy coffee and a doughnut. Upon calling the shop, the first version was verified and the story with the surveillance photo of the robber would be above the fold on the front page of the Friday Star-News. Walking by Howie's office, Ernie was sleeping on his back with his paws up in the air alongside Howie's desk.

"See you tomorrow Howie. Come on Ernie."

Howie couldn't resist a parting shot, "Those robberies really have legs, don't they?"

"You can't be serious? What next, pajamas stolen from a dryer at the Laundromat? Bye Howie. Ernie, let's go!"

With an eager Ernie seated on the front passenger's seat, they waited in the line of family vans and SUVs for Isabella. Jan was prepared for what promised to be a grilling about her evening with Charlie. As Isabella opened the car door, Ernie licked Isabella's face then jumped into the backseat. Jan gave her daughter a big kiss and hug. "Hi Sweetie, how was your night at Dad's?"

"Cool but Dad had lots of questions about why you were going to Chicago in the middle of the week."

"What did you tell him?"

"Not much. Told him work stuff and to see a friend. And you met this hot guy."

"Isabella, how could you?"

"Chillax! I didn't say anything to Dad about Charlie."

"Thank you. We had a great time! We had dinner at a very cool steak restaurant called Carmichael's, talked a lot, walked around his neighborhood, just lots of fun."

"Where did you slee...?"

"Stop, Isabella, please—enough!"

Upon returning to their apartment Isabella took Ernie for his afternoon walk as her mom headed upstairs hoping to find a sweet email from Charlie. She recognized Charlie's email but her eyes focused on another email. CLICK, and "Oh my God!"

Jan
2,977
Deuxieme acte
LR

"Shit! Again! What the hell! 2,977! Deuxieme acte!" Shaking, Jan tried to gain some composure as her daughter walked into the apartment.

"What's up? You look like you've just seen a ghost?"

"What does deuxieme acte mean? Do you know?"

"Deux as in two?"

"Yes."

"Second act. Why?"

"Oh, I just needed to translate something in an email.

Do you have homework?"

"Oui, I'm going to do it now. Come on Ernie."

Jan, who hadn't moved for five minutes, was out of breath. Another email! Why? What was this? What was Leonard doing? Why not just say it when he was alive? What the hell was the number 2,977? The second act of what? She thought of Charlie but still called Howie first. With Isabella home she tried not to shout into the phone, "Again, it's happened again! I got another email from Leonard!"

Howie was not as restrained, "You shittin' me? What does it say?"

"Four short lines—again."

Jan
2,977
Deuxieme acte
LR

Howie's voice was so loud she had to lower the volume on her phone, "2,977—what the fuck is 2,977? Deuxieme acte is second act. Makes no sense. What kind of game is this? What's he doing and why? Fuck me!"

"Howie, what do we do?"

Lowering his voice, he tried to calm down, "Slow

down—girl! Let's think this through. I'm on my way to a Chamber dinner. We'll talk first thing tomorrow. Forward the email to me and don't do anything crazy. I know you, but try to relax. And, have you told him yet?"

Faking naiveté she asked, "Him who?"

"Your spy—him."

"No, I called you—first. But, I'm going to call him."

"Whatever, call me if anything else happens. Otherwise, see you tomorrow morning."

"Thanks, Howie."

23

Jan was overwhelmed. It was starting to play out like a Ludlum novel and she was starting a relationship with one of the main characters—the spy. It sounded like a great movie but she didn't like the part she was playing. She called Charlie's new number. No answer, no voicemail, just ring, ring, ring. As she hung up she held onto her phone waiting for it to ring.

After making sure she saved the original email, she forwarded a copy to Howie. Now, following her pattern, she Googled 2,977. On the first page of nine million entries she found it was a Senate Bill, a rat gene, a mobile authentication code, and something having to do with robotics. Nothing resonated, but then again, she didn't know what she was looking for. Where the hell was Charlie? Just as she started to continue her search, her phone rang and she could see it was his new number. "Charlie, I got another email from Leonard!"

"What! Another email? What does it say?"

Jan
2,977
Deuxieme acte
LR

"What the hell does 2,977 mean and what's the connection to second act?"

"Guess I'm the only one who doesn't speak French. I've Googled but haven't come up with anything, yet. You're the spy. What's going on? Why did Leonard set this up? What's he trying to tell us? It's the same questions we've had for days only now there's even more to consider."

"I only wish I knew. I don't have a clue what's going on?"

"I'm so frustrated Charlie, we don't even know his

real name."

"Yes, we do."

Surprised, she had to lower the excitement in her voice not wanting to alarm Isabella, "When did you find out? How? What is it?"

Then she could hear Charlie's other phone ring. He quickly responded, "Sorry, I've got to take this call—right now. Oh, hope you liked my email! Bye."

Charlie's email, she totally forgot her other email. CLICK!

Coop, yesterday couldn't have been any better. Everything about you excites me and I can't wait to see you again. Oh, btw, I'm happy you left your toothbrush. Your Cowboy

Reading his words brought a big smile briefly to her face before the reality of Leonard's second email crashed her back to earth with a thud. Then she thought of what Charlie said. They now knew Leonard's real name. When Ernie came running into the kitchen she knew Isabella couldn't be far behind, "Who were you talking to?"

"Howie then Charlie. How about a salad for dinner?"

"C'est parfait!"

"Great! You're hungry. I still can't believe my eleven-year-old is teaching me French. Do you want to chop some vegetables?"

"Your eleven-year-old is almost twelve and I think I'm going to finish my homework. Let me know when it's ready. I'll teach you French. Papa Lenny's mom taught him, he taught me and I'll teach you."

"Wait, how did you know Leonard's mom taught him French?"

"He told me. His mother was a French teacher. Didn't you know?"

"No, I had no idea. What else did he tell you?"

"Let's see. There's the Grateful Dead, President Kennedy, French and he was born in Cleveland."

"Really, he was born in Cleveland! That explains the ball cap he always wore. Thanks for sharing, Bella. I'm sure Papa Lenny was glad he could share things with you."

Thanks to her daughter, Leonard's bio was filling out. Now if there were only more details about his work with the NSA. Never in the years she knew him did he play any kind of mind games. He was always very direct. He never talked much about himself or his past, except to Isabella. God knows she tried to pry out more details, more history. Now he dies and the games start. What's the point? What's he doing—dead? Why?

Back on her computer, she re-started her search where she left off, 2,977. Luckily she ventured past the first page because in the middle of the second Google page she found an entry that left her speechless.

September 11 attacks: 2,977 victims.

As her heart and mind raced, Jan took some deep breaths in hopes of calming herself. Could Leonard somehow be connected to 9/11—too? This was beyond crazy. It couldn't be a coincidence. So excitedly perplexed, she didn't know what to do next.

24

Fifteen hundred miles away Charlie boarded a plane. He reflected on his relationship with Jan and her connection to Leonard Rosen that brought the two of them together. He was treading on thin ice asking questions about Rosen to friends at the Agency, but it did lead to discovering Rosen's real name, Isaac Stone. Yet, knowing his real identity didn't provide Charlie with any additional info on Jan's neighbor except to turn up several

NSA operatives who knew of Isaac Stone. Their comments were consistent and spoke of Stone's reputation as a brilliant genius and pioneer in intelligence analysis, algorithmic problem solving, software and search engines.

Charlie was frustrated he couldn't get a handle on the Isaac Stone affair. Nothing seemed to make sense which in a rather obtuse way made perfect sense. Isaac was pointing Jan in a specific direction for a reason. Based on Isaac Stone's relationship with her and Isabella it was safe to assume he had a plan, something extraordinary. The Kennedy assassination was a generation defining event. It altered history but it was old news. Who cares? There had to be more. Regardless of Isaac Stone's connection, why would he construct such an elaborate puzzle? After landing, Charlie searched for a safe environment and called Jan.

When she saw it was Charlie she skipped hello, "I loved your email, now what's his real name?"

"At least I like your priorities. It's Isaac Stone, but I don't know if it helps? I asked around and no one admits to knowing him. Several agency associates admitted hearing about him but they just confirmed what we already know about his genius."

Her voice started to crackle, "I've discovered something. I'm scared Charlie. I don't want to believe it!"

"What? What is it? Tell me!"

"Hold on! Charlie, 2,977 was the number of victims from 9/11. Could Leonard, I mean Isaac, know something about 9/11 and the Kennedy assassination? What's the connection? Why involve me—Charlie? Why me? I'm scared!"

"Whoa! Talk about the ultimate puzzle. I'm just as baffled as you. I don't have any answers, just the same questions. The one assumption it's safe to make is Isaac Stone had to have a very good reason for all this. Why all the cryptic code? Why the trail to follow? You're the last person in the world he'd ever want to jeopardize. I've got to be very careful. Somebody very powerful at the Agency has shut down anything to do with Isaac Stone. Perhaps that explains why he's been so cryptic. Now, when am I going to see you again?"

"Soon, I hope. Isabella's with Rick this weekend. What about your boys?"

"They're with their mom. I'll drive down. I'll rent or borrow a car. I'll call you tomorrow but count on me coming down Saturday morning."

"Great! In the meantime, I'll keep working on Leonard, I mean Isaac. Oh, by the way, I discovered Leonard Rosen was a former Cleveland Indians 3rd baseman, Al Leonard Rosen, which makes sense since Isaac was from

Cleveland. And Isabella also told me his mother taught French which explains why he was so in love with the language. Obviously, Leon..., I mean Isaac confided to my daughter. Charlie, I'm lost, totally lost. I need you!"

"Hang in there. Stay strong. We must assume Isaac knew exactly what he was doing. I'll call you tomorrow."

25

Tossing salad was a good metaphor for what was going on in her head. The questions, all the questions. What did Leonard, aka Isaac Stone, want her to do? What was his motive? Why did he die? Finished with the salad she couldn't stop thinking, weighing options and trying to solve the email puzzle."

"Bella, dinner's ready. Ernie—you too!"

"What were you doing on 9/11, when the planes went into the towers?"

Once again Isabella caught her mom off guard, "What? Where did 9/11 come from? Isabella, were you eavesdropping—again?"

"I can't help it. Sound travels."

"I was getting ready for class. Then, I watched the

news all day. The whole country was numb with dis-belief. Bella, did you ever hear Papa Lenny talk about 9/11."

"Hmmmmm, I don't think so. Pourquoi?"

"Just curious."

"La salade est grande! Wait, he did say something! I think he said it shouldn't have happened."

"Are you sure?"

" I think so, shouldn't have happened."

Cleaning up after dinner she couldn't help but think about the significance of what Isabella told her. "It shouldn't have happened." Connect that to Kennedy. Did Isaac Stone think both acts were preventable? Could he have known about them beforehand? Is that possible? How could he have known? They were almost forty years apart. As her imagination raced wildly, she had to sit down. For the first time since Isaac Stone's death she felt the enormity of the situation. Was it plausible her quiet, frail neighbor foresaw the two most significant events in the past fifty years before they happened? No, he couldn't have! Could he? She had to call Howie.

"Howie, you still up?"

Sarcasm was Howie's specialty, "It's 7:30. I'm old but not that old. You must really have something special to interrupt my Jeopardy."

She led with her theory, "What if Isaac Stone knew about the Kennedy assassination and 9/11 before they occurred? What if he pre...?"

"Wait, who the hell is Isaac Stone?

"Oh, sorry, Charlie discovered Leonard's real name."

"Well, that's helpful but don't go crazy with your theories."

"I can't help it. Isabella said Isaac told her 9/11 shouldn't have happened. Now connect 9/11 with Kennedy."

"Aren't you assuming a boatload of shit? How the hell did you connect 9/11 to all this?"

"Oh, sorry, I forgot to tell you! Everything's been moving so fast. I did a search of 2,977. Guess what? It's the number of victims killed in 9/11!"

Howie shouted into the phone, "Holy fuckin shit! You fuckin kidding me! Those are the two most significant events of my life. Could Rosen, or whatever his name is, be involved with both? Do we know when he worked for the NSA?"

"I don't know but I'll find out. I'll ask Charlie, but for now let's assume Isaac knew something about both events. Does it make sense? Does Leonard, I mean Isaac, want his story told to bring down our entire intelligence community? Is this all about payback. I'm thinking as I'm talking. Howie, what do you think? Could Snowden know about this? Could he? Should we contact Snowden?"

"Slow down, you're moving too fast for me. Forget Snowden. Who knows if he's in Russia or even still alive? Let me think about your theory, let me think. We've got a real name; I'll make more calls. Listen, I know I suggested this before but I want to make sure you journal all this. We'll run it in the Star-News one day. You'll win whatever they call the award they give to esteemed journalists from small town papers. Seriously, this could make Watergate look like a college fraternity prank. Stay on it! Trust your instincts!"

She appreciated his suggestion, "I've written some and I'll write more. I promise! Thanks for the reminder. I can't wait for you to present my plaque."

"Goodnight Cooper! You've gone into my House-wives. Not that I'll be able to concentrate on anything but this fuckin puzzle."

"Goodnight Howie."

She did need to get back to her journal. Not for Howie's sake but because she understood the scope of what was unraveling before her. She also hoped it might organize her thoughts. The goal was to realize Isaac Stone's intent. She was now convinced it could change history.

As with most nights, tucking in her daughter and kissing her forehead goodnight was a highlight of her day. And, as soon as she turned off the lights Ernie jumped onto the bed and snuggled next to his best friend.

Propping up her pillows Jan continued to write in her journal for more than an hour alternating between pages about Leonard Rosen, aka—Isaac Stone, and Charlie, aka—the spy. She couldn't help wondering how each story would end.

26

She was wide awake at 5:30, a half hour before her alarm. What seemed like the weight of the world kept her from getting much sleep. Although her theory about Isaac seemed to make sense, she didn't want to convince herself it was true by incessantly repeating it. She needed Howie's and Charlie's objectivity. Then a welcome interruption took her out of her circular mindset when Isabella and Ernie came running into her room and jumped onto her bed.

"Hey guys. You're up early. TGIF."

"Ernie was snoring. He snores when he lies on his

back with his legs up in the air."

"What a coincidence! Your dad snored, too."

"What about Charlie?"

"I mention your father and you bring up Charlie. Bella, how does your mind work?"

"When are you going to see him—again?"

"As a matter of fact, this weekend."

"So cool, j'aime Charlie"

"I'm glad you like him. Now please put on your sweats and take the big snorer for his walk."

Jan followed Ernie into the Star-News office. As he began his rounds she walked straight to Howie's office. As usual he was on the phone but motioned for her to sit down.

"Thanks Dale, let me know what you find. That was my Pftizer, ex-CIA. I asked him to find out what he could about Isaac Stone. I called my Barker, FBI, earlier. If anybody can help it's my guys. Let's see what they come up with."

Amused at Howie's use and placement of the pronoun "my", Jan offered her theory, "What if 'my' Isaac predicted both the Kennedy assassination and 9/11 but for whatever reason no one listened to him? Does that make any sense? Does Isaac want to expose and bring down our intelligence establishment? This would dwarf

Snowden!"

"Keep honing your theory, but don't get carried away, too many loose ends. We need to fill in some blanks before we connect any dots."

"That's a good line, Howie. I might use it. Oh, I'm going to call Sheriff Mills. I want to find out more about Leonard's, I mean Isaac's death. It might help to know what he died from? He never complained but he wasn't the picture of health—either. I don't know who his doctor was, but it should be easy enough to find out in this town. Let me know what your well-connected buddies say."

"Where's Ernie? Do you specifically tell him to stay out of my office?"

"No, he just gets better offers. I'm sure he'll get to you after he visits the rest of the crew. Get him some good treats, you tight wad."

After leaving Sheriff Mills a voicemail she called Charlie. While she waited for his return call, she thought of her upcoming weekend. Raleigh wasn't Chicago, but it would give them some time alone. Then her phone rang.

"Good morning Charlie. I miss you."

"Miss you too. Sorry, can't talk now, but I'll try and call you later. Bye."

Disappointed at first, she was at least relieved he called her back, said he missed her and would call later. It was nine in the morning on a workday. She forced herself not to overreact. Then her phone rang again.

"Hi Jan, Sheriff Mills here. Thanks for your articles on the robberies. They helped, we got our man!"

"Good morning Sheriff. Congratulations, fantastic you caught the robber. I want to get more details from you but that's not why I called. I have a few questions about Isa..., I mean Leonard Rosen. Did you find out the cause of death or any info about any health problems?"

"Sorry, can't help. The cause of death is listed as natural causes. The VA came in right away, with all sorts of official paperwork, picked up the body, handled everything. Made it easy from our end."

"Who did you deal with at the VA, do you remember?"

"Hold on, I think I still have his card. Here, here it is. Charles Montgomery—nice guy. You met him, right?"

"Yep, I met him. Thanks, Sheriff. Can you send me a copy of the death certificate?"

"Sure, I'll drop off a copy."

As soon as she hung up she heard Howie, "Can you come to my office, and bring Ernie."

"What's up?"

"I got a call back from my Pfizer, CIA. Here Ernie, look what I've got for you, a super biscuit. Geez, leave my fingers! Don't you feed him?"

"What did your CIA guy say?"

"He said Stone was either the most brilliant mind in intelligence history or a total kook depending on who you believed. Stone wasn't much for structure, or politics, or the normal back stabbing that goes on in the intelligence community. He did his job, and never complained, or made waves. No one was smart enough to challenge him so they just ignored him. Hell, he worked under nine administrations. Half of Washington coveted his opinion, the other half found him crazy, probably because they couldn't understand him. Stone had quite the reputation."

"Makes sense and could explain why no one listened to him about Kennedy or 9/11. Don't you think?"

"Be careful. Don't bias your reasoning. It's possible but not definitive—yet. Lots of holes to fill in but the outline's getting clearer. I'm still waiting to hear back from my Lou, FBI."

"Oh, just so you know and don't feel hurt I didn't tell you, Charlie's coming down tomorrow morning for the weekend."

"I already guessed. Only wish Isaac Stone was as

easy to read as you."

"And, you'll be happy to hear Sheriff Mills caught the doughnut robber. Know you'll want a front-page story and mug shot. I'll get right on it after I go to the market, stop at the cleaners, get my nails done and pick up Bella."

"It's amazing you ever find time for work?"

"Bye Howie. Let's go, Ernie."

27

She had time to run errands before she picked up Isabella. Nails would be last, save the good Mother-Daughter bonding. The market was the first stop for cheese, wine, bacon and eggs for the morning, and fresh coffee. The cleaners were in the same shopping center. The gift shop was the final stop before picking up Isabella. She grabbed a half dozen scented candles and started to think about clothes and bedding she needed to wash. The line of cars was moving quickly and as usual, Ernie saw Isabella first.

"Hi sweetie, how was school?"

"Bonjour, school was cool! Is Dad picking me up in

the morning?"

"Yes at 9:00. What do you want to do tonight?"

"Can we watch the Grateful Dead DVD? Please?"

"Sure but you'll have to wake me if I fall asleep. And make sure Ernie doesn't howl like he did last time. Did I tell you Charlie's coming down tomorrow morning?"

"You already told me. So cool."

"Since I've got my sandals on let's run the big snorer around the block when we get home."

"You're going to give him a complex. He knows we're talking about him, don't you Ernie."

After their walk and tossing her best sheets into the washer she boiled water for their pasta. She also grabbed her journal to give her something to do while the Dead played their 6 twenty minute songs. Now who was calling her.

"Hi Jan, I'm so sorry but something's come up and I'm leaving for L.A. in ten minutes. I'm not sure when I'll be home but I'm afraid I can't make it tomorrow. You know I'd much rather be with you."

She couldn't hide her disappointment, "Dammit Charlie, I want to see you! Is this what it's going to be like? God, I can't deal with this! I was really looking forward to our weekend."

"I'm really sorry!"

She dropped her phone on the kitchen floor, sat down and started to cry. She knew it wasn't going to work. She knew it.

"Mom, what's wrong? Why are you crying?"

"I'm okay, just disappointed. Charlie can't come."

"Why not?"

"He's got to work."

"That sucks!"

"I'll be okay, but you're right, it sucks!"

This was one of those times when the best medicine was a hot cup of tea, a blanket and the warm bodies of Isabella and Ernie on each side. She blankly stared at the Dead's concert flick without hearing the music. Her mind was consumed with Charlie and where their relationship was going. She knew it wasn't going to work. Charlie wasn't available. Not with his job. Any woman would always be second.

Mom, Isabella and Ernie were all sleeping long before the Dead finished their last song. After dragging Isabella to bed, she took Ernie for a short walk. On the way back upstairs she passed Isaac Stone's old apartment and thought about the last two weeks of her life and how everything had been turned into a chaotic conundrum. First, the grief of Isaac's death, then Charlie, then emails and finally the enormity of Isaac's crazy puzzle. She was exhausted with a splitting headache as she crawled under the covers. Instinctively, Ernie who normally slept with Isabella, was already on her bed resting his head on her pillow.

28

Jan woke in almost the same spot she fell asleep. Ernie was still next to her—snoring. With no motivation to get up, she stayed in bed until 8:00. She could have stayed there all day but Isabella had to get ready for her dad. "Time to get up Bella. Your dad's going to be here soon. I'm going to take Ernie out but you better get ready."

"Oui."

Walking Ernie by his favorite tree she noticed the Apartment FOR RENT sign on the lawn in front of her building. Who could possibly replace Isaac Stone?

"Mom, are you going to be okay. What are you going to do today?"

"I'm fine. I've got lots of stuff to catch up with. You have fun with your dad. There he is. I hear him walking up the stairs."

"Hi Rick. How are you?"

"Everything's good, and you?"

"It's been a hectic couple of weeks after Isaac's, I mean Leonard's passing."

"Who's Isaac?"

"Oh, it's a long story. You don't have time for it now. Have fun with your daughter. Bye Bella. Give me a hug."

"Au revoir, Je t'aime."

Fourteen hours after she washed them Jan put her damp sheets in the dryer and then sat down with her journal. The past two weeks were so chaotic she welcomed the time to take a deep breath, reflect and hopefully gain some insight. With ever faithful Ernie by her side, she began writing and didn't stop for three hours, eighteen pages later. Needing some fresh air, she picked up Ernie's leash. "Come on boy, let's take a walk to the park."

The memories were still raw. Looking at the empty park bench brought tears down her face. The somber mood was interrupted when Bailey, a golden retriever friend of Ernie's, came running towards them. At least Ernie was happy and had someone to play with.

If the morning was for reflection, she decided the rest of the day would be for creating a plan to solve the Isaac Stone mystery. Sipping a cup of hot tea, she began listing the questions she needed answered to help explain who this man was and what he was trying to accomplish.

How old was Isaac Stone, and did he have a middle name or initial?

Where did he go to school?

Any relatives, friends, or co-workers?

When was he hired by the NSA and how long did he work there?

Was there anything in the public record, anything published?

How and why did he end up in Raleigh?

Could any of his idiosyncrasies: The Grateful Dead, the Cleveland Indians, his affection for President Kennedy, love of the French language or his favorite movies provide any insight or clues?

Had he been sick? If so with what and who was his doctor?

Why was it so difficult to find answers to such simple questions?

Jan sighed after writing the last question. This approach made sense. Learn and understand as much as possible about this mysterious genius, hope to gain insight, realize his motive and hopefully his objective. With Ernie, exhausted from his play date, already sleeping at her feet she grabbed a blanket, a pillow and took the opportunity for a rare afternoon nap.

As much as she wanted to stay curled up on the couch it was 5:30, Ernie was hungry and needed to go out. After taking care of Ernie, she Googled Isaac Stone. No surprise, over 1.8 million entries with nothing even remotely relevant on the first three pages. The phone interrupted her search. Who was calling? She didn't recognize the number.

"Guess what. I'm calling on my new iPhone Daddy got me."

"Aren't you the lucky girl."

"What are you doing?"

"I'm relaxing and playing on the computer. What else have you two been doing?"

"We went to Pizza Katie's. We're going to watch a DVD tonight. Je t'aime."

"I love you too, Bella. Thanks for calling."

Jan knew Rick enjoyed spoiling their daughter and they talked about getting Isabella a smart phone. Isabella was old enough and Jan liked the thought of always being connected. She wondered if Isabella had told Rick about Charlie. Now who's calling?

"Hi Jan, I miss you and wish I was holding you right now."

"Charlie, I miss you too. I wish you were here next to me on the couch, but I'm afraid. Charlie, I'm afraid you're not available, not with your job. Is that what happened with Kathy? What's the divorce rate for spies?"

"Please, let's leave Kathy out of this. I understand your hesitation. My job's different, I know. Can't we just see where things go. I want to be happily married, not married to my job."

"Charlie, it's what they demand of you. They're impossible! How can there be any normalcy? How can any woman be more important than your job? And, where the hell are you?"

"Can't we see, take it slowly. I'm not in love with my job—believe me, I think about the crazy demands all the time and how it affects me and especially my boys. Can't we try. I want to try."

"Oh Charlie, I wish I could touch you."

"I'll be flying home from California tomorrow. I'll call you when I land. I wish I was holding you and looking in your eyes."

"Be safe, Charlie."

Two thousand miles apart they felt much the same. Relationships are difficult enough. It wasn't about their chemistry, their connection, their passion for one another. Jan hoped she wasn't rushing into a relationship. After all, they barely knew each other. She only hoped it didn't come down to Charlie having to choose between her and his career. As if the Isaac puzzle wasn't overwhelming enough, she had absolutely no idea how she was going to resolve Charlie.

29

The apartment always seemed empty without Isabella, especially on Sundays. After starting tea she turned on her computer—three emails. Charlie and Howie would have to wait. There was something more important. CLICK!

Jan
Un, deux, trois?
Listen
Isaac

Her heart raced and her mind moved even faster. Un, deux, trois? Why a question mark after the three and it was signed Isaac not LR. Then a very scary thought hit her. Could Charlie be sending these emails? Is this his way of explaining something he can't tell her. Is he leading her somewhere. Does that make sense. She had to call Howie.

"Eight on a Sunday morning; this better be good!"

"I got another email, four lines."

Jan

Un, deux, trois?

Listen

Isaac

"It's signed Isaac. Un, deux, trois? with a question mark, then the word listen."

"Some bastard's fuckin' with us!"

"Howie, do you think it could be Charlie? What if he can't tell us because of his job? Could this be his way of telling us if he can't say anything?"

"What? Now you're confusing me. You haven't told him about this one, have you?"

"No, I always call you first."

"Don't tell him. At least not until we know more."

"I won't, not now, but what should we do? I'm scared."

"Are you going to be home or are you going to church?"

"I'm not going anywhere."

"I'll be over in a half hour. Venti soy latte?"

"Thanks, better get me an extra shot."

She was shaking. Reference to Isaac, not LR, implied somehow, someone was tracking or listening to them. What the hell did the word "listen" mean? Who's sending these emails? She trusted Howie— unequivocally. That left Charlie or someone else.

Howie arrived with her soy latte, a big biscuit for Ernie, his new best friend, and his laptop. Jan was almost hysterical as she welcomed Howie, "Thanks for coming over. I'm a little unnerved. Well, more than a little. I'm scared shitless. The ramifications of this are too much for me to even think about. I've got an eleven-year-old daughter. I can't be part of some espionage plot. I won't! What should I do?"

Howie tried to soothe her nerves, "Relax, we'll figure it out—eventually. What bastard is writing these emails and why? This whole thing has taken on a life of its own. Let me see the email!

"Here, look for yourself."

"I need a copy. Can you forward it to me."

"Sure."

I'm baffled at the timing of the change from LR to Isaac. Who knew? It's either got to be Charlie or else someone is hacking into our computers or has your apartment or the office bugged. Guess that could be Charlie, too."

It wasn't the response she wanted to hear, "Howie, do you really think it's him. I can't believe he's making up his feelings for me. Tell me I'm not being a naive fool. It can't be part of his job, can it?"

"God, I hope not, but let's not rule anything out. Not yet. I'm going to call my Pftizer again tomorrow. In the meantime, we need to be careful!"

"What does be careful mean? Charlie already has me calling him at a different number because he says the old number isn't secure. Maybe it's just the opposite."

Howie grabbed her arm and moved towards the door whispering, " I think Ernie needs to go out, and I've got to leave—anyway. Walk with me."

Once outside, Howie explained what being safe might entail starting with what they just did—move outside and away from what might be a bugged apartment. "If Charlie's a part of this, well, he's been in your apartment and who knows what he might have bugged and done to your computer. If it's not Charlie, then someone else could have done something. Either way we've got to be careful. I'm going to call my Barker, FBI and ask him to send his people down ASAP to run a security check of your apartment, our office and our computers. Until then, we need to be extremely careful."

Nervously Jan asked for some Fatherly advice,

"Howie, I don't like any of this! It's too spooky and I'm scared! Is there anything more we can do? Should we stop trying to find answers and let it go? What should I do when Charlie calls? What do I tell him? Should we report this to someone? There's got to be someone who can take over!"

"And who might that someone be? I've got my guys from the FBI and CIA looking into things. Who else would you like to call?"

"I don't know, the President, the NY Times, Oprah, Anderson Cooper, 60 Minutes. I don't know but this is too big for us, isn't it? What about the latest clue? 1, 2, 3? What the hell does that mean. Listen, listen to what?"

Still trying to settle her down Howie tried to be the voice of reason, "We've got to think this through. Let's see where things go. Regarding your spy, it's your decision but it seems to me you've got a built-in excuse. Make that the reason. You can always tell him the truth; you can't envision having a relationship with a spy. That is the truth, isn't it?"

"Sort of. Logically I know it won't work but then there's the hope that maybe things will change. Getting back to the latest clue. What's your take?"

"Hell if I know! I'm trying to think of what trois means assuming Kennedy is #1 and 9/11 is #2. Listen,

listen to what?"

"We're on the same page. Hate to be sarcastically redundant but I don't have a clue. Howie, I can't take much more of this. I can't!"

"I understand. You didn't ask for any of this, but you must assume Isaac knew exactly what he was doing. There's a reason for everything he's done. Everything! Regarding your spy, understand those dice are loaded. If you want a fling, screw your brains out but don't fall in love with the guy and please watch what you tell him until we figure things out."

Reluctantly, Jan agreed, "I guess you're right. Thanks, Howie. I don't know what I'd do without you."

Changing the subject Howie reached down to pet Ernie, "By the way, have you noticed how Ernie seems to be showing me more love."

"Keep feeding him those super-sized biscuits and he'll keep loving you. And you're giving me relationship advice. God, we both need help!"

30

Jan dreaded Charlie's call. She wasn't sure what to

say or if she should just end their relationship, at least until the Isaac puzzle has been solved or disappeared for good. Then she thought of Isabella. She was the only reason Jan ever needed. She couldn't and wouldn't endanger her daughter. The madness must stop! Goodbye Charlie. Of course, hoping the phone wouldn't ring guaranteed it did.

"Hi Jan, we just landed. I miss you."

She tried to be indifferent, "Hi Charlie. How was your trip?"

"Work, nothing unusual except for something you'll be interested in."

"What's that?"

"I ran into a guy who knew Isaac Stone."

"Really, what did he have to say?"

"He confirmed what we already know and then gave me a little more. He said Stone had a long running battle with the Agency over what they did with the information and recommendations he provided. Apparently Stone never understood the politics of the NSA and it haunted him for almost fifty years."

"Do we know when he started and when he left the NSA?"

"I think so. Started in the middle of 1963. Oh, one other interesting tidbit. He apparently spent a year at

MIT when he was sixteen before starting at the NSA. Retired from the NSA in 2011. I miss you! I could drive up right now."

She tried but couldn't pretend everything was okay, "Charlie, I don't think this can work. I don't think I can deal with your lifestyle. It's too much for me and I've got an eleven-year-old daughter! I'll never be part of anything that could place her in danger. I'm sorry. I'm not strong enough! I like you, a lot, but I don't know how we work this out and I don't want to get hurt. It's better we end things now. I don't want to fall in love and then have my heart broken. Its best we just let it go. I'm so sorry!"

This wasn't what Charlie expected or wanted to hear, " I need to see you, hold you, talk to you! Can't we talk about it in person?"

She tried to be strong, "Charlie, you're not listening. It can't work! I can't be in a relationship with a spy who has no idea where he's going to be tomorrow or what he's going to be doing or what danger lies around the next corner. You're at their beck and call. I can't live in fear of phone calls in the middle of the night telling me my husband has been killed in some subversive plot. I can't, Charlie, I won't! I can't live like that!"

"So that's it! It's over! I really think we have a future."

"A future! Call me Charlie after you've quit your job,

for good, with no regrets. Above all, do it for your boys! They need their father. I'm sorry Charlie. I'm so sorry. I've got to go. Goodbye."

Tears rolled down her cheeks as the emotions overwhelmed her. Her routine, often boring life had turned from a roller coaster ride into a nightmare. She'd become a nervous wreck. Leonard Rosen, Isaac Stone, The Kennedy Assassination, 9/11, a 3rd something, the NSA, a spy she could love but couldn't. It was overwhelming! The tears continued joined by shaking and another headache—something she never got before Isaac died. Poor Ernie didn't know what to do except lick the tears from her face.

She couldn't move for a half hour. Numb, exhausted and with a splitting headache there was no stopping the what-ifs. It wasn't in her DNA. Her mind kept spinning. She wanted to drop everything connected to Isaac Stone but she just couldn't.

Now she knew when and how long he was with the NSA. She also knew he went to MIT and had ongoing problems with his bosses at the NSA. Why would Charlie throw out this information if he was part of the puzzle? It didn't make any sense. She was about to call Howie when she heard Ernie's bark. Seconds later Isabella came running into the apartment and gave her mom a big hug. Ernie, not to be left out, jumped up and hugged them with his two front paws. Then Isabella pulled her new iPhone out of her pocket and called her dad.

"I'm inside. Mom's here. Thanks for all the clothes and my new phone, Daddy, je t'aime!"

"I love you, too, Isabella. Say hello to your mom. Talk to you during the week."

Checking out her daughter's new phone she tried to disguise her misery. "Wow, you really scored! Your dad mentioned he wanted to get you a phone. Did he talk to you about some ground rules?"

"No, what kind of rules?"

"Figures he'd leave that for me. Let's talk about it later. Look at Ernie; he sure missed you. Will you please take him for a walk and talk to him about his snoring.

"Wait, your face is all red, have you been crying? What's wrong?"

"Oh, just typical girl stuff. I got a little emotional after Charlie and I talked on the phone. I'll be okay. Sometimes things get complicated. That's all. Thanks for looking out for your mom. I love you."

"Je t'aime."

While Isabella took Ernie for his walk, Jan called Howie. "Howie, Charlie called. He told me he ran into somebody who knew Leonard—I mean Isaac. He found out Isaac started with the NSA in the summer of 1963 and worked there until 2011. And, Isaac went to MIT when he was sixteen for a year before he went to work for the NSA. Apparently, Isaac had ongoing issues with the hierarchy at the NSA and their politics. Does it make sense Charlie would tell me all this if he was the person sending the emails?"

"I don't know. What I do know is that you need to be careful and don't get too attached to this guy."

"Don't worry, I've already taken care of that."

"Good. Oh, the FBI is coming to the office tomorrow and then needs to secure your apartment. Where you calling me from now?"

"Shit, I didn't think. I'll talk to you later. I hear Bella and Ernie running up the stairs. Bye."

Isabella was anxious to show off her new clothes and her mom was a more than willing audience for a fashion show and the welcome change of mood. Moments like this kept reminding Jan how quickly Isabella was growing up. She was becoming a teenager, now with a cell phone. It was a welcome diversion to spend time focusing on her daughter rather than all the craziness in her life.

"Sweetie, are you hungry?"

"No, we had a big lunch. What about my phone?

What rules?"

"They're not really rules. Let's call it common sense. Like no texting in class, or late at night. And, you have to turn your phone off when we're eating or at a movie and before you go to bed."

"But you don't do those things. You're still bummed out about Charlie. I understand."

"Isabella, sometimes you…"

Pieces of the puzzle were coming together but the last email threw a monkey wrench into everything. It didn't make sense but it had to if Isaac sent it. Didn't it? Charlie couldn't be sending the emails, could he? If so why give her new info about Isaac? Plus, he changed to a different phone and constantly warned her about who they were dealing with and precautions they needed to take. It seemed more likely others were tracking them, not Charlie.

Two impossible puzzles: Isaac Stone and Charlie. Was there a connection between them? Overwhelmed with confusion, Jan turned to more immediate concerns. "Isabella, what are you doing?"

"I'm playing with my phone. It's much simpler than yours. Everything makes sense. Now I see why Papa Lenny loved Apple."

"Well I'm glad you've got it figured out. I've had the

same phone for three years and I still have trouble with it. Maybe I need an iPhone."

"Oui, oui!"

"Bless your dad. He loves to spoil you. You scored Sweetie!"

"You know I can get Dad to buy me almost anything. I think it eases his guilt."

Yet again, her daughter was very perceptive, "I hope you haven't said that to him."

"Please, why would I take away all his fun? When are you going to see Charlie? I like the two of you together."

"Isabella, sometimes I think you're twenty-one, not eleven. Let's take Ernie for a nice long walk."

"Nous allons toujours prendre soin les uns des autres."

Her French was getting better but not that good, "Translation please."

"We'll always take care of each other."

Jan couldn't stop the tears as she hugged her daughter and whispered in her ear, Oh, Bella, I love you so!"

After eating about half of her salad Isabella retreated to her room and her new iPhone giving Jan a chance to relax and reflect. She forced herself to stay off her computer and instead turned on 60 Minutes to find, eerily, a segment on the NSA. The story reinforced everything she'd discovered and detailed the secrecy of this spy enterprise. Emphasis was placed on their hierarchy, lack of oversight and of course, Snowden. The point was well made how ineffective congressional oversight has proven in dealing with all our intelligence agencies.

Tired, she went into her daughter's room to get Ernie, "Isabella, that's enough on your phone. I'm going to take Ernie out and then I think I'm ready for bed. You'd better get ready, too."

"Are you okay? You haven't seemed yourself lately. Is it Charlie?"

"God, you know me so well. Men and relationships can be difficult. It's something for you to look forward to."

31

Physically exhausted, she couldn't escape her splitting headache. She tossed and turned for hours finally getting to sleep slightly past 2:00. Morning came much too soon. Then she remembered the FBI—today! The FBI, what the hell has happened to her life?

"Bella, is Sandy's Mom picking you up from school?"

"I think so but I'll call you."

"Perfect, now you can call me. That's so cool! Come on Ernie, let's drop Isabella off and go to work."

Normally the safest of drivers, the speedometer hit 60 rushing to the office. Of course, Howie was on the phone, but motioned her to sit down as he waved a biscuit at Ernie. Before he was off the phone she placed an Isaac cheat sheet in front of him.

Isaac Stone (aka: Leonard Rosen)
Born—Cleveland, Ohio, Feb. 6th, 1945
16 yrs. old— MIT
NSA 1963—2011 (48 years)
2011 until his death (lived next door)
72 yrs. old (died)
Passions—Computers, Grateful Dead, Cleveland Indians, John Kennedy, French language, Spielberg movies
Events—Kennedy assassination, 9/11, 3...???

Howie quickly scanned the page as he ended his call, "What's this?"

"It's what we know about Isaac Stone."

"You've become quite the detective. I hope you're keeping that journal. Can you make me a copy of this?

Oh, the FBI is going to be here at 10:00. They're going to scan our office for bugs and check our computers. Then they'll do the same at your apartment."

"I'll have to go home to let them in."

"You really don't need to go. They can let themselves in."

Shaking her head, she wasn't going for it, "No, no way! The FBI isn't going to be snooping around my place without me! Why don't you come over, too?"

"In case you didn't notice I've got a newspaper to run."

She couldn't resist raising her troubling question, "Howie, it doesn't make sense to think Charlie's part of this. Why would he tell me new information? What would that accomplish? And, he's always warning me about being safe and uses a different phone to call me. Why would he do all that if he was somehow complicit?"

Howie quickly shot back the obvious answer, "The exact reasons why you don't think he's involved are the reason why he could be involved. That's basic Spy 101."

"You don't think one of your contacts could be leaking any of this. Do you?"

Defiantly, Howie left no doubt how sure he was of his guys, "I trust those guys with my life."

"That's what I assumed but I needed your assurance.

I'm stuck on the latest clue. Is #3 something that's happened or something that's yet to occur? I don't know where to go with this clue. I wanted to get on my computer but I assume I can't use it until after the FBI gives us a clean bill of health."

"You assume correctly. Let the new clue settle. You'll figure it out. Oh, the FBI checked your flip phone or whatever you call it. I gave them our mobile phone numbers. They called me earlier to say they're all clean."

"But, what about email. I need to check my email."

"Get it off your phone."

"That's such a pain and it's not a flip phone; it's a Blackberry. I like the keypad."

"Whatever."

Back in her office, CLICK!

Jan, I understand your concern. I justify the demands of my job and the costs to my personal life by service to my country. But I'm tired of disappointing my boys and the strain it puts on my life. I've thought of quitting many times but am always sucked back in. Now I have you, us to think about. Can we at least talk? Please. I miss you. Your Cowboy

She re-read the email but before she could think about

how, or if, to respond, two obvious FBI agents walked into the office with large metal briefcases. Naturally, Ernie was there to greet them. After Howie introduced himself he gathered the rest of the Star-News crew and politely told them to get lost for an hour.

The agents had small, innocuous, rectangular objects that plugged into the ports of the computers. Then they scanned all the offices with devices that looked like metal lint removers, plugged a meter into every wall socket, inserted a device into the phone outlets and another device into each of their phones. Finally, they turned on the computers and ran some type of software that took about fifteen minutes. The results: a clean bill of health, nothing had been compromised.

The agents met Jan and Ernie at her apartment and followed the same protocol deployed at the Star-News. The results were identical: a clean bill of health including Isabella's Mac Book. After thanking the two polite men, Jan returned to the office.

"Well, Howie, everything looks secure. I'm not sure whether that's good or bad news."

"Why, do you think that points the finger at your spy?"

"I don't want to think so, but I don't know. I'm totally confused. I'm more frustrated than I've ever been in my life! What do you make of everything? What do you think?"

Shaking his head and pulling his glasses halfway down his nose Howie displayed his frustration, "I've been mixed up with some crazy stories before but nothing like this. It feels like we're characters in a suspense novel or actors in a movie. Only we don't know what the hell we're up against or the ending."

"I know. When I add up everything nothing makes sense and I have no clue where we're going or how it will end."

"I have no fuckin idea— either! None! I called my Pftizer and my Barker again and gave them the Stone bio. Let's see if they turn up anything."

"I still don't know what to do with Charlie. I haven't told him about the latest clue. Suggestions?"

"Hold off until my guys check him out—again."

"I'll try to wait but..."

"No buts and please wrap up the doughnut robbery story."

"How could I forget that story. What a relief Sheriff Mills nailed the guy and got a confession. All of Raleigh and its doughnuts are safe again!"

32

Finishing the doughnut story took all of thirty minutes and Jan quickly directed her attention back to Isaac Stone. Out of desperation she searched for Isaac Stone, born Feb. 6, 1945 in Cleveland, Ohio, but ran into a dead end. She needed his mother or father's name or the hospital where he was born. A search of the MIT's website for Isaac Stone was no help and MIT's very sophisticated social media site also turned up nothing.

Shifting gears she discovered a Celebrated MIT Alumni website specifically recognizing noted MIT alumni. Bingo! There she found Richard W. Schneider. Hoping this was the man in the photo with Isaac she dug deeper and called in Wikipedia.

Their entry for Richard W. Schneider was fascinating with far too many common threads between Isaac Stone and Richard Schneider to be coincidental. Unfortunately, Schneider died in 1997.

A New York native, Schneider earned his B.S. in mathematics from Ohio State University in 1940 at the age of

19. He then served in the U.S. Navy as a signal/radar officer on the U.S.S. Enterprise, an aircraft carrier that was a leading fixture in the Pacific during World War II. He subsequently earned his M.S. degree from Ohio State in 1947 and his Ph.D. from MIT in 1950.

Schneider joined the faculty at MIT in 1951. He played a major role in the revisions of the mathematics departments graduate programs. He retired in 1992, but remained active as an emeritus professor, teaching mathematical information theory and algorithmic problem solving.

Schneider made important contributions in computational theory, algorithmic equations and computer coding. As an outgrowth of his work on mathematical properties, Schneider co-developed a program for the disparate folding of information. Schneider's accomplishments earned him numerous awards and honors and he is remembered as both a mathematical and computer genius.

Richard Schneider died in 1997 after a two-year battle with cancer. He is survived by his wife, Ruth Schneider, of Akron, Ohio, and their two children, Marvin Schneider, and Rose Schneider Milnick.

Amazingly, Schneider never filed for a patent or copyright always asserting his efforts be open to anyone. His work and passion were teaching, research and his students. His country reaped the benefits of his efforts.

It all made sense. Pieces of Isaac's life were coming together. Could following the Schneider trail help unravel the Isaac mystery? Jan was about to find out but first she had to tell Howie. As usual, she started talking before she entered his office, "Howie, I think I've finally come up with something tangible. I discovered Isaac's mentor at MIT. Isaac had a photo of the two of them on his wall next to Kennedy and Jerry Garcia."

"How the hell did you come up with that?"

"I searched a bunch of MIT sites and found a list of well-known alumni. I recognized one name, Richard W. Schneider from the inscription on the photo Isaac had on his wall. It fits, but Schneider died in 1997. I don't know if his wife is still alive but he has two children. I can't wait to call them."

"Don't get too excited. The MIT connection was fifty years ago. The kids might not have been born. Your best bet is the wife, if she's still alive. Or maybe MIT has something that connects this Schneider with Stone."

"I haven't had any luck trying to find a birth certificate for Isaac. I need the Mother and Father's name and a hospital would help, too."

"I think I can help you with that. My Barker, FBI, should be able to figure that one out. They can access info we can't. I'll call him."

"That's great. When?"

"My God woman you just told me about this Schneider connection. I'll call my Lou but see what else you can dig up. Have you noticed how Ernie's so happy and relaxed here with me. Guess he's a good judge of character after all."

"Sure Howie, just don't get him fat from all those humongous biscuits you keep feeding him." Back in her office, the Sheriff's envelope on top of her desk had to be a copy of the Leonard Rosen death certificate. There was a name, date, time, location, cause of death (natural), and address of deceased. There was no doctor's name, no social security #, no Father or Mother's name, no occupation, no next of kin. Nothing new, but what did she expect? After all, Leonard Rosen wasn't his real name.

The rush she felt while uncovering the MIT connection between Isaac Stone and Richard Schneider soon dissipated realizing it was a total shot-in-the-dark. Her ringing phone was a welcome distraction.

"Bonjour."

"Hi sweetie. Is Sandy's Mom picking you up?"

"Oui, oui. We're going to the office store to get poster

board for our next project. You're going to pick me up at Sandy's at 5:00, right?"

"I will. See you then."

Burned out, she still got back on her computer. Then, one word turned frustration into hope: Facebook, and her best shot, Schneider's daughter, Rose Schneider Milnick. And, there she was and her brother Marvin, too! Amazing people don't use the privacy settings. Within five minutes she was loaded with enough information to hopefully locate Rose and Marvin. Unfortunately, the only evidence of Richard, and his wife Ruth, appeared to be from a few old family photos.

Now what? What premise should she use to approach Schneider's children, Rose and Marvin? Why is she contacting them and what's she looking for? Her paranoia had overcome her judgment. Just tell them the truth. Isaac Stone, her neighbor, recently passed away and he had a photo of their dad and him on his wall. Since she couldn't locate any relatives or friends of Isaac she wondered if they knew him or had ever heard their dad talk about him. But, the Schneider's would have to wait till tomorrow. It was time to pick up Isabella.

"Bonjour. Guess who we're studying now? President Kennedy! I'm so excited. Miss Simpson asked me to speak to the class about him because she remembered our project."

"That's great! What did you say?"

"I said the people loved him, he was young and handsome and had a beautiful wife, Jackie and he represented hope for the future."

"That's perfect. Did you remember things Papa Lenny told you?"

"Oui, and the more I find out the more I see why Papa Lenny loved him. We saw a bunch of photos of him and Jackie and their kids on the big video screen. My favorite was the one with his little boy under his desk."

"That's mine, too! His son was nicknamed John-John. That's one of the most famous photographs in history. Tragically, he was killed in a private plane crash in the late '90s."

"Do you think things would be different if President Kennedy had lived?"

"Bella, that's a question people have been trying to answer for more than fifty years. Sadly, we'll never know."

33

Passing FBI scrutiny gave Jan a sense of security walking into her apartment. She could now talk on the phone and use her computer without wondering who might be listening. Dinner was the furthest thing from her mind but she always worried Isabella didn't eat enough, "How about mac and cheese for dinner?"

"Parfait!"

"I'll call you when it's ready."

While the water boiled, she turned on her computer to find another email from Charlie.

Jan, I can't stop thinking about you. I need to talk to you in person. I've also got more information to share. Please call or email me. Charlie

What other information was he talking about? She didn't like how he dangled the information carrot to entice her. She'd been so preoccupied today she hadn't had much time to think about him. She did know there were two questions she needed answered. First, was Charlie spying on her? Her gut said no but she wasn't sure. The second question was more problematic. Could she and Charlie have a healthy long term relationship if he stayed a spy?

"Mom, the water's boiling over!"

"Thanks, I was reading an email. Come on, let's eat. I'll mix in the cheese. Here, is that enough for you?"

"That's plenty, why do you worry about me eating? I'm not skinny, am I?"

"No, of course not. You're perfect! I'm sorry, it's a Mother's prerogative."

"What about Charlie?"

"I'm not sure. I just don't know. We'll see."

"It's time you found a husband. You're smart, and beautiful and fun. Maybe you're looking for someone perfect who doesn't exist."

"Okay. Is that from Dr. Phil or the Billion Dollar Matchmaker?"

"No, why do you think things I say come from TV? The girls were talking about it at lunch last week."

"Excuse me! Let's eat. Then you can get to your homework."

While Isabella supposedly did her homework, but actually played on her iPhone, Jan searched for Rose Schneider Milnick's phone number. Thanks to the wealth of online resources, it was relatively easy to find. She'd call tomorrow from the office.

Then her thoughts turned to Charlie. It was one thing to say it was over but far different to say her feelings towards him were gone. She was torn. After going through different scenarios, she decided the first answer she needed had to come from Charlie. If he couldn't or wouldn't answer that question truthfully and decisively, they obviously had no relationship—no future. "Charlie, are you spying on me?"

She needed to look him directly in the eyes, read his facial expression, hold his hand. Spy or no spy she felt she'd be able to tell if he was lying. She carefully crafted her email wondering if she was being a naive fool.

Charlie

I'm sure you can understand my reluctance to continue our relationship. We have great chemistry and a wonderful connection, but I just don't think our lifestyles are compatible. I understand why you're drawn to your job and you do a great service for our country. However, it would seem to make a relationship, at least the kind I want, impossible. I'm so frustrated and confused but I have a few questions I need to ask you in person. I'd also like to hear about your other information. Isabella's

going to be with her dad Wednesday night. Schedule permitting why don't you drive down
   Jan

As she clicked "send" she wondered if the email was "too cold" and what type of response she'd get from Charlie? In less than a minute she received her answer.

Can't talk now but Wed night @ 6:00 works. Can't wait to see you! C

She couldn't help but second guess herself. Everything in her life was chaotic, almost bizarre. She had no alternative but to trust her rattled instincts. She was mentally and physically exhausted and after Ernie's walk crawled into bed hoping for the good night's sleep she so desperately needed.

34

So much for good intentions. She tossed and turned most of the night. How could anyone function on two hours of sleep? Throwing on sweats she made sure Isabella was up then grabbed Ernie's leash for his morning walk. Not surprisingly the FOR RENT sign was still in front of her apartment building.

Anxious to get to the office and call Schneider's daughter she rushed Isabella out the door without even mentioning breakfast. "Let's go Bella. I need to get to the office. It's my day to pick you up from school, Sandy—too."

"Am I going to Dad's tomorrow night?"

"As far as I know, why?"

"Dad said he would help me get a special ringtone for my phone if it's okay with you."

"Sure, you and your dad work it out."

"Great! See you after school. Au revoir Ernie!

As usual, Ernie's entrance drew a much warmer welcome as they walked into the Star-News. Howie was drinking his coffee and reading the NY Times. "Good morning Howie. I've got a phone number for Schneider's daughter. Found her on Facebook with lots of photos and info. Her brother's still around, too. No mention of her mom, though."

"Well that's a start—nothing to lose. Where does she live?"

"A small town outside Akron, OH. I also want to tell you I've decided to see Charlie tomorrow night. He's driving down. I've got important questions to ask and need to do it in person. I hope I'm not being a naive fool."

"Just don't think you can read him or change him. Come on, he's a spy, he lies for a living. But, after considering everything I don't think he's spying on you. It doesn't add up to me, either. The relationship thing is a different animal. It's never going to work. Not with a spy—impossible. If he wants to find another job, I'll be the first in line to say congratulations."

"That's fair. Thanks, Howie. I'll let you know what I find out from Schneider's daughter."

"I know you want to call this woman in Akron but please finish your stories for the paper first, and aren't you forgetting something. Where's my Ernie?"

"Wave one of those super-sized biscuits and whistle—I'm sure he'll come running."

As has been the case since Isaac's death, her Star-News assignments were finished in a few hours. Now it was time to call Rose Schneider Milnick.

"Hello."

"Hi, Mrs. Milnick."

"Yes, who's this?"

"My name's Jan Cooper and I live in Raleigh, IL, a small town south of Chicago. Mrs. Milnick, I found you on Facebook and I hope you can help me. Was your father Richard Schneider, the MIT professor?"

Not sure what to expect, Jan got the answer she needed.

"Yes, why, why do you ask?"

"Well, for the past six years I've lived next door to a retired computer genius who I believe was a student of your dads many years ago. My neighbor recently passed away without any known relatives or friends. On a wall in his apartment was a photo of him with a man who I believe was your father. I'm trying to track down any information I can about my neighbor. Is your mother still alive?"

"Oh no, she passed years ago. Who was your neighbor?"

"His name was Isaac Stone. As far as I can tell he went to MIT for a year back in the early 60's and then went to work for the NSA."

"Gee, I wasn't born until 1958. Isaac Stone doesn't ring a bell, but my Dad taught for more than forty years and there were so many students. Is there anything to set this Isaac Stone apart?"

"Only that I think he was the youngest information analyst ever hired by the NSA and that he went to MIT at sixteen."

"That doesn't help much. Most of my dad's students were very bright. I'd like to help you but I don't know how."

"What about your brother Marvin, do you think he might remember anything?"

"No, I doubt he'll be able to help. I'm the family historian and keep all the family records. Do you have the photo of your neighbor with my dad? Can you scan it and email it to me?"

"Everything was put in storage by the VA but I'll try to get it, scan it and email it to you."

"My garage is full of alphabetized boxes of my dad's old papers and stuff. It's well organized. I'll check the S's and see if there's a Stone. I've got your number and I'll give you a call back and text you my email address."

"Thanks Mrs. Milnick. I appreciate all your help. You've been very kind."

"Please call me Rose. I'm glad to help. My dad lived for his students. He'd want to help."

"Thanks again and please call me Jan. I look forward to talking with you soon. Bye."

The photograph, where's the photograph of Isaac and Schneider? The movers must have taken it with everything else from Isaac's apartment and supposedly put it in storage. She wondered if there was any way to get the photo back. Charlie was her only hope. She decided the best strategy was to be somewhat devious and ask for all three photos—Kennedy, Jerry Garcia and Isaac and Schneider. This should remove any focus on what she wanted. She could also use the excuse she wanted the photos for Isabella.

Charlie, we have a favor to ask. On the wall above Isaac's computer were three photographs. They were of John Kennedy, Jerry Garcia and a photograph of computer guy with Isaac. Isabella has asked if we could get those photos? She wants to hang them on her bedroom wall. If you have access could you bring them with you tomorrow? Thanks, Jan

Hopefully, Charlie won't find her email a strange request and he has access to Isaac's possessions. Ernie was lying next to Howie's desk as she entered his office.

"I talked to Schneider's daughter. She was very sweet. Her mom's been dead for years and she didn't think her brother would be able to help. The good news is she has all her dad's old records and files in her garage—alphabetized in boxes. The bad news is she didn't remember the name Isaac Stone. I'm trying to get the photo of her dad and Isaac from Charlie. If I can, I'll scan it and email her a copy. In the meantime, she's going to look through her dad's stuff. We can only hope she turns up something."

"Good work, Sherlock. I hope you gave Charlie a good reason for wanting the photo."

"Not to single out one photo, I asked for all three and told him Isabella wants to hang them in her bedroom which I'm sure she'd want to do."

"I like it. The more we learn about Stone the closer we are to solving this. You're keeping a record of all this. Right?"

"Yes, boss. You'll get your story. How many biscuits did you have to give him this morning?"

"Biscuits, who? What are you talking about? Oh, Ernie's down there, didn't notice him."

"Sure Howie." Returning to her office an email from Charlie was waiting.

Not sure I can get access to storage locker but I'll try. Look forward to seeing you tomorrow. C

At least it wasn't a no. Tomorrow night would tell her a lot about Charlie, and hopefully Isaac.

35

Jan spent the rest of the day planning feature articles for October and the holiday season and choosing which syndicated columns to run. For once, mundane work was a welcome relief. Through lunch and well into the afternoon she enjoyed being almost hypnotized by routine work. Her phone call brought her back to her new reality.

"Hi Jan, this is Sheriff Mills."

"Hi Sheriff. Thanks for the death certificate."

"You're welcome, but that's not why I'm calling. I was at the local Rotary lunch yesterday and ran into Doc Harmon. Low and behold, out of nowhere he tells me he's sorry to hear about Leonard Rosen. Turns out he treated him for prostate cancer. I didn't pursue Rosen's medical history but thought you'd like to know."

"Thanks Sheriff. I'm glad you called. That might help explain things."

Prostate cancer. How bad was it? Why wasn't it listed as the cause of death? Hopefully Doctor Harmon could provide some answers. "Doctor Harmon please, this is Jan Cooper."

"Are you a patient?"

"No, Aronson's my doctor but I know Doctor Harmon."

"Let me see if he's available."

"Hi Jan, it's been a long time."

"It has. Doctor Harmon, as you know, our neighbor and good friend, Leonard Rosen recently passed away. In fact, my daughter Isabella and I found him hunched over on a bench at the park. I know he hadn't been the picture of good health but I never knew he was that sick. He didn't have any relatives as far as we can tell. My daughter was very close to Leonard and I promised her I'd try to find out why he died. Sheriff Mills told me you'd been treating Leonard. Did he die from prostate cancer?"

"I didn't see the body after he passed and hadn't seen him for probably three months. The cancer was getting worse but I can't say it caused his death. Leonard had problems: high blood pressure, bad cholesterol, occasionally an irregular heartbeat and even throw in a little gout from time to time. I prescribed him a half-dozen different medications. I hope that helps and gives Isabella some closure. By the way, thanks to you we've got a new member of our family."

"Really, I didn't know you and Mary had another

child."

"No, no, four's plenty, but we rescued a two-year-old lab. We all love him. He looks a little like your Ralph."

"Thanks Doc, but I'm sure you mean my Ernie. I'll pass the compliment on to him."

"Of course, it's Ernie. I'm bad with names but could never forget that sweet face. Stop by and say hello the next time you're in to see Doctor Aronson."

"I will, and thanks for your help."

As she put down her phone she wasn't sure whether Dr. Harmon's information was helpful or not. Isaac had numerous health problems and the prostate cancer may or may not be the cause of death.

Her phone ring was a welcome call from her daughter, "Hi Bella."

"Bonjour, I'm at Sandy's. We're practicing putting on our make-up."

"Thanks for calling, sweetie. Make sure you wash your face thoroughly before you come home. You know how I feel about make-up on you. I'll pick you up in twenty minutes. Bye."

Because Howie was talking on his phone as she left the office she didn't have a chance to tell him about her conversation with Dr. Harmon, but it could wait till to-morrow. It was time to pick up her daughter.

"How was school?"

"Fun! I like the 6th grade."

"Good, I did too! Bella, I spoke with Dr. Harmon today. I don't know if you remember him. He's in the same office as Dr. Aronson. Anyway, he was the doctor who was treating Papa Lenny. He told me Papa Lenny had health issues including a common type of cancer. I wanted to tell you."

"Merci. I miss Papa Lenny."

"I know Bella, I do to."

After taking Ernie for his late afternoon walk the Cooper's retreated to their computers. Jan was almost relieved she had no email. She did have a pile of snail mail—mostly junk. There were a few bills and a postcard reminder that Ernie was due for his yearly physical. While their turkey meatloaf, potatoes and steamed vegetables finished cooking Jan brought her journal up to speed. Howie will be happy.

"Bella, dinner's ready."

"Be right there."

"I hope you like the meatloaf."

"Tres savoureux!"

"Translation, please!"

"Very tasty."

"Charlie's driving down tomorrow for dinner if his

work doesn't get in the way."

"I know you like him even if he does live in Chicago. Why would work get in the way?"

"Well, he gets assignments all over the country."

"Mom, I'm okay with him staying the night. You need some action. I'll keep my door closed."

"I appreciate your candor and I'm glad you approve but we'll have to wait and see. Okay?"

"You're blushing, aren't you?"

"I think it's the meatloaf. It's a little too spicy."

36

Up before her alarm—again, she threw on her sweats, whistled for Ernie, and whispered to Isabella it was time to get up. Returning to her apartment after Ernie's dance around his favorite tree, she jumped into the shower. Without having to be reminded, Isabella had her little square backpack suitcase all packed for her weekly visit to Dad's.

"I like that outfit on you. Your father must have bought that for you."

"I picked it out but he bought it. I showed you last

week, remember?"

"Oh, that's right, you did. Well, you have fun tonight and call me later, okay?"

"Sure."

Since it was Jan's turn to bring in the morning snacks she stopped for doughnuts on the way to the office. As she ordered the usual dozen mixed and dozen glazed she was amused to see her story of the robbery taped to the donut case.

Howie, as usual, was in the office before her. Ernie ran ahead anticipating his biscuit. "Howie, yesterday I didn't get a chance to tell you about my conversation with Dr. Harmon. Sheriff Mills told me, by accident, he discovered Dr. Harmon was Isaac's doctor. Apparently, Isaac had a bunch of health issues including prostate cancer and high blood pressure. He also had high choles-terol and gout. He was taking a cocktail of pills, but Dr. Harmon wasn't sure of the cause of death."

"That's interesting but not sure what it means unless you're suggesting this was a homicide?"

"You said it—not me! I don't even want to go there! God, Howie, it can't be, can it? I can't handle that!"

"There's one other possibility but it's not pleasant. Perhaps Isaac was really sick or felt he was dying. What if he took his own life?"

"Oh great. Two possibilities! Murder or suicide!"

"Don't jump to any conclusions! Since the NSA picked up his body we'll never know. Hopefully your spy will have photographs for you tonight. He's still coming, isn't he?"

"Last I heard he's coming but he's disappointed me before. Oh, I got caught up with work yesterday."

"Good, then keep your journal up to date."

"Oui!"

"What happened to yes. English only in this office—please."

"Sorry, Isabella's influence. You know how she loves French."

Jan was more than bothered by Howie's suggestion of possibly homicide or suicide. She couldn't and wouldn't go there. It was way too conspiratorial with too many repercussions—all bad.

Because she had no idea how to solve Isaac's latest clue she went back to the MIT Alumni website. Anything to take her mind off Charlie or how Isaac might have died. Twenty minutes of search produced nothing but confusion. Realizing her dilemma she found an Information number for MIT.

After being passed among three phone voices she realized whatever she was trying to accomplish wasn't going to happen. She needed the name of someone of authority at MIT if she was going to get anywhere. Hopefully Howie could help but he was out of the office at another one of his so-called community luncheons.

"Ernie, where have you been? You just made me think of something I need to do right now. I'm calling your vet to set up your annual check-up. I bet you're excited to see all your friends."

The gym rather than lunch was enticing. Forty minutes on the elliptical and twenty minutes of weights did the trick. She felt invigorated, cleared her head and worked up a good sweat. She missed her workouts and needed to get back to the gym more often.

A hundred miles to the north, Charlie searched through a storage locker in a nondescript unmarked warehouse. Forty legal sized boxes lined one wall and they were too small to hold the photographs. Furniture filled the back and middle part of the 12x30' locker. Then braced between a mattress and boxes of bedding Charlie found the three bubble wrapped frames. Photographs secure in the rented SUV, he headed south slightly before 4:00.

37

Jan waited patiently for Howie to finish his call. She needed help with MIT before she left the office. "I tried to get some info on Schneider from MIT. Talk about a wild goose chase. I was wondering if you might know anyone who could help?"

"MIT, let me think." Then a big smile consumed his face, "I once dated a gal who was a Dean of something there. Amy, yes Amy! Very bright gal with huge boobs. Let me work on it."

"You dated her and she'll still talk to you. Will wonders never cease."

"Listen—you. Never mind, you've got your own problems. What time is your spy coming to town?"

"About 6:00. I'm nervous. There's lots riding on this!"

"Just don't mix sex with truth. Call me if you need anything. Understand?"

"Thanks Howie. Let's go Ernie."

Dinner at home seemed like a recipe for a good conversation. No distractions, not tonight. She picked up a couple of steaks, baked potatoes and asparagus plus she still had all the goodies from last week's cancellation. "Come on Ernie, we've got to get ready for your buddy Charlie."

What to wear was complicated. Too sexy and too tight didn't translate well for a serious conversation. She chose a thin black T-shirt and cotton khaki shorts. Then shifting from rather cool to hopefully steamy hot, she changed her sheets. The candles were in a cabinet, ready as needed. Although she had already taken a shower in the morning and one at the gym, she took a third. As she was drying off her phone rang. No Charlie, don't do it again, don't! She nervously looked at her phone screen and was ecstatic to see it was Isabella.

"Hi sweetie. Are you with your dad?"

"Oui, we're going out to eat and then Dad's going to help me with my phone. I hope you have a fun night and say hello to Char…"

"Thanks Bella but let's leave it at that for now. Say hello to your dad and I'll talk to you in the morning."

"Bonne chance."

Jan tried to stay busy while she waited for Charlie. First she brushed Ernie, a task normally done by Isabella. Then she organized her silverware drawer and recycled dozens of paper shopping bags she'd been saving for years for no reason. Finally, she just stood in front of her kitchen window, peering out between the curtains, waiting for him to arrive.

Even Ernie was confused by her behavior. To see what she was looking at he placed his two front paws on the kitchen counter and pushed the bottom of the curtain up with his nose.

And, there he was. Jan was not only excited about seeing him but couldn't wait to see what he pulled from the SUV. But all he had was a small gym like bag. That was it. In seconds her excitement turned to disappointment. No frames! No key to unlock the Schneider mystery! Then as if willed by a mystical power, Charlie stepped to the back of the rented SUV and opened the rear door. He had them! They were packed in bubble wrap. Sensing a small victory she couldn't contain her excitement and started to jump up and down like the cheerleader she once was! She yelled for Ernie and ran downstairs! Trying unsuccessfully to be cool she couldn't contain how happy she was to see him, "Hi Cowboy, need a hand?"

"Hi Jan, hi Ernie. God, I missed you! Can I get a big hug?"

Forgetting the reason Charlie was in Raleigh she wrapped her arms around the spy she wanted to love. "I missed you! Looks like Ernie did, too! What have you got?

"Just my toothbrush and a few things. Oh, I found the photographs you wanted for Isabella."

"That's great! Let's go upstairs."

As they walked upstairs she second guessed her questioning of Charlie's loyalty. After all he'd given no reason to doubt his integrity. Although he could be spying on her all his actions said it wasn't him. Her overriding question was whether it was possible for the two of them to have a relationship? As they walked into her apartment, the questions had to wait as they stood, hugged and kissed.

Feeling him getting aroused, Jan decided they'd better have their talk before it got any hotter. "God Charlie, it seems so long since I've seen you. So much has happened. I'm so glad you're here where I can see you, touch you and talk to you in person. Please Charlie, please sit. I've got to ask you something before we go any further."

Charlie sat down but held onto her. "Gee, you cut right to the chase. I know my job's a big obstacle to overcome and I've been thinking about it, a lot."

"No, Charlie, this question isn't about whether our relationship can survive your job. That comes later."

"Then what is it? What?"

"Charlie, I'm new to all this spy stuff. First Leonard dies and you ride into the picture with the NSA. Then cryptic emails, Leonard becomes Isaac with some type of connection to the Kennedy assassination and 9/11. Charlie this is too overwhelming for me. I don't know if I can keep my sanity and I worry about the danger. I'm a single Mom with an eleven-year-old Daughter. The first two emails were confusing enough but the third email was even more bizarre and very threatening because someone knew we discovered the real identity of Leonard Rosen. It's like someone is following everything we do. Charlie, give me your hands. Look me in the eyes and tell me you had nothing to do with any of this crazy shit."

As Charlie tightly held her hands he made his plea, "Is that what you think? That explains our conversations or lack of them. My sweet, sweet Jan. I came here tonight to tell you I'm falling in love with you. I'm not spying on you. You must believe me, I don't know any more than you do. I want you! I need you!"

And in just a minute her angst disappeared. She felt he was telling her the truth. Her deepest fear had almost been removed and the utter relief brought Jan to sobbing tears.

"Oh, Charlie. I'm so sorry to have questioned you but I'm so scared. I'm afraid of who we're dealing with. Isaac's Doctor didn't shed any light on why he died.

Charlie, could somebody have killed Isaac or could he have committed suicide?"

"Wow! I hope you don't think I had something to do with his death. Guess I'd worry, too. But you've got to believe me, I'm not involved. I'm as bewildered as you. Please bring me up to speed."

"I will. I'm sorry. Just hold me Charlie—please."

Charlie wrapped his arms around her and held tightly as she released all her pent-up emotions. Ernie, never to be ignored, pressed against them. He doesn't like it when I cry. He knows something's wrong. It's okay, boy."

As Ernie joined them on the couch she brought Charlie up to speed on her conversation with Doc Harmon, the whole MIT thing with Schneider and his daughter, the FBI screening and Isaac's latest clue. "Charlie, have you ever seen anything like this? Is this the kind of shit you deal with every day?"

"Absolutely not. I've seen some crazy scenarios but this is beyond anything I've ever seen. The emails have me confused. This last one brings its own confusion. Is #3 something that's already happened or something yet to happen? And, how did he know to sign it Isaac? How did he know when? That's almost beyond comprehension. The email sender must be Isaac before he died or someone else—now. Neither scenario makes a lot of sense because we have no idea what the motive might be. That's locked in the puzzle."

"But Charlie, if Isaac sent them, how would he know when we discovered his real name? That's what throws me."

"You're right on point but don't underestimate Isaac Stone. The people I spoke with told me he wasn't just the smartest person in the room; he was the smartest person in any room. It makes no sense to think someone would kill Stone, make it look like natural causes and then send you emails."

"Can you see why I'm a wreck? My quiet life's been turned upside down and inside out! I've tried my hardest to keep all this from Isabella. I can't, I won't put her in danger! Ironically, my relationship with you has given me some ground cover."

"Our relationship, let's get back to our relationship."

"We can talk about it later. Can we just go for a little walk? Will you hold me and kiss me like you did in Chicago?"

"That's a great idea. I'll grab Ernie's leash."

As they walked out the door she had to ask, "Charlie, are you really falling in love with me?"

Ironically, Charlie's answer came precisely as they passed Isaac's old apartment. "I think I've already fallen." Their kiss lasted until Ernie started to whine.

As in Chicago, a short walk took a long time. Ernie even grew tired of standing during their kissing breaks and laid down at their feet. Emotions took time and space to breathe.

Back in the apartment, Charlie washed up as Jan strategically positioned candles hoping to create some ambiance. Dinner seemed superfluous. Instead, they decided to share a bottle of wine, microwave popcorn and dig into a half-gallon of Mint Chocolate Chip. As they sat on the floor nibbling popcorn and sipping wine the conversation took an unavoidable turn.

"Charlie, is it possible for a spy to be in a healthy relationship? You've had experience and you must have friends."

Charlie didn't pull any punches, "You have every right to be concerned. It's difficult. Most unfortunately—fail. I know the odds are stacked against it."

"It's more than concern. It's a deal breaker. I'd go crazy worrying about you and then there's all the secrecy. Above all how would it affect the kids?"

"What if I quit?"

"What? Whoa Cowboy, not so fast! Don't quit for me! Don't put that responsibility on my shoulders! Don't do that! Quit for yourself and for your boys. They're the innocent victims of all this. They need their dad around for a long, long time!"

Charlie nodded, "Of course, you're right. What if I quit for all the right reasons?"

"Then, I could fall in love with you!"

Instinctively, they both knew their biggest issue had not been resolved. But now it was time to blow out the candles, put the melted ice cream in the fridge and savor each other.

Their passion was beyond sexual rising to a point of intimacy neither had felt in a long, long time. Jan felt totally satisfied, and more importantly, totally safe. Charlie felt understood, appreciated and excited—again and again! They half-dozed off for more than an hour when she realized Ernie still needed to go out. Charlie, ever in sync, found Ernie's leash.

Walking out the door and past #11 Jan whispered, "Charlie, I want the white picket fence. I want the family vacations each summer. I want to grow old, gracefully, with the person I'm meant to be with. I want it all, Charlie. Can we have that? Is it possible?"

"I hope so, Coop, I sure hope so. I love you!"

"Cowboy, I love you, too!"

38

Jan slept better than she had since Isaac passed. Charlie was still asleep next to her when she woke. She wasn't sure if it was Charlie or Ernie snoring but the whistling wind sound was soothing. With Charlie sleeping so peacefully next to her she couldn't help but wonder if he could let go of his job? Could this be the man she was destined to be with the rest of her life? Could they be in love after only a couple of weeks? Her life had become a quagmire of complex, impossible questions. She desperately needed more answers.

"Good morning Cowboy. How'd you sleep?"

"Good morning. I slept like a baby. Does Ernie snore?"

"That's funny, I wasn't sure who was snoring since you both do. Can I make you some coffee?"

"Please, just black."

"You're easy."

"Am I really?"

"Charlie, do you have to leave right away or can we talk?"

Assuming they must have already covered all the pressing topics Charlie readily agreed, "Sure, I've got a little time."

"Great! I'll fix breakfast. I've got bacon and eggs."

"Perfect. I'll take Ernie out."

As soon as Charlie and Ernie left Jan rushed to the bathroom to brush her teeth, comb her hair, wash her face and touch on just a hint of fragrance. Since they had just slept naked together she threw on nothing but fresh black panties and a pink t-shirt. She hadn't cooked breakfast for a man in ages. It felt wonderful!

"Boy, he sure likes that one tree."

"Yeah, he's a creature of habit but aren't we all. Why don't you give him a biscuit. They're in the cupboard next to the fridge."

"Here Ernie! Good boy! He's such a great dog."

Jan's ringing phone had to be her daughter. "Good morning Bella. How was your evening?"

"We had so much fun. I got a ringtone. I can't wait for you to hear it. Is he still…"

"Isabella, what did I tell you? We'll talk later. I'll pick you up."

"Bonjour."

"That must have been your daughter."

"Yes, that was my precocious eleven-year-old. Sometimes I think she's twenty. She's coaching me on relationships which is very interesting since she not quite into boys—yet."

"I know what you mean though with my boys it's all about sports and video games."

"Sit and let's eat."

"I love the smell of fresh coffee and bacon in the morning. I can't believe how incredible you look. Do you always look this hot when you wake-up?"

"How sweet! Guess they call it beauty sleep for a reason. Charlie, can we talk about Isaac?"

"Sure."

"Here, let me fill your cup. What's your take? Where's it going? What about 1, 2, 3 and listen. Any ideas?"

"We know Stone was brilliant. That's a given. It's possible he predicted the Kennedy assassination and 9/11 or at least saw things that led him to believe the events were going to happen. It's also very plausible that he's leading us on this path because he wants us to discover something else. Understand everything's changed since Snowden in 2013 and he wasn't even an NSA employee. He worked for Booz, Allen Hamilton, a sub-contractor. Believe me, what Snowden revealed is just the tip of the iceberg."

"That's comforting to know. How did things change

after Snowden released his bombshell?"

"I only know what I've personally seen. Security is much, much tighter. We're scrutinized, all the time. Isaac's lucky to have retired before Snowden came out. I have a theory."

"What? What is it? Tell me!"

"He knew you. He knew how you think, how you process information and what you'd do once you got the emails. He understood your perseverance, how your mind works, and your resourcefulness. Does that make sense? I really think they came from Isaac. It's almost as if he chose you."

"Chose me? Chose me for what? I don't follow. You said he'd never jeopardize us, didn't you?"

"I did and I still believe he never would but..."

"I hate buts, Charlie. Why did he die? You don't think he was murdered?"

"Murdered, absolutely not! Not the NSA's style. If they wanted him dead, he would have just disappeared one day. How he died and why he died is troubling, but I'd be very surprised if it was murder."

"Why do you think the emails are so cryptic? If he trusts me why didn't he just tell me? Why wait until he's dead? What's the big secret? Do you think they'll be more?"

"Yes, I definitely think they'll be more. He was probably cryptic because he knew he had to be since the NSA was monitoring him and he didn't want to leave a trail and endanger you and Isabella."

"Charlie, didn't you say your boss told you the Rosen case was closed? You thought that was odd, right?"

"Yes, but now I'm guessing it's because the NSA doesn't want anyone digging up any of Stone's old files. They might prove more than troublesome. Disaster is probably a better description and the last thing they want is another Snowden that's much, much worse."

"Will you come to the Star-News with me and talk with Howie? He's trying to help me solve this mess. He's got great sources. I think it would really help."

"Sure! When?"

"As soon as possible. I need help and insight from both of you. When I'm alone with my thoughts I seem to falsely prove my own theories and go in circles. I'll check his schedule and let you know."

Looking at his phone Charlie finished the last of his coffee, "Sorry, but I'm afraid I've got to go"

"Charlie, everything's moving so fast. I'm not used to this pace. I'm usually, make that always, much more cautious, more deliberate. Are we going too fast? Can we be in love this soon? We haven't even known each other for three weeks. Does it make sense for us to have a serious relationship while this Isaac jigsaw puzzle hangs over us?"

"Everything's not a function of time. I felt our chemistry and a strong connection to you that very first day. You're like this wonderful gift that's come into my life, and I love it. And I love you! We need to be very careful but I think we're stronger working together."

"Oh Charlie, sometimes you just melt my heart. Thanks for always being so patient with me. I love you."

39

Jan was relieved. Fifteen hours with Charlie couldn't have gone better. He not only answered both her questions but his answers were home runs. Not in her wildest dreams did she think the last thing she would say to Charlie this morning would be, "I love you."

It took all of two minutes for her to second guess herself. Would he really quit his job? Could they have fallen in love in a couple of weeks or was it lust and circumstances. Was she in love or did she just love the idea of finally being in love? Was he Mr. Right or Mr. Right-now?

"Come on Ernie, let's go to the office. Ernie, what do you think of your friend Charlie? I know you like him but do you like him for me?"

Entering the Star-News, Ernie ran right to Howie's office and what's become his morning bribe. As Howie gave Ernie a chicken flavored biscuit he quickly appraised Jan's evening by the big smile on her face, "Well, I don't have to ask you how your night went. Your face has that sex glow!"

"Good morning to you, too. My night couldn't have gone better. Thanks for asking. Let's go Ernie. I've got lots of work to do."

"Very funny! Both of you sit! You're not going anywhere and neither is he. Sit down and talk to me."

"Howie, I held his hands, looked in his eyes and asked him if he was spying on me. His answer was immediate, decisive and sincere. I totally believe him. I'm sure he's telling the truth. I don't think he knows anymore about Isaac than we do. Less actually since I had to tell him about Schneider and what we know about Isaac's health. I'm not being naive, I'm not. Really, I'm not."

"Need I remind you part of his job is lying effectively. He's had lots of practice but if you're positive."

"I'm sure. He also said he's going to quit his job. That would answer my other big question. Howie, he could be the one."

"Lord have mercy! Some hot sex after a couple of weeks and now you're ready to settle down, get married and paint that picket fence. It's a TV movie or at least a reality TV show. If you tell me you're going to Vegas over the weekend, I'll puke!"

"Not to Vegas but I did suggest the three of us get together to discuss Isaac. I think it'd help, don't you? You both have much more experience than me and approach from such different backgrounds. Does that make sense?"

"I can't argue with that assumption. Set it up. I assume you got your photo?"

"Yep, I almost forgot. It's in the hall. Let me get it. Here, look."

"Wow, is that Isaac? He's a young teenager. I can't quite make out the inscription. It looks like share your mind..."

"It all figures. The word 'share' is significant since Schneider apparently believed in sharing all the benefits of his brilliance passing up a fortune in royalties and patents. I'll reduce the photo and email it to his daughter. You never know."

40

"Hi Bella, hi Sandy. How's school?"

"C'est bonne. How was last night?"

"Let's talk about that later but first I've got a surprise for you."

"What? Tell me."

"Charlie found the three photos your Papa Lenny had on his wall and brought them for you. Do you remember them?"

"Oui. John Kennedy, Jerry Garcia and the computer guy with Papa."

"Exactly!"

As they pulled up to Sandy's house Isabella reminded her girlfriend, "Bye Sandy, remember what we talked about."

"For sure, girlfriend. Bye Ms. Cooper, bye Ernie."

"Bye Sandy. What's she supposed to remember, Bella?"

"You'll see later. It's a surprise."

"Hey, I hope you're hungry? I've got steaks and baked potatoes and asparagus and ice cream."

"Didn't you and Charlie eat? Mom, you're blushing."

"We had a fun night. Let's leave it at that. I'll take your stuff upstairs if you take Ernie for a walk. Then we can hang up the photos—if you want."

"Oui, oui. I can't wait to hear everything. Let's go Ernie."

Jan laughed, then almost choked, at the thought of a steak dinner with Isabella while discussing her sex life. Then she tried to prepare simple answers for the inevitable third degree sure to come from her eleven-year-old therapist.

"Bella, which photos do you want to hang."

"John Kennedy for sure and probably Jerry Garcia. I don't know about the other one."

"Why don't we hang up two for now?"

"Cool. Do you have nails?"

"You mean the picture hangers? Where's that song coming from? Is that the Grateful Dead?"

"Isn't it the coolest thing you've ever heard? Dad helped me download Truckin' for my ringtone."

"Oh my God! That's just great!"

"You're forgetting something."

"I put the potatoes in. What?"

"Charlie. Aren't we eating Charlie's dinner tonight? That's so rad. You skipped dinner and just...!"

"Isabella, please. Do we really need to have this conversation?"

"Oui—Oui—Oui!"

"Alright, but..."

"Mom, tell me everything! Where, how..."

"Oh, Isabella. Next thing you'll be asking for a video."

"You made a video. Let's watch it after dinner. I won't tell anyone, I promise."

"Isabella, stop it—right now. Where do you come up with those wild fantasies? I hate to disappoint you and your vivid imagination but there's no video. A video, come on Bella, I'm your mother."

It was hard enough keeping things from Charlie; keeping things from Isabella was impossible. She was relentless and extremely perceptive. She obviously inherited both from her mother. As they sat down to dinner Jan knew Isabella wanted more details about Charlie.

"I hope you're hungry Bella. Charlie wasn't hungry last night so we ate light. Okay, I know you're waiting for more details. I like him but I've been afraid his job will make it impossible to have a serious relationship because he travels so much and at the last minute. Last night he told me he's considering quitting his job. I don't know how serious he is, we'll see. You know he's an attorney like your dad. Remember, we've only known each other a few weeks. We'll see where things go. Take it slow. Relationships take time. There you go. Is that what you want to hear?"

"Not really. But you like him a lot, right?"

"Yes. You know he has two sons, Max and Harry. Max is twelve and Harry's 9. You should have fun with that."

" I think I already knew that. If he quits his job would he work in Chicago?"

"I don't know. Remember to thank him for your photos. I know he had to go to a lot of trouble to get them for you. Is that all you're going to eat?"

"I ate. Thanks for sharing. I know it's hard for you. One more thing. Is he a good kisser?"

"Isabella, enough, please. Here's ice cream. Ernie, it's your lucky day, have some steak."

The Truckin' ringtone couldn't have come at a better time and sent Isabella scurrying into her room for girl talk with one of her BFFs. Jan was relieved she got through the interrogation without having to lie while also keeping Isabella isolated from the Rosen/Stone mystery.

She recognized the #330 area code. It was Rose Milnick with good news. She found Isaac Stone amongst the S's. Turns out, he was one of her dad's favorite students and they developed an algorithmic problem solving formula that became the foundation of modern intelligence gathering. Like her father, Isaac wasn't motivated by money or material things and they just gave their program to the U.S. government.

"Rose, that's amazing! Your dad and Isaac actually worked together in the early 60's. Their research explains why Isaac was hired by the NSA. It makes sense. I can't thank you enough for helping me with this."

"You're most welcome, my dear. I think Dad would have saved a copy of their research paper. If I find it or anything else, I'll give you a call."

"Thanks so much Rose."

This appeared to be another piece of the Isaac puzzle but Jan wasn't sure how important because they already knew about MIT and the brilliance of Schneider and Isaac. This confirmed what they already knew.

As she started to catch up on her journal she couldn't help but be amazed at how her own process for connecting disparate bits of information had evolved. Did Isaac know this would happen? Was it part of his plan? Was she fulfilling his objective? Was it even remotely possible Isaac could have known this would happen? Just as she started to write she had to close her journal because Isabella and Ernie ran into the room, "Do you think you and Charlie are going to get married? Where would we live?"

"What are you talking about? Sit, you too, Ernie. Let's talk. We need to have a girl-to-girl talk about relationships. First there's chemistry, how much you're attracted to someone. Then there's the connection, how well you relate to one another, how you get along. These are the easy ones, but then there's compatibility. That's lifestyle, beliefs and goals. That's usually the deal breaker. You need all three C's for the relationship to work. Charlie and I have great chemistry, that's what you've seen. I think our connection's good—too. But, and it's a big but, our compatibility is still very much up in the air. That takes time to figure out. Does all that make sense?"

"That's pretty good. You should write a blog or advice column for the Star-News. What about sex. Aren't you going to talk about sex?"

"No, we'll save that discussion for another time. Understand I'm not getting married without you and I discussing it first. That's a promise."

"Am I too young to fall in love?"

"My eleven-year-old daughter. Is that a hypothetical question or a real-time question? Is there a boy you like at school?"

"Yuck, I'm just teasing you. The boys at school are so immature. I promise to let you know when I meet a boy

I really like."

"I love you, Bella. Now get ready for bed."

Ironically, explaining things to Isabella gave Jan better insight into her own questions, doubts and timeframe. Maybe she did need more time for her head to catch up with her heart. As she got ready for bed she couldn't help but wonder where Charlie was sleeping.

41

Trying to solve the Isaac mystery ranged from interesting to fascinating to bizarre to horrifying. The overriding question remains why and what? Jan knew more about Isaac, accepted his genius and realized he had a Kennedy connection and might have known about 9/11. But, why did he die, why the emails, and why her? Then throw in Charlie and a third event.

No wonder she couldn't sleep and was wide awake an hour before her alarm. She took Ernie for an early walk, started her coffee which somehow has replaced tea, and turned on her computer. There was an email from Charlie.

Coop, ILU. c

She didn't have time to savor the moment when her daughter came skipping into the room, "Bonjour, you're up early, too."

"Good morning, Bella. TGIF. Have you thought about what you want to do over the weekend?"

"Let's go to Chicago!"

"That's timely and I'm sure just coincidental."

"I could stay with Dad and you could stay with Charlie."

"I'm glad you like Charlie but please, give it a rest. Besides, don't you think it might take lots of planning?"

"You can do it. We could drive up tomorrow morning and come home Sunday afternoon. Easy peasy!"

As Jan tried to think if it would be possible she gave Isabella her stock answer, "If only things were that simple. What's easy peasy? That's not French, is it?"

Ever persistent Isabella tried to simplify her plan, "It means very easy or simple, I think. All the girls say it. Don't think it's French. I'll call Dad, you call Charlie."

"Thanks, but I'd better call them both. It's hard to pin Charlie down on anything and I'm not sure if he's got his boys or not. We'll see. I'll let you know later. Now, please get ready for school."

As Ernie ran into Howie's office for his morning bribe Jan thought of the logistics of pulling off Isabella's suggested road trip.

"Good morning Howie. What have you got for me?"

Howie gave his usual 'sit down' hand gesture, "Wait till you hear this. I talked to my Pftz. He discovered a very interesting bit of information. Stone warned of possible terrorist jet attacks to New York and D.C. before 9/11 but they were continually ignored by the hierarchy at the NSA. After the warnings were tragically proven correct Stone was livid. Eventually, some of Stone's intelligence leaked and became public, although he was never specifically mentioned by name. The NSA explained it as being impossible to process all the voluminous intelligence they constantly receive."

"Stone was victimized by political and bureaucratic bullshit, and what's worse, for the second time in his life! He was beyond angry, totally frustrated, full of guilt and basically shut himself down until he retired! That's why all his files, all his work at the NSA was placed under the veil of the National Security Act or whatever the fuck it's called. Can you imagine what he must have been thinking? Can we even grasp what was going through Isaac's head? Those fuckin' bastards!"

Jan was enraged. "God, Howie! Poor, poor Isaac!

What a burden to live with. His findings were ignored, not once but twice! The two most significant events of a generation and they wouldn't listen to the smartest man at the NSA! The thought of being able to prevent 9/11 and the Kennedy assassination is mind boggling. It's beyond belief!"

Then Howie did something Jan had never seen him do before. He stood up next to his chair as if to emphasize the significance of what he was about to say, "Think of the consequences! The ramifications of 9/11 are unprecedented! It's cost our country tens of thousands of lives, trillions of dollars and supercharged a global war on terror. I'm surprised the NSA let Isaac live. Or did they? Wonder what your spy boyfriend would say about that?"

"I'm speechless, I'm numb! I'm mad! I'm frustrated! It's all so unbelievable! He was my neighbor—our friend. He was a quiet, gentle man, but he was capable of changing history—perhaps more than anyone in our lifetime—if they had only listened to him! God, my news seems like such minutia compared to what you've just told me."

"What, what were you going to tell me?"

"Please sit, you're making me nervous. I spoke with Rose, Schneider's daughter. She found some interesting stuff in her dad's 'S' box. Schneider and Isaac worked together creating a new algorithmic problem solving formula. Rather than commercialize it they just gave it to the government. The timing fits. It seems Isaac was hired soon after by the NSA. Howie, should we write this story with what we now have? Syndicate it? Don't we have to make this public? Who should we call?"

"Good grief girl, slow down. Nothing's finished, what we know is history. There's got to be more or Stone could have released everything before he died. He could have asked you to write the story. There's got to be more! Lots more, has to be. Take his last clue. Did #3 happen or is it going to happen? What's Isaac trying to tell us? What could it be?"

"Howie, it's all so unbelievable. The same man predicts the Kennedy assassination and 9/11 and he was my neighbor! How? Why? We're sitting on the story of our lifetime!"

"I'm not arguing with you. There must be more. Maybe more than #3? Stone must have more for us. I can't imagine what's next but there has to be a next."

"What more could there possibly be? Why me? Howie, why me?"

"I suspect we'll find out, soon enough. Now get out of here. I've got to make some calls. Ernie's fine where he is."

With her anxiety continuing to boil Jan had to flip the switch to the weekend. First she called Rick. It was okay with him, though he was curious why such a spur of the moment visit, and wondered where she was staying. With a friend wasn't quite the answer he was looking for or believed.

With Rick's cooperation resolved it was time to call Charlie. She would have to wait for his return call. Isabella's road trip rested in his hands, wherever they were.

When she saw her email icon pop up she hoped it was from Charlie, not quite! CLICK!

Jan
Truckin' got my chip…
Salut Ernie
Isaac

"Howie, Howie, again, another email!" Ernie beat him into her office. As Jan re-read the screen over and over, Howie did the same. What the hell was this? Howie closed her office door.

"Truckin', how did he know Isabella downloaded the ringtone? He couldn't—could he? Ernie? Isaac loved Ernie. Why Ernie? Why Salut? Chip, what kind of chip? There's a reason for everything in his emails."

"Fuck me! What the hell is this? Truckin'? Ernie? Salut? Chip?"

"Oh, did I tell you? Rick just bought Isabella an iPhone and helped her download the Grateful Dead song Truckin' for her ringtone. How in the hell could Isaac have known that? It just happened. We talked about it but... Do you still think Isaac's sending the emails? It's impossible! He couldn't have known. The timing, how could he have known."

"I have no fuckin idea! It's all too bizarre. Now my Ernie? What's that about?"

"He loved Ernie but everyone loves Ernie. Howie, how did Isaac anticipate the timing for all this and sync his emails before he died? Is that possible, even for Isaac?"

"The Grateful Dead ringtone could be possible, I guess, because he and Isabella probably talked about it, but how would he know exactly when? I have no fuckin clue what the reference to Ernie might mean. Forward a copy of the email to me. I don't care if it's 11:00 a.m., I need a drink. I've got a bottle of scotch in my desk. Can I pour you one?"

Jan felt her stomach gurgle, "I'll pass. I've been specifically trying not to expose Isabella to any of this but now I've got to ask her some questions about the ringtone, Ernie and Isaac. Wish me luck. She usually sees right through me."

"You're going to need luck. I'll make some calls if I can figure out who in the hell to call. Let me know what your spy has to say."

Before Howie was out the door of her office she finished dialing Charlie. Waiting for his return call Jan wondered what connection Ernie could have with anything? Thank God her phone rang.

"Charlie, I got another email from Isaac. Its four lines."

Jan
Truckin' got my chip…
Salut Ernie
Isaac

She explained the Truckin' reference to Charlie who, like Howie, was totally dumbfounded. He had no answers and didn't want to even speculate why Ernie was in the email.

"Jan, your behavior theory could be right-on. That might be the key to all this. Stone knew you well, had plenty of time to study you. He could have anticipated your actions, as unbelievable as that sounds."

"He probably assumed I'd bring Howie into this and he even might have known about Howie's sources but how the hell could he know about you? You didn't know him, did you Charlie?"

"Absolutely not. Never met him. Never even heard of him before all this."

"Charlie, it's as if Isaac's still alive or has an accomplice."

"I'd rather not speculate, but whoever is sending you the emails is counting on you acting in a certain way."

"Charlie, are you going to be home this weekend? Do you have the boys?"

"I'll be home. It's supposed to be my weekend with the boys but they're going with Kathy to her parents for their 40th wedding anniversary. Why?"

"Isabella suggested we take a weekend road trip to Chicago. She can stay with Rick. Do you want a house guest?"

"I'd love one. I'll be home later tonight. What time do you think you'll be here tomorrow?"

"Probably around noon by the time I drop Isabella and Ernie off at Rick's."

"Bring Ernie here."

"I will if it doesn't raise too many questions with Rick."

"I understand. I'm really excited to see you."

"Me too. Is my toothbrush still there?"

"Right where you left it. See you tomorrow. Can't wait!"

As Jan set her phone down she took a deep breath and drank a bottled water hoping to settle her stomach. Everything was happening so quickly, too quickly. She reflected, yet again, how her quiet, peaceful, often boring world had been turned upside down by quite possibly the biggest story imaginable intertwined with the most meaningful relationship since her marriage. As she flipped through the pages of her journal she was amazed at how it read. Conflicted, challenged, frustrated, emotionally fried, it was also the most exciting time of her life.

After telling Howie of her weekend road trip to Chicago she thought of everything she needed to do. First she'd finish her Star-News assignments. Then find a hot new pair of jeans she so desperately needed. Luckily, the one boutique in Raleigh that had her size was on the way to Isabella's school.

"Bonjour! Are we going?"

"We're going!"

"Yeah! Road trip!"

42

What a beautiful morning for their road trip to Chicago. Unfortunately for Mom, Isabella brought all six of her Grateful Dead CD's. Turning down the volume while cruising the open road seemed like the ideal time for a conversation about Papa Lenny.

"How's that ringtone working out? Do your friends know it's you?"

"Sandy knows because she's heard the song when she comes over but my other friends can't figure it out. Why?"

"Just curious. Did you and Papa Lenny ever talk about it? I mean getting that ringtone?"

"I don't remember. Maybe we did, but not really. He had a Grateful Dead email sound. He said he would show me how to download it. I miss him."

"I know, me too. Don't let me forget, Ernie goes for his yearly checkup on Tuesday. I made the appointment after school so you can go with me. If I remember you and Papa Lenny took Ernie last year."

"I remember. Ernie passed his checkup with flying

colors and Papa Lenny got the info he needed about Ernie's chip." Mom, watch where you're driving!"

As Jan steered the car back into her lane she tried to settle her nerves and racing heart. Truckin', the chip, Ernie. Is it...? Could it all fit together? But how did Isaac know they'd go to the vet. She was bursting to tell Howie and Charlie. "Did Papa say anything else about the chip? Did the vet put the chip under Ernie's coat?"

"Maybe, but Papa asked questions. Said he would handle it. Why? I get computer chips and Ernie's chip confused. He might have. He seemed to ask lots of questions about Ernie's chip. What are you and Charlie going to do?"

"I don't know, what are you and your dad going to do?"

"Dad likes to take me shopping. Maybe the Apple store? Maybe a movie. I brought the Close Encounters DVD just in case. I've watched it a couple of times since it was Papa Lenny's fav. You know I haven't said anything to Dad about Charlie, but I think he knows."

"I appreciate you not talking about Charlie. I'll talk more to your dad—later. Close Encounters was Papa's favorite movie. Interesting. You have a great time with your father. I love you."

Jan was anxious as she approached Rick's. This was

her first serious relationship since their divorce. It felt awkward and was more than symbolic since she was taking Ernie with her to Charlie's. Then again, this is her ex-husband who knows her better than anyone. He might not know the name of her new boyfriend but surely he's figured out there is one. She had to have a conversation with Rick, just not today.

43

Jan arrived right on time and Charlie was there to greet her. As soon as he opened her car door Ernie jumped out and gave Charlie a big doggie hug. If you believe in canine intuition Charlie was a keeper. Nudging Ernie away it was her turn. Arm in arm, Ernie at Charlie's side, they walked to his apartment.

"I'm so glad you drove up. You look great, feel great. And, I'm glad you brought Ernie."

"Judging by his response the feeling's mutual. I'm glad we came, too. I miss you Charlie and we need to talk. But hold me first, please."

As Ernie smelled his way through the apartment Jan and Charlie sat down to catch up. "Charlie, my life is in chaos. I'm scared. I'm confused. I'm overwhelmed. The enormity of what we're discovering leaves me numb. I need you to help me get through this. It's too much for me."

Rubbing her shoulders Charlie tried to console her, "I understand what you must be going through. This is perplexing to me and I live in this world. You've been amazing through all this."

"But there's even more. Isabella shed some light on Isaac's last email. Apparently, she and Isaac talked about ringtones. Isaac had some type of Grateful Dead email notification. God, you're not going to believe what she told me about Ernie. I forgot last year Isaac took Isabella to the vet with Ernie, but that's not all. They talked about a microchip for Ernie and Isabella remembers Isaac knowing lots about the chip. Remember the email? Truckin' got my chips. Those are the opening lyrics to the song. Charlie, there's more. The vet didn't put the chip in Ernie, Isaac did. At least that's what I've pieced together. Ernie goes in for his annual checkup on Tuesday. What could be on that chip? Am I off on some crazy tangent? Is it possible? First he knows about the ringtone, now Ernie's appointment. What do you think? Am I crazy? Am I going off the deep end?"

Charlie kept massaging, "No, you're not going off

any deep end. Your behavior's been remarkable, but Isaac knew it would be. Stone knew the date of Ernie's last checkup. I'm certain doing something with the chip would be a piece of cake for him. The vet visit should tell us a lot."

Thanks for the massage, it feels so good, "Could Isaac have planned this—all of this—everything? Is that possible? How could it be possible?"

"I don't know. I'm as bewildered as you. I've never seen anything like this and I'm not sure anyone else has. Not to change the subject but can I feed you? Are you hungry? How about a sandwich? I picked up some deli stuff."

"Perfect!"

Lunch was pastrami on rye with coleslaw and dill pickles. Charlie's suggestion for a walk after lunch to the nearby dog park met everyone's approval. Ernie, like Isabella, liked her Cowboy.

"I've got to research dog microchips when I get home. Charlie, do you know anything about how they work?"

"Forget when you get home. Let's check them out when we get back to my place."

"Great idea. So, you're convinced Isaac is sending us the emails?"

"Yes. I don't think the NSA is overly concerned about

the revelations of what we've discovered becoming public. They're accustomed to stuff like this. They've got an entire department devoted to just discrediting conspiracy theories. Anyway, Isaac's story must be known by a few in the hierarchy at the NSA. It makes Isaac an unsung folk hero but it's not really a difference maker—not anymore, not after Snowden."

"And you work for these people."

"Not for long!"

44

Walking back to Charlie's apartment they shared a sense of common purpose. Jan was surprised, relieved and elated Charlie brought up leaving the NSA. Plus, the tone of his comments about his employer were scathing. The possibility gave Jan the encouragement she needed. Back at Charlie's apartment the search for dog microchips was a piece of cake, especially considering Jan's recent Internet forays.

The microchip is the size of a grain of rice injected between the dogs shoulder blades. It comes in a sterile applicator and takes a few seconds to inject. The process is similar to a vaccination. Radio frequency identification (RFID) implants provide the permanent ID and don't require a power source. When a scanner is passed over the dog, the microchip gets enough power from the scanner to transmit the microchip ID#. The microchip normally lasts the life of the dog. The ID number can also be programmed to reach a website.

The Ernie Truckin' chip clue made more sense but there was still no clear path to where it might lead. Charlie was confident Isaac could have manipulated and reconfigured this dog chip technology with ease.

It was almost 4:00 when Jan rested her head in Charlie's lap. She was exhausted. As Charlie gently twirled a fingertip through a lock of her hair they both fell peacefully asleep.

Two hours later Jan felt a wet nose on her cheek and it wasn't Charlie's. Somehow Ernie was laying between them on the couch. As she began to shoosh Ernie off the couch Charlie opened one eye. "He's okay. He can't hurt this couch. What time is it? Wow, we took a two-hour nap. I sure sleep better with you. I know this quaint little romantic café a couple of miles from here. How does that sound?"

"Sounds great. I'm not super hungry but romantic sounds inviting. I'll change." Jan put on her new jeans that were so tight she had to do a couple of squats just to walk in them and a slinky silk blouse. She could pass for a fitness model and Charlie did a triple take with his mouth wide open as she walked into the living room. The new jeans worked. They never made it out of his apartment.

After an hour of intense sensuous pleasure, they showered—together. An often-awkward experience was anything but as they took turns soaping up and rinsing each other with obvious emphasis. Fascination with each other's dimples added humor to their water fun. Charlie fingered the two little indentations on Jan's lower back slightly above her butt while she tried to fit a nipple into the dimples on the sides of Charlie's face.

Pretending to want a closer look at her dimples, Charlie knelt on the shower floor and maneuvered Jan so her lower back was directly in front of his eyes. Then he playfully turned her body around and reciprocated the oral pleasure she'd given him. Only Jan wasn't satisfied once or twice. After the third time, she lifted his head and suggested, "I think three times are more than enough."

Physically exhausted and out of hot water they toweled each other off and relaxed on the couch sipping water then wine. Faces flush from both the number and intensity of orgasms they smiled at each other with utter contentment and no need for words. Her phone broke the mood.

She knew it had to be Isabella, "Hi Sweetie. How are things going?"

"Great, et le votre?"

"If you asked me how my day's going, it's been fun, fun, fun. Charlie says hi and Ernie misses you."

"Give them both a big hug from me. Wowser!"

"Thanks for calling, Bella. I love you. See you tomorrow at noon."

"Charlie, I can't imagine having a more wonderful child, but she's growing up so fast. I don't want to miss anything. Do you ever feel that way about your boys?"

"All the time. I don't see them as much as I'd like but that's going to change."

The quaint romantic café could wait for another time. Charlie lit the candles he could find, put on his recently purchased Barry White's greatest hits and they just curled up on the couch talking about places they'd like to go and things they'd like to do—together. Isaac Stone brought them together but they both felt the need to build and define their relationship free of the consuming mystery before them.

Jan was sleeping so comfortably Charlie didn't want to wake her and carried her to bed. After taking Ernie for a walk he climbed into bed and snuggled. He couldn't help but wonder what their relationship would be like if they had met under different circumstances. Realizing it was an impossible question he quickly joined the woman he hoped would one day be his wife in peaceful sleep.

45

Charlie watched Jan wake with a big smile. Amazing what nine hours of sleep does for the human body. "Good morning. You must have needed a good night's sleep. Do you remember last night?"

"Good morning Cowboy. What time is it? Boy, I did sleep. The last thing I remember is you trying to impersonate Barry White. Oh, and raving about the dimples on my lower back, a feeble excuse to play around with my butt and my nipples."

"I do love those dimples, your nipples and your tight little butt. Our chemistry, sexual and otherwise is off the charts."

"You're not going to get an argument from me although I'm a little sore. Guess I haven't used some of those muscles in a long time."

"You're a funny girl. I hope you don't blame me for your soreness. You're the one with all those crazy yoga positions."

"I know my way around a yoga studio. I hear it's a great place to meet women. We'll have to take a yoga class."

"This is Chicago, home of Michael Jordan and Walter Payton. We still play real sports in this town. I'd rather pick up my yoga directly from you."

"Charlie, are you really thinking of quitting the NSA?"

"I am. I know you want me to do it for myself and my boys but you're obviously a big part of my decision."

"What's it like quitting the NSA?"

"It's not easy. They prefer we don't leave."

"Is that why Isaac Stone never left?"

"That I don't know but I'm surprised he stayed so long especially considering the circumstances we believe are true. How about some breakfast? There's a funky spot called The Egg and I a couple blocks away. They have an outdoor area where people bring their dogs. I want to show Ernie what canine Chicago has to offer."

"You sold me and your buddy will follow you anywhere. We both thank you for always being so thoughtful."

They walked hand in hand with Ernie alongside Charlie on a beautiful morning. Jan had never felt this comfortable with any man, not even Rick.

French toast, bacon and eggs and a cinnamon roll were a great combination they split. An extra order of bacon went to Ernie. Sipping their second cups of coffee they couldn't avoid talking about the Isaac Stone puzzle. Tuesday would be interesting. No telling what they might find on Ernie's microchip. Walking back to Charlie's apartment the conversation got more intimate.

"What would you do if you didn't work for the NSA?"

"Probably practice law or maybe private security. Guess I should start thinking about what I want to do with the rest of my life now that I think I've found the person I want to spend it with."

"There you go again, raising the goose bumps on my back and buckling my knees. Do you really think we have that kind of future?"

"I'm sure of it."

"I need something from you—right now! I need one of your long sidewalk kisses. You can even rest your thumbs on my dimples."

46

Jan packed her things and walked out to the living room to find her two guys rough housing on the floor. She stood quietly for a minute soaking up what it would be like to be married—again. Always planning, she needed to hear more, "Charlie, what's our plan?"

"Plan! I hope we're moving forward. I want to be with you. I want you to meet my boys, too!"

"I'd love to meet them, that's important. I don't want to be just in lust. Don't get me wrong. The sex is fantastic but I want a real commitment. Is that where we're going? Can we be in love, this soon? I'm sorry. I don't mean to be this insecure but my emotions are sort of raw these days."

"I understand. January Cooper, I love you. The whole Stone thing would be impossible for most people to handle and I think Stone knew that. Do you ever think Stone chose you?"

"No, but I guess he might have in some way. I love you Charlie, but I don't want to be in love with you and have to fight for you with the NSA."

"I'm going to check on the steps I need to take to exit the Agency. I'm sure you can appreciate its sort of a delicate thing."

"I get it. When will I see you again? Tuesday is Ernie's checkup. We should know more about Isaac's latest clue after Ernie's trip to the vet."

"I'll try to drive down one day this week. I loved having you here and thanks for bringing Ernie."

"I'd better get going. I've got to pick up Isabella."

"Let me take your bag. Come on boy, let's go."

As they waved goodbye Jan couldn't help but wonder if, and when, their quasi honeymoon would end? It was impossible to get a grip on reality with her world turned upside down. Was Charlie what she needed now, what she wanted for her future or both? Her life was one question after another except for the beautiful young girl standing on the curb waving.

"Hi sweetie, I missed you. Give me a hug."

"Bonjour."

"Hi Rick. How was your weekend? Bella, will you run Ernie a little before we leave?"

"Oui."

"We had a great time. She's become quite the little shopper. She must have inherited that gene from you."

"I hear she's got a dad who spoils her rotten."

"I can't help it. She's the most precious little girl in the world but she's growing up so fast. How's your new boyfriend? I'm guessing he lives in Chicago."

"I thought you might ask. He lives here and he's an attorney, too, although he's not practicing now. I avoided telling you about him until I thought it might become serious. His name is Charlie."

"His name is one of the few things I've picked up from our daughter. You should be flattered she's so protective of you, even with me."

"I just never want to put her in the middle of anything."

"I understand and totally concur. I'm happy you may have found someone. You deserve it."

"Thanks. A lot's been going on lately. I'm so glad we've got such a civil relationship. Thank you for that and being such a great dad to our daughter."

As they drove away emotions got the better of Jan, again, and she started to cry. She tried but couldn't hide the tears from her daughter. "What's wrong? Why are you crying? Was it something Dad said?"

Jan shook her head, "No, sweetie. Your father was wonderfully supportive when I told him about Charlie."

"Did something go wrong with you and Charlie?"

Still shaking her head Jan tried to convey her feelings.

"No, we had a great time. Sometimes emotions are hard to explain. There, I've stopped."

"Bonne. Tell me about your weekend."

"Oh Bella, it was wonderful. We talked, we played, we went for walks. You should see Ernie play with Charlie. It's so cute. I like him a lot. He says he's going to quit his job. I hope so. We'll see."

"Thanks for sharing. I love you."

"I love you, too, Bella."

Jan only wished the drive home didn't include non-stop Grateful Dead music but a singing Isabella and a howling Ernie seemed to enjoy it so she hummed along as her mind wandered amidst all that was facing her.

Ernie started to bark when he saw the familiar markings of Raleigh. Once home, Isabella took him for a walk while Mom took their bags upstairs. Noticing the FOR RENT sign on the lawn in front of their building immediately brought her back to her new reality. Her emotional cocktail included hope, fear, excitement, frustration and love. Then when it seemed nothing more could be added—surprise!

"Mom, how are things going with the Isaac Stone puzzle?"

"What! What was that?"

"Don't you think I know?"

Trying to stay calm Jan asked in what she hoped was a normal voice, "Know, what do you know?"

"Come on, I know you, Uncle Howie and Charlie are trying to figure something out."

"Where did you pick up the name Isaac Stone?"

"It's a small apartment and I'm your daughter. I know you're being protective of me. I won't get in the way. I promise."

"Oh Bella, I should have realized you'd figure something was up. It's very complicated and none of us have any answers."

"Who is us?"

"Your Uncle Howie, Charlie, and me."

"Was Papa Lenny in some kind of trouble?"

Jan knew she had no recourse but to tell her inquisitive, perceptive daughter the truth or at least part of it. "No, no, I don't think so. This has to do with the government agency your Papa Lenny worked for and Isaac Stone was a name Papa Lenny used before he moved here. It's all about information he may have known. Information he may have discovered. Your Papa Lenny was so smart he could see and figure things out no one else could. The three of us are just trying to solve a little puzzle we've discovered that's very complicated. Does that make sense?"

"I guess. Is President Kennedy part of the puzzle?"

Jan didn't want to go there but she wasn't asking the questions, "Maybe, possibly."

"Wow, this is like the JFK movie!"

"Oh God no, but you're right about something else. A big part of my job as your mother is to protect you."

"Oui, but you don't need to close doors or run outside to make phone calls, anymore, okay?"

"Deal. I love you Isabella. Give me a big hug."

"Je t'aime aussi, you can tell me everything."

"Thanks sweetie, aren't I the lucky one!"

Jan pondered whether she had one more or one less thing to worry about and whether she should be relieved or dread having to give her daughter updates. She couldn't help but wonder if some of Isaac's brilliance had rubbed off on Isabella. The remainder of the day was spent catching up with chores and getting ready for the week. Isabella finished her homework while Jan brought her journal up to speed. All were asleep in the Cooper apartment by 8:30.

47

Jan, alone with her thoughts, surprisingly slept well. Up with her alarm she found Ernie lying comfortably next to Isabella. Although his eyes were closed his tail was wagging and he was ready for his morning walk.

Getting ready for school and work was routine this Monday morning as was Jan's computer check of the news and email. She hoped her one email was from Charlie, not Isaac. CLICK!

Jan, absolutely loved our weekend. I'm going to follow through on what we discussed and will also let you know my schedule and when I can drive down. Talk soon, ILU, c

Charlie had a romantic side Jan found irresistible. She especially appreciated the ILUs and believed him when he said he was going to explore leaving the NSA. Her response came easily.

Oh Charlie, I loved our weekend, too. Thanks for fol-

lowing through on our discussion and can't wait to see you again. ILU, Coop

After dropping Isabella at school, Jan stopped to pick up doughnuts. She was amused to find her articles on the robberies still taped to the front of the doughnut case.

When Jan opened the Star-News door Ernie ran straight to Howie's office and his morning treat. After placing the doughnut boxes next to the coffee machine, she grabbed a glazed and headed to see Howie.

"Good morning. Here's a glazed. How was your weekend?"

"Thanks. Even though my cholesterol's pushing 320, I still love those glazed. I've got some news but first tell me about your weekend with 007."

"He's convinced the emails are coming from Isaac. He says if the NSA wanted Isaac dead he would have just disappeared. We also researched dog microchips for Ernie's trip to the vet tomorrow. And somehow Isabella pieced together our conversations and last night asked me to explain the Isaac puzzle."

"What did you expect, she's a mini-you. But aren't you forgetting some details about your weekend?"

"God, you're as bad as she is. We had a great time, very romantic. He says he's going to quit the NSA."

"Really! Huh. Interesting. We'll see."

Jan wanted to hear Howie's news, "What do you have?"

"I spoke with my MIT Amy. Did I mention she's a beautiful blonde—brilliant, huge tits, too. What was I thinking?"

"You've conveniently forgot you've been married three times. Skip the regrets. What did she have to say, Romeo?"

"She says Isaac Stone was a child prodigy and that most people who knew him and Schneider credited Isaac with coming up with their algorithmic whatever it was called. She said Isaac is amongst MIT folklore although you won't find him in any of their media materials. Supposedly, they offered him a teaching job on several occasions. I could have married that woman. I loved to rest my head between her boobs and then do that windshield thing!"

"Please, enough of your sexist car analogies. How long since you've seen her?"

"Only about twenty-five years. She's been married twice and has two grown kids. Oh, by the way, my Pftz checked out your lover boy. He couldn't find anything, which I guess is good."

"I'm not sure what he expected to find. I think my

evaluation was more telling. Keep me posted on when we can meet with Charlie."

"Now get out of here and do some work. My Ernie seems to have found a home in here with me. Guess he likes to be where the real action is."

"Oh please, give me a break. We'll see how long he stays once you run out of those flavored king-sized biscuits and you'd better be careful how you use your favorite pronoun 'my' around MY dog. He's very sensitive. Oh, I don't want to burst your bubble about your Amy, but I've got one word for you to consider—gravity."

"Hahaha, very funny. And, don't forget your journal."

Jan's boring, tedious daily work at the Star-News was once again a welcome diversion from her frantic new life. Simple and routine now had considerable merit. Every time her phone rang or she received an email she feared—now what? Then, as if in sync with her thoughts, her phone rang.

"Hi Jan, this is Rose Milnick. I had a chance to go through more boxes."

"Hi Rose, thanks for getting back to me so quickly. What did you find?"

"Well, most of what I found was related to Grateful Dead concerts my dad and Isaac went to. Seems they got together most every year in the late 60's and 70's, put on their tie-dyed t-shirts and would rendezvous at a concert. I've got a bunch of photos but most of them aren't marked. One has a caption on the back from a concert at Barton Hall, Cornell, May 1977. My Dad was a true Deadhead."

"That's amazing. Isaac loved the Grateful Dead, too. He'd listen to them all day long while he'd play on the computer. Luckily, for me, he wore headphones. My eleven-year-old daughter has picked up his love for the group and just downloaded a Truckin' ringtone for her cell phone."

"That's a cute story about your daughter. I never cared for The Dead. I remember my mom hated them, too. That's probably why he'd rendezvous with Isaac. Oh, I forgot. There's a notation on the back of a photo of the two of them from 1960 something where Dad writes, 'Isaac, my brightest, you will change the world.' Believe me, that's saying a lot. My dad had many brilliant students and I've never seen or read anything like that before. They collaborated on many projects through the years. I hope this helps."

"It certainly does. I can't thank you enough, Rose."

"Glad to help. Isaac was obviously very special to Dad. Stay in touch."

"I will. Bye Rose."

Fascinating information, but unfortunately nothing new. Isaac had a Deadhead accomplice and further corroboration of his genius. Jan was about to share the news with Howie when he and Ernie walked into her office.

"I was just coming in to see you. I got another call from Rose Milnick. She found more info on Isaac. Her father and Isaac were both Deadheads and went to concerts together. More significantly, she found some photos where her dad referred to Isaac as the brightest student he ever had. Not earth shaking news but reaffirms things."

"Well, I've got some news, too. My Amy called me back. She searched but couldn't find any records at all for Isaac Stone but he's mentioned in several mathematical and scientific studies as a co-author. Seemed he'd been collaborating with a half dozen MIT professors on various projects since he was eleven. Get this, there's no record of him ever going to school—anywhere."

"His legend keeps growing. Who was this man who lived next door to me?"

Jan pondered the psyche of Isaac Stone. Calling someone a genius was not often associated with understatement but in this case it seemed true. Maybe he was the smartest person in any room. The more they learned about his credentials the more almost anything having to do with his ability to predict the future seemed possible.

Was he doing just that with her, now, after his death!

Once again Jan chose the gym over lunch. Charlie gave her another reason to stay in great shape. Only today she added pelvic thrusts to her routine.

It was 2:00 by the time Jan got back to the office. She was warmly greeted by Ernie, who obviously enjoyed his lunch at the Star-News. Howie was out at yet another of his fried chicken luncheons. With almost an hour until she had to pick up Isabella, she pulled out her journal. The Isaac side had grown to more than thirty pages while the best Charlie could do was ten. Starting from opposite ends of her journal Jan wondered when and how each story would end and merge.

"Hi sweetie, how was school."

"Tres bien."

"Bella, did you know Papa went to lots of Grateful Dead concerts with his college Professor, the other man in the photo we haven't hung up yet?

"I didn't know that but I knew he went to lots of Dead concerts. Did you know they did more than 2,000 concerts? Can we go see a Dead concert? Please!"

"They're still touring? Didn't Jerry Garcia die years ago? Wasn't he one of the original band members and I think their lead guitarist?"

"You sure you're not a Deadhead. Did you and Daddy

ever go to one of their concerts?"

"No to both questions but I think your dad secretly always wanted to go. I think you should get him to take you. I'm sure he'd love it. God knows you have enough of their t-shirts."

"You're so funny. I know when you're kidding. You do know that?"

"You know me too well. Now, please take Ernie for his walk. He's got to work off all those biscuits your Uncle Howie keeps feeding him."

This Monday night at the Cooper's was pleasantly routine without any unexpected emails or disappointing phone calls. Jan pondered what tomorrow's chip adventure might reveal. Ready for bed, she first checked her email. CLICK!

Jan, didn't want today to pass without telling you I love you. c

It was almost the perfect goodnight kiss.

48

Jan slept well, until 4:00 am. Then she couldn't get back to sleep, her mind wandering between Ernie's vet visit and the likelihood of Charlie quitting his job. Two and a half hours later she woke her daughter.

"Good morning Bella. Time to get up. Come on Ernie, let's go for a walk. You've got a big day ahead of you."

As Jan walked Ernie around the block she couldn't help but wonder, again, what Isaac might have in store for them this afternoon. After Ernie lifted his left leg at his favorite tree Jan passed the FOR RENT sign in front of their apartment building.

"Sweetie, remember we take Ernie to the vet for his annual check-up after school."

"Oui."

"Last year you and Papa Lenny took him. Remember?"

"Didn't we talk about this before? We got his chip so we can find him if he gets lost. Easy peasy!"

"Again, with easy peasy! I assume you mean simple. You don't remember anything unusual about the vet visit, do you?"

"Not really. Papa Lenny did the talking. He knew a lot more about the microchip than the vet's nurse. Didn't I tell you?"

"I'm not sure but it doesn't surprise me. See you later."

Following his new normal, Ernie ran straight to Howie's office as the door to the Star-News opened. By the time Jan joined him the biscuit was devoured and Howie was somehow engaged in a one-sided conversation with Ernie about his MIT Amy. Shaking her head in disbelief Jan couldn't resist, "Now I know you've gone off the deep end. Is Ernie coaching you on relationships?"

"Very funny. You know they've done all sorts of studies on the therapeutic value of talking to dogs. Besides being good listeners they provoke our own soul searching."

"Is that right?"

"You got anything for me?"

"Ernie's check-up's this afternoon and hopefully it'll provide the answer to the chip clue." Returning to her office Jan checked her computer. Thankfully—nothing! Since Charlie didn't have his boys last weekend she wasn't sure what their status was for this weekend.

Hi Charlie, your email last night was like the sweetest goodnight kiss. Big day for Ernie at the vet this afternoon. I love you, Jan

49

Finished with her Star-News work by 11:30, Jan checked her gym class schedule and decided to take the noon spin class when she discovered Brandy, one of her favorites was teaching. As she left the office she had to smile at the sight of Ernie lying on his back alongside Howie's desk. Yep, no doubt the Star-News nerve center.

Invigorated from her workout and still humming the Bruno Mars song that played on the spin room sound system, she didn't feel like working when she got back to the office. She hoped her one email was from Charlie.

Jan, know more tomorrow about weekend. I Miss you & ILU. Talk later. c

It was the best Jan could hope for. She grabbed Ernie, waved goodbye to Howie and headed to pick-up Isabella. "Hi sweetie. How was school?"

"D'accord, mais trop de math."

"Translation, please."

"Okay, but too much math."

No surprise, the vet was five minutes from Isabella's school. Housed in what looked like a remodeled barn, it was extremely pet friendly including front and back lawns with lots of trees. Ernie marked what he could. The waiting room was full of mostly quiet patients and their anxious owners. Jan, Isabella and Ernie sat between a pug, a pair of Siamese cats and owners who remarkably resembled their pets. While Jan completed the annual status of "Your Pet Questionnaire" Isabella tried unsuccessfully to introduce Ernie to the cats.

After only a ten-minute wait, the vet assistant called out Ernie Cooper. As if he was receiving a medal Ernie proudly strutted into the exam room with his equally proud owners. Lisa, the vet assistant, welcomed Ernie, took his weight and temperature, entering Ernie's stats in his folder. Mr. Biscuit lover was a couple pounds heavier than last year. Of course, Jan blamed Howie.

"Was that your grandfather who brought Ernie in last year? He sure gave me a tutorial on microchips."

"No, that was my neighbor, Leonard Rosen. Tragically he passed away a few weeks ago."

"I'm so sorry to hear that. He seemed like such a nice

man."

"He was, he was. I assume that's the scanner you're holding. What exactly does it read?"

"Well, Ernie has 15 digits, the ISO Standard. Here, you can see the digits in this small screen. His unique number is 981121102121102. This number is registered with your contact info in case Ernie's ever lost."

"Hold on Lisa, I want to write the number down for my records. Let me make sure I have the numbers right, 981121102121102."

"That's it but you should already have the number. Mr. Rosen gave it to me."

"He did? Really? Are you sure? Can anyone create and install their own number?"

"I don't know. Didn't know they could, but I guess it's possible. Mr. Rosen knew the number and definitely knew what he was talking about."

"Let me check the number one more time: 981121102121102."

"There's one more thing Ms. Cooper. He told me the first three digits, the 981, are the manufacturer's identification number. Guess there's more than one manufacturer."

"Really. Lisa, was there anything else Mr. Rosen told you about the microchip."

"No, I think we've covered everything except I remember he spoke French with your daughter. I took three years in high school but couldn't translate what they were saying. Your daughter translated for me."

"Welcome to my world. She has to translate for me, too."

"Lisa, just so I'm perfectly clear. You didn't put any microchip in Ernie. It was already there and Mr. Rosen knew the number and gave it to you. Does that mean he placed the chip between Ernie's shoulder?"

"I guess he must have unless you had another vet."

Their vet, Paul Carmichael's appearance was somewhat anticlimactic. Not surprisingly, Ernie's in very good health. Even his weight, despite all the biscuits, was almost ideal, somewhat of a surprise considering all he's fed during the day. Preoccupied trying to figure out what the fifteen characters could possibly mean, Jan deftly deferred Dr. Carmichael's questions about Ernie to Isabella. Before he married, Jan and the doctor had gone out—once. For lots of reasons it wasn't a match but Dr. Carmichael was still a little too flirtatious for her comfort level. After Ernie got his biscuit he strutted out of the exam room showing off a playful sense of pride.

"Mom, what was all that stuff about Ernie's chip?"

"Since I wasn't with you and Papa Lenny last year I

wanted to find out more."

"It seemed like lots of questions. Funny how I couldn't get a word in with Lisa but you let me do all the talking with Dr. Carmichael. Didn't you go out?"

"Once, a long time ago. I'm surprised you remember. Very casual, no chemistry. He's been married for years. Let's take Ernie to the park." Isabella's nod coincided with Ernie's bark recognizing where he was headed.

50

What the hell was #981121102121102? Was it a combination of something? A phone number, a code or password? It could be anything. Maybe it wasn't about the chip number at all. She needed help. "Howie, write down this number: #981121102121102.

"What's this?"

"It's Ernie's chip number."

"You fuckin kidding me. Give it to me again."

"Its #981121102121102."

"Let me make sure I got it right, #981121102121102. I'll have my FBI Barker run it through their computers. Maybe it's a combination of different numbers or a code or something. Did you Google it yet?"

"No, I'm at the park but I will once I get home. Any other suggestions?"

"This is all about how your mind works, not mine. Go with your instincts."

"I'll try, see you tomorrow. Call me if you come up with anything."

"I assume my boy Ernie was given a clean bill of health."

"Yes, your boy Ernie's the picture of health."

Back home Jan started her Google search with the 15-digit number. Surprise, a Google search came up empty. No matches, nothing. She entered another 15-digit random number and again, no matches. Then she Googled '15-digit number' and got 24.7 million matches. The ten entries on page one included a unique phone number, fifteen transcendental numbers, a 15-digit number limitation on Excel, a 15-digit random number generator and coupon codes. Page two was more of the same, dominated by various phone codes and some credit cards using fifteen digits. The phone numbers and credit cards were certainly possibilities but didn't seem quite right. She needed Howie's input. "Howie, there's nothing, absolutely nothing, zilch. I'm totally lost. Help me!"

"Hold on. You'll come up with something. You're

usually lost, frustrated and then—bingo. Isaac is counting on you and he hasn't been wrong, yet."

"I hope you're right. Isaac probably had more confidence in me than I do in myself."

It was almost 6:00, dinner time. Isabella was in her room, simultaneously on her Mac and iPhone with Ernie, as usual, at her side. Isabella nodded when her mother suggested a chopped chicken salad for dinner. Walking back to the kitchen, Jan's phone rang.

"Hi Charlie, can you talk?"

"I can. How did it go at the vets?"

"I got the 15-digit number. Of course, I Googled it but got nothing. Zero. Zilch!"

"What's the number?"

"#981121102121102. Wait, wait, I forgot, how did I forget. Maybe, that's the key. I can't believe I didn't remember. That's it! Now, the number looks totally different. Oh, my God, there's two separate six digit numbers. Oh, my God, this has to be it."

"Jan, Jan, calling Jan! I'm here. What the hell are you talking about? What did you forget?"

"Sorry Charlie. I'm a little excited. I forgot the vet assistant told us the first three digits were the manufacturer's identifier. If you leave off the first three digits you get twelve digits. But, here's what feels like Isaac. The twelve remaining digits can be split into two identical six digit numbers. Now the fifteen-digit number becomes #121102. I can't wait to follow-up on this. I'm so excited. Thanks, Charlie."

"What are you thanking me for? I didn't do anything."

"I'm sorry but I just have the feeling we're going to be able to figure this out."

"What clue, figure what out?"

"Isabella, I'm on the phone, please feed Ernie."

"Charlie, you still there?"

"I'm here. Sounds like you have your hands full. I can't wait to hear everything. I'm out of town until Friday and if you call me I might not be able to return your call. Unfortunately, I won't know about the weekend till Friday. I love you."

Uncomfortable to say 'I love you' with Isabella in the room Jan said what she could, "Back at you, me too. Bye Cowboy."

"Je suis tres heureux pour toi."

"Isabella, you've been eavesdropping—again. Translation, please!"

"I was coming to eat not listening. It means I'm very happy for you. What clue?"

"Thanks for feeding Ernie. We're trying to figure out the puzzle, that's all. I'll finish making our salad. You hungry?"

"Un peu."

"I've heard that before."

51

Finished with dinner and dishes, Ernie and Isabella retreated to the bedroom and Apple world. Jan rushed back to her computer and Googled, #121102. And there it was. She couldn't breathe! Her heart raced! She didn't know what to do, so she just sat and took a half dozen deep breathes. Where this might lead was beyond comprehension. After flushing her face with cold water, she called Howie.

"Howie, I can't believe it! Wait till you see this. It's unbelievable! The implications. This could be the biggest discovery in human history! I can't believe it. I've had to put a dish towel around my face to muffle my voice. I'm so excited, I can't breathe!"

"Slow down. Slow down and talk to me."

"I wish you could come over but Isabella's asking too many questions as is. I don't want her to know what I've just discovered. I can't believe I'm talking to you from the corner of my kitchen with a towel wrapped around my head and phone."

Gaining a modicum of composure she first explained how she forgot the first three digits in the chip were the manufacturer's identifier. Then she told Howie to look at the remaining twelve digits and notice they were two identical six digit numbers, #121102. "Wait to you see what that number means! Just wait! I'm going to email you a compilation of what I've discovered. You might want to take one of those relax-a-pills now. Call me after you've read it and settle down."

Back to her computer and Google, she decided to copy and paste the relevant info about #121102 into a word document she could send Howie.

A fast radio burst (FRB) is a high-energy phenomenon expressed as a short-lived radio pulse lasting only a few milliseconds. The origin of fast radio bursts is unknown, but there is speculation these signals might be signs of extraterrestrial intelligence.

Fast radio bursts are a function of the date the signal was recorded or YYMMDD. June 26, 2011 would be FRB 110626. The first FRB discovered was FRB 010621. Then a team of students from McGill University, reviewed data from the Arecibo radio telescope in Puerto Rico and discovered a FRB detected in 2012 did not conform to the previous pattern.

– FRB 121102 – was followed by several bursts identical to theoriginal signal. By running data through a supercomputer at McGill, FRB 121101 was discovered to release a total of 10 identical bursts indicating the FBRs were not random one-off signals This offered further proof that extra-terrestrial life did exist.

Snowden raised hopes of extra-terrestrial existence in a scientific podcast called Star Talk. He concluded if we are receiving electronic messages in multiple radio bursts the likelihood of extra-terrestrial life is almost a certainty.

The UFO community believes amongst Snowden's hoard of NSA files are a number of documents detailing the NSA's listening and recording of signals often referred to as 'black projects' or secret space programs.

52

It only took Jan fifteen minutes to create a document containing the significant parts of a dozen or so articles on FRB 121102. There were lots more but she wanted to send Howie what she had, now. Ten minutes later her phone rang.

"Holy fuckin' shit! My hearts pounding out of my chest! Do you know what this means? The NSA listened to everyone and everything for fifty years and Isaac heard it all, everything, all of it! Plus, he had access to all the files, all the data, everything, from everywhere. And, he was so much fuckin smarter than anyone else who ever heard or analyzed the data! He knew! He figured it out! He knew! He had to know. He knew more than anyone—ever! He heard more than anyone—ever! Unfuckin believable! Do you realize what he discovered? There's life out there! We're not alone! I've got to take another pill and have another drink."

"Howie, I'm shaking! I'm sweating! I'm a total wreck! Where's this going? What do we do? There's got to be more. What else? Where's it going? There must be more. How is this going to end? I'm not going to be able to sleep. Kennedy, 9/11 and now extraterrestrial life from God knows where. We're not alone. Holy shit! We're not alone. Howie, my pulse must be over 180. This is too big for us! It's too much! We need help. The President! He should know, shouldn't he?"

"Slow down! Think! We need to think! Isaac could have packaged everything and gotten it to the President if he wanted, but he didn't. He had to have a good reason. Think! Isaac knew what he was doing. We must assume that."

"Mom, when are we going to watch the movie?"

"Five minutes. Bella, give me five minutes, please."

"Holy shit! Howie, I forgot all about the movie we're going to watch. You won't believe it! Isabella says it was Isaac's favorite."

"What movie? Nothing can top what you just emailed me. What movie?"

"Close Encounters of the Third Kind! Isaac's favorite movie was Close Encounters of the Third Kind. Isabella has the DVD. Isaac gave it to her. That's what we're watching tonight. Spielberg, should we contact Spielberg? Come over and watch it with us."

"I'm not going anywhere! I feel like shit, like I've been run over by a truck. I'm going to stay close to the toilet and medicine cabinet. I remember the movie. Liked it except for that French actor. What's his name? Truffle, something like that. Jan, we need to think. You need to think. What we do will probably be the most important thing we'll ever do in our lives."

"Thanks for adding even more pressure on me. That's the last thing I need."

"Did you tell your spy, yet? Did you tell him or email

him what you sent me?"

"No, not yet. I need more time to think about what I'm doing and he's going out of town. Do you think there's more clues in Close Encounters? And, how could you not like Francois Truffaut? That sexy voice, that accent. Obviously, it's the French part of him you don't like. Stay home, but watch the movie. I have a feeling it's important."

"Got to go. That double bacon cheeseburger I had for lunch is coming back up to haunt me. See you tomorrow."

Jan made popcorn while Isabella took Ernie for a walk. The DVD case read 132 minutes which translated to half the movie for Isabella. Pillows in place on one end of the couch and Ernie on the other, Mother and Daughter snuggled up to enjoy the Spielberg classic.

"Sweetie, do you know what The Third Kind means?"

"I think something about UFO's and aliens. Papa Lenny told me. Funny, he didn't talk much about movies except for this one. He had lots to say. He liked the guy with the French accent. Me too. I want a boyfriend who talks to me like that."

"Welcome to the club. The actor was Francois Truffaut and he was a famous director, too. The First Kind is a sighting of a UFO. The Second Kind is physical evidence that proves extraterrestrials, the existence of alien life and the Third Kind is actual contact with some type of alien life. Did Papa Lenny talk about that?"

"Oui, I remember. He repeated the same thing before and after we watched the movie. He said if there were aliens we wouldn't be able to recognize them. He said movies are made to sell tickets and people want aliens to look a little like us."

Jan couldn't remember how old she was when she first saw the movie but knew watching it this time would be very, very different. Isabella lasted less than an hour. Jan stopped the movie, helped her daughter to bed and then went back to the couch and Close Encounters.

Thanks to Google and her computer Jan discovered much that made watching the movie even more fascinating. Composer, John Williams wanted a seven-note sequence, but it was too long for Spielberg so they settled on five notes. Williams supposedly brought in a mathematician to compute the number of five-note combinations they could make from a twelve-note scale, over 134,000. The unmanageable number was reduced to 100 options from which they decided on the five-note sequence for the movie.

Apparently, Spielberg wanted non-human beings for aliens but an orangutan idea didn't pan out and most of the small aliens were local elementary school girls from Mobile, Alabama, where the scenes were shot.

Jan discovered all sorts of other interesting facts about the filming of Close Encounters but she couldn't decide what might be relevant and instead bookmarked the articles for future reference. In awe of the timeliness of the movie Jan absorbed every scene. Was it part of another clue from Isaac? After taking Ernie for his walk and peeking in to see her daughter fast asleep she collapsed on her bed. Totally exhausted, a cocktail of unanswered questions kept her from getting to sleep.

53

"2:45, who the hell's calling?"

"Hello, is this Jan Cooper?"

"Yes, who's this?"

"I'm Sandy Stevens at Raleigh General. Howard Nafzinger was brought in by ambulance about a half hour ago. He's had a heart attack, but he's conscious. He's still in the ER but should be going to recovery soon. He was able to call 911. You're listed in our files as the person to call in case of an emergency."

"I'll be there in fifteen minutes!"

"Isabella, sweetie, wake up. Isabella, I need to talk to you!"

"What! What's wrong? Are you okay?"

"I'm okay, but Uncle Howie had a heart attack and was taken to the hospital. I've got to go. Will you be okay here with Ernie? I'll call you from the hospital."

"No, no. I'm going. I'm going with you. First Papa Lenny, now Uncle Howie. I'm going. I don't want Uncle Howie to die. I'm going."

There was no way Jan could stop her daughter from going, nor did she want to. In less than ten minutes, they threw on sweats, grabbed flip flops, baseball caps and a confused Ernie and were on their way to Raleigh General. Parked in a loading zone, Jan cracked two windows for Ernie, and Mother and Daughter ran into the hospital hoping for the best.

"How can I help you?"

"We're here to see Howard Nafzinger. I just got a call he had a heart attack."

"Your name?"

"Jan Cooper."

"Okay Ms. Cooper. Mr. Nafzinger was just taken to recovery. Dr. Stricker was the attending physician in the ER. Let me check if he's available. He can brief you further. Wait, there he is. Dr. Stricker, these ladies are here to visit Mr. Nafzinger. Do you have a few minutes?"

As he looked down at the chart he was carrying Dr. Stricker introduced himself to Jan, shook her hand and said hello to Isabella. His first words were exactly what Jan hoped to hear. "He had a heart attack but he's going to be okay. It was probably triggered by the Scotch he was drinking combined with pills that had an expiration date of August 2003. He also said he's been under a great deal of stress. The first words out of his mouth as he was being wheeled in were, call Jan, call Jan! We did and here you are."

"Thank you Doctor. Can we see him? Is he awake?"

"I just left him. He should be all wired up in a few minutes. Hospital rules prohibit your daughter from going with you but I think we can make an exception considering the circumstances. Let me take you to his room. All I ask is that you make this brief, he needs rest. He's on an IV and we're monitoring all his vital signs. Before he leaves here, Dr. Kumar, our cardiologist, is sure to have a serious conversation about his life style. If it doesn't change he might not survive another attack. Hopefully you'll be able to help him make those changes. Obviously, you're very important to him."

As the Dr. knocked on the door to Howie's room and

announced he had a couple of visitors Isabella ran to his bedside and reached for his free hand. "Uncle Howie, I love you. Mom and I have been so worried. I don't want to lose you." As she kissed him on the forehead, tears flowed down Jan's face. She was overcome by a wide range of emotions accentuated by the love and compassion she just witnessed from her daughter.

Howie mumbled, "Oh Isabella, thank you. I love you, too."

As Jan leaned down to kiss his forehead she whispered, "Thank God you're going to be okay. I need you now, more than ever."

"I'm not going anywhere. Just do me a big favor."

"What, tell me."

"No more glazed!"

"Perfect! I couldn't have asked for better words from you! We were both terrified when the hospital called. You're lucky. Take this as your wake-up call. Isabella and I need you around for a long, long time, and don't worry about the office. I'll take care of everything and brief the troops. I'll pick you up when you can come home."

"Thank you. You're the only family I have." And, as he held their hands this often gruff, usually sarcastic man who was boss, Father and friend was crying.

54

Ernie's nose peered outside the partially open car window, and his bark voiced his displeasure at being left alone for almost an hour. Jan, numb as she crawled into the driver's seat, took two deep breathes. What next? What more? It was 4:30, and the dark early morning didn't physically change being wide awake. Her mind raced but couldn't focus. As she pulled out of the hospital lot she got some solace from her daughter who put an arm over her shoulder.

Arriving home, Jan held up her groggy daughter as Ernie stopped at his favorite tree. The still present FOR RENT sign jolted her back to reality. Once inside their apartment Isabella plopped down on the couch and immediately fell asleep. Ernie would have joined her if he wasn't hungry and still bewildered over the sudden change in routine. Jan paused at his box of biscuits. Screw the biscuits. She was going to make pancakes for the two of them.

Ernie devoured his three slightly buttered pancakes in one big bite. Jan needed a little more time, lots of maple syrup and a strong cup of coffee. She quickly wrote down six things she had to do at the office. Then she sent an email to the staff detailing Howie's condition. Since she'd already composed the email in her head it only took a couple of minutes to type and send. She emphasized he was resting comfortably and was out of immediate danger. She closed by asking everyone to be present for a 10:00 staff meeting where she would give an update and answer questions.

55

Sixty-eight-year-old Howard Nafzinger has covered all the biggest news stories of the past four decades. Yet, every story added together couldn't match what he read in Jan's email last night. Awake and relieved to be alive he needed to get out of the hospital—now. The nurse noticed Howie was awake, "Oh, Mr. Nafzinger, you're up. What can I help you with?"

Howie was his old self, "Nurse, come a little closer so I can read your name."

The nurse didn't move but smiled, "Uh-huh, I think this is close enough."

Howie shook his head, "I can make out the capital D, which seems appropriate but my vision is still blurred. Just a little closer, there's got to be another D there! I won't bite."

Nurse Davidson smiled at her flirtatious patient, "Mr. Nafzinger, if I get any closer my chest will be smack in the middle of your face."

Howie was disappointed he couldn't convince this buxom beauty to play his game, "Well, I do have a nose for the news. Okay, Nurse Davidson, I need to get out of here. I'm leaving."

As the nurse pulled up the zipper on her white top to the base of her neck, she raised the tone of her voice, "You're not going anywhere! You just had a heart attack. You didn't drive to the ER. You took an ambulance. You just can't walk out of here! It doesn't work that way. Your cardiologist, Dr. Kumar, will be here soon and talk to you. I'm sure he'll release you when it's safe for you to go home. You're lucky. It could have been much worse."

Howie wasn't buying it. "Nurse Davidson, you don't understand. Unless this is a prison, I'm leaving—NOW!"

Losing her patience and having faced this situation before Nurse Davidson followed hospital procedure, "Let me text the Doctor. Please don't get up or disconnect anything. I'll stay with you and keep you company until he gets here."

Howie started to appraise his physical condition and all the attachments to his body ignoring his dizziness. "What are all these wires and tubes? I assume you're monitoring something."

"We're monitoring everything—all your vitals. You're still in danger. You know I've subscribed to the Star-News for years. It's a good paper."

The compliment out of left field surprised him, "Well I appreciate that, but I'm still leaving."

Nurse Davidson decided it was time to get out the heavy artillery, "Sir, if I have to sit on you I will. Better yet, I'll get Reuben, our 350-pound nurse's assistant to watch over you until the Doctor gets here."

With the realization leaving was going to be more difficult than anticipated, Howie changed his tone, "Okay, then how about a sponge bath while we wait for the Doctor! I feel a little clammy."

"Mr. Nafzinger, unfortunately, for you, that's not going to happen with me but that's a specialty of Reuben's. I'll text him for you."

Howie knew the conversation was going nowhere but he rather enjoyed it—so he continued, "That's okay. You just remind me of my second wife. She was a beautiful woman."

"And you remind me of my grandfather who was a wonderful man."

"Perfect retort, Nurse Davidson, right on point!"

As Dr. Rajesh Kumar entered Howie's room Nurse Davidson whispered into the Doctor's ear, handed him Howie's chart and left to attend other patients. The tall, handsome, dark skinned doctor talked as he reviewed Howie's chart, "Well, Mr. Nafzinger, I see you're awake and alert. Your chart looks okay but you're not out of the woods just yet. You're lucky. Many people don't get a second chance. Consider your attack a wake-up call. Your life and how long you live rests entirely with you. Clean up your diet, watch your blood pressure, your cholesterol, get more exercise and control your stress level. We'll also set you up with a monitoring device."

Liking Dr. Kumar's bedside manner Howie tried again, "Look Doc. I've got a newspaper to run and it's imperative I get to my office, now."

As he put the chart down the Dr. tried to reason with his stubborn patient, "Mr. Nafzinger, you don't understand the severity of what happened to you. You're more than likely going to be okay but we still need to monitor you. You're not going anywhere. You're still in danger. You're probably going to be here 3-5 days. Better get comfortable."

Howie wasn't going to be denied and tried the legal angle, "Get me any release you need signed and I'll get out of your hair and won't have to sue anybody."

"You're very persistent. You do understand the chances of you having another incident are highest within 24 hours of the first."

"I'll take that risk."

"You will, but I won't. Is it that important you get to your office? I'm sure somebody can cover for you. What can possibly be more important than your life?"

"Doc, unless I'm mistaken you can't keep me here against my will. Write it up as left for religious reasons. I'm leaving."

Dr. Kumar didn't physically stop him, "Sir, please don't pull out the tubes your IV and the sensors. Please."

Howie's mind was made up and he was going back to the office. He couldn't sit in a hospital bed when the biggest story of his life was waiting. He tried to stand only to quickly lose his balance. Dr. Kumar caught him from falling. "I've got you Mr. Nafzinger. Let's get you back in bed. I purposely let you try and stand to make you realize you're in no condition to go anywhere. Understood?"

A reluctant, but beaten down Howie nodded, "Okay Doc, but you're going to need more than 400 lb. Reuben sitting on me to keep me here much longer."

The doctor laughed, "400 lb. Reuben! Who's that? The only Reuben who works here is 125 lbs. soaking wet."

Howie was now even more impressed with Nurse Davidson, "Doc, give Nurse Davidson a raise. She's outstanding!"

Smiling over the Nurse Davidson remark Dr. Kumar was relieved to convince his patient he wasn't going anywhere, "By the way, I'm glad you appreciate Nurse Davidson. We're getting married next month."

Howie smiled, "Well isn't that just great. I underestimated you Doc. Not only are you a very wise doctor and a psychiatrist to boot but also a great judge of women. Congratulations!"

"Thanks. I'll convey your thoughts to my fiancée."

"Thank you Doctor."

"You're welcome and we really do like the Star-News."

56

There was no normalcy to this Wednesday morning. Jan sat for an hour and just pondered all that was her world. It wasn't an attempt to organize; it was an attempt to keep her sanity. As she stared into nowhere a familiar wet tongue licking her face snapped her back to reality. "Ernie, I love you, too. Let's go for a walk."

Returning from their walk Jan couldn't help but pause and stare at Apartment #11. In a matter of seconds, she started to tremble, then shake. Thankfully Ernie was there to help settle her nerves as she unlocked her apartment door. Surprisingly, Isabella was up and in the shower.

Howie was all Jan and Isabella talked about on the drive to school. "Hopefully we can visit Uncle Howie in the hospital after I pick you up from school."

"Oui, oui!"

Raleigh's status as a small town was driven home again when Jan walked into the doughnut shop. Before she could even order she was bombarded with questions about Howie from not only the girls behind the counter but also from two customers. She couldn't wait to tell Howie about his rock star popularity. Then, as if an ironic sign, Jan was told the shop had run out of glazed doughnuts.

As soon as Jan opened the Star News door Ernie ran to Howie's office expecting his morning biscuit. Before she could get to Howie's box of treats she was peppered with questions from the four staff members in the lunch room. Her answers were concise and hopefully enough to satisfy the worried troops until 10:00. "He's going to be okay. I'll give you more details at10:00."

Ernie devoured his biscuit in seconds and then followed Jan to her office. After taking care of a few Star News details Jan instinctively called Howie's cell phone. She didn't bother to leave a message, instead she called the hospital. Told Howie was resting she left a message all was well at the office and she'd call back later.

With both Charlie and Howie unavailable Jan felt desperately alone. Then knowingly, Ernie sat next to her, tilted his head and placed a big paw in her lap. This was Ernie's remarkable gift of unconditional love at just the right time, and it never failed.

The staff meeting went smoothly. Jan elaborated on Howie's condition and promised to keep the staff updated by email. The several staff questions specifically related to Friday's paper were easily answered. The biggest reaction came when, in hopes of helping Howie, she asked they not bring doughnuts or pastry to the office. "'Enjoy the doughnuts, no more after these are gone." Sheepish grins were exchanged by half the staff munching on doughnuts. The meeting ended without further questions.

Back at her desk Jan turned on her computer, proofread upcoming stories and then called Howie. This time, he answered and asked Jan to stop by. Today, Ernie would stay in the office with his friend Shirley, the circulation/advertising manager.

Jan walked into the hospital, past the receptionist and directly to Howie's room. She heard the TV before she saw him sitting up in bed. "Wow, it's great to see you awake. How do you feel?"

"I've felt better, and I can't tell what the hell they're giving me through all these tubes. The cardiologist and his fiancée, my Nurse Davidson, are fantastic. Maybe you should do a story about them. How did the staff meeting go?"

"Easy peasy!"

"Wait, what did you say? Easy what?"

"Easy peasy. It means very easy or simple. Isabella says it all the time. Guess I picked it up from her. Sort of descriptive, don't you think?"

"Whatever."

"One day you've got to tell me why you dislike the French. I've got to tell you what a celebrity you are at your favorite doughnut shop. Somehow their staff knew about your heart attack by 7:45 this morning. Then, while they were asking me how you were doing two customers said they heard about it, too. Small world, small town. Do you know how long you're going to be here?"

"No, the Doc's supposed to come by soon. Stick around, he told me probably 3-5 days. Jan, my dear friend, thank you and your precious, thoughtful daughter. I haven't cried since my mother passed away twenty years ago."

Sentimentality wasn't a character trait of her boss and she appreciated his candor. Their conversation was interrupted by the knock at the door.

"Good afternoon Mr. Nafzinger."

"Hi Doc. Doctor Kumar, this is my star reporter and wonderful friend, Jan Cooper."

"My pleasure Ms. Cooper. How you feeling Mr. Nafzinger. Any pain, discomfort, nausea, dizziness?"

"Negative. Feel better. Slept well."

"That's great, let me look at your chart."

"When can I go home?"

"Everything's improving. Keep getting better and

we'll try to get you home Friday or Saturday. I know how anxious you are to get home but you need to stay at least to Friday. Okay, or are we going to spar again?"

"Doc, after what happened early this morning I respect your opinion. No argument this time."

"Good. I'll stop by later today. Try to relax. Ms. Cooper, I enjoy your stories."

"Thanks Doctor. I appreciate that. Howie, Isabella wants to see you. I hope you can handle the two of us later this afternoon."

"Absolutely. Please come by, but tell the staff not to bother. When does your spy get home?"

"Hopefully, Friday. I'll bring your friend Ernie to visit when you get home. I don't want him to forget you."

Jan thought Howie was smiling at her until she turned around and saw the nurse walk into the room. After glancing at her watch, Jan kissed Howie's forehead and excused herself. "I'll see you later this afternoon and you be nice to Nurse Davidson."

As much as Jan wanted to go to the gym she needed to get back to the office. Ernie was at the door to welcome her. Her normally orderly desk was strewn with newspapers, notepads, and her journal. It mirrored what was going on in her head. Totally out-of-character she opened a Red Bull. After tending to business she was glad it was time to pick up her daughter. "Come on Ernie."

"Hi sweetie, how was school?"

"OK. Are we going to the hospital?"

"That's exactly where we're going. Uncle Howie really wants to see you."

Ernie relaxed in the back seat as Jan and Isabella walked into the hospital and directly to Howie's room.

"Hi, Uncle Howie. How do you feel?"

"Isabella, it's so great to see you. I'm feeling a lot better and should be able to go home in a few days. Easy peasy!"

"Oh my God! How did you...Mother!"

"You said it to me, I said it to Uncle Howie and you got it back. Full circle, easy peasy!"

"Uncle Howie, can you watch movies here? We watched Close Encounters of the Third Kind."

"That's what your mother told me. I've seen it and enjoyed it. What did you think? Do you believe in extraterrestrials?"

"Oui, oui. Papa Lenny did—too. We watched movies together when I was younger."

Jan had to chuckle at her daughter's perspective. "When? How much younger? Do you have other movies or did Papa Lenny keep them? Do you remember which movies?"

"Hmmmmm, let me think. This must be part of your puzzle. When you ask me lots of questions that aren't about my iPhone, school or what I want to eat it's about the puzzle. Uncle Howie, you're in on this too, aren't you?"

"Isabella, you're just like your mother. When did you start high school?"

"Uncle Howie, you're so funny. I'm glad you can laugh."

As Nurse Davidson entered the room Isabella and Jan said their goodbyes, "I'll stop by in the morning and update the staff with another email. I'll give you a call tonight, too."

"Thank you, I'm so happy you stopped by to see me. It made my day. Jan, thanks for everything. Don't know what I'd do without you. I love you both."

Holding hands as they walked to the car, Ernie's bark and the tip of his nose out the partially open window welcomed them. Jan recognized her daughter was troubled, "Bella, what was that like for you to visit Uncle Howie and see him connected to all those tubes."

"Uncle Howie's means a lot to me. He'll be okay, right?"

"Yes, he should be but he needs to make some life-style changes. That's where we can help. Let's do it together. Okay?"

"Oui, I can't lose him—too."

57

The drive home was interrupted by a stop at the park and a pizza pickup from Katie's. After dinner Isabella retreated to her room and homework and Jan sent out another staff email.

She didn't recognize the phone number, "Hello."

"Hello, Ms. Cooper, this is Dr. Kumar. I'm sorry to call at dinner time. Can you talk?"

"Yes, of course. It's not Howie! Is he okay?"

"Yes, he's recovering nicely. We didn't get a chance to speak at the hospital but I wanted to discuss something with you."

"Sure, Doctor. What is it?"

"Do you know if Mr. Nafzinger is under a lot of pressure at the paper, is he worried about something or under a lot of stress?"

Jan was conflicted over how to answer, "Think we're okay at the paper. We have been working on a rather important story. Do you think that could have triggered his heart attack?"

"I'm not sure but in talking with him I get the impression something's going on. I know how close you are to him. Is there something else that might be causing unusual stress?

"There's that one story. We talk about it all the time. I thought it was his diet and lack of exercise."

"Those are certainly extremely important. You're the closest person to him and I'd appreciate it if you'd try to ease him back to work. I know he can be stubborn but I'd suggest he work from home for at least a week and then maybe half days at the office for another week. Is that possible?"

"I'll certainly try and think it's doable. He's awfully stubborn, as you've discovered but he needs to get healthy."

"That would be great! I appreciate your help. You and your daughter mean the world to him and I think he'll listen to both of you. Thank you, Ms. Cooper. Please call me if anything comes up or you have any questions. Have a good evening."

"Thanks so much for you call, Dr. Kumar. We'll do all we can."

Jan felt like a deflated punching bag. Her world was ready to explode. Her terrible headache returned. There was no Howie, and probably no Charlie to talk to. She sat at the kitchen table and couldn't move. Instinctively, Ernie was at her side with his face in her lap. There was no better medicine.

"Who called? Ernie heard you and jumped off the bed. Are you okay?"

"Yes, I'll be fine. It was Dr. Kumar. He had suggestions on how we can help Uncle Howie. It was very kind of him to call. He thinks Howie should take it easy for a couple of weeks, maybe half days. Bella, I'm exhausted. How about you?"

"I'm tired, too. Looks like an early night for both of us."

"Isabella, I'm so proud of you. I love you."

"Je t'aime."

Jan got a pillow, a blanket, her journal and ever faithful Ernie and propped herself up on the couch. Without Howie or Charlie, it was up to her. She opened her journal and let her imagination run wild with thoughts of what the third event might be. Radio waves from somewhere in the universe? Isaac had been listening, hearing everything for fifty years. Life elsewhere in the universe. We are not alone. Isaac heard something. What's #3? What did he hear? What could it be? Isaac, I hear you. I hear you!

"Mom, who you talking to? "

"Gosh, I'm so tired I was probably talking to myself. It's been a long, stressful day. Glad you've got your PJs on. You're ready for bed and I will be as soon as I take the big snorer out. Goodnight sweetie. I love you."

Jan grabbed Ernie's leash and her phone, walked pass #11, then called Charlie before Ernie reached his tree. Howie was out of reach, at least temporarily but she had to share her thoughts with someone. She knew Charlie probably wouldn't return her call but that didn't matter. Eyes on the face of her phone, hoping and waiting, didn't produce a ring.

Back in their apartment, ready for bed, Ernie was unsure where to sleep. Jan decided for him. Tonight, she needed him. "Come on Ernie, come on up."

With her phone alongside her pillow and Ernie wedged between her feet, Jan hoped to quickly fall asleep. Wishful thinking. Her news was historic, monumental, earth shaking. "Charlie, call me. I need you!"

58

"Mom, wake up! You're going to be late."

"What, what time is it?"

"It's almost 7:00. You never oversleep. I'll take Ernie out but get up, don't go back to sleep."

Normally it takes Jan forty-five minutes to get ready. This morning, she cut that in half. Tossing a couple of energy bars in her purse and her computer bag over her shoulder she followed Isabella and Ernie out the door. "Bella, want to visit Uncle Howie later? I know he'd love to see you."

"Oui, oui."

"I'll see him during the day and we can go back to the hospital after dinner."

"Oui."

Jan paused, sat, and watched her precious daughter as she walked towards the school door. Only the gentle horn beep from behind interrupted her pleasant train of consciousness. Driving to the office her thoughts turned to Charlie. The red light gave her an opportunity to check her phone even though no alert light flashed. No voicemail, no emails. "Shit!"

Everyone at the office was in the coffee room. Anticipating their questions Jan gave an update knowing they'd tell the rest of the staff. On the way to her office Ernie made an abrupt right turn into Howie's office searching for his friend and morning treat.

Jan left Ernie in the office and headed to the hospital. "How you feeling?"

"Better, hope I can get out of here soon. How's everything at the office?"

"Your boy misses you. Everything's good, tomorrow's paper is all set."

"Enough of the small talk. Tell me what's really going on."

Jan swallowed hard and tried to be vaguely honest, "I still have no idea what Isaac's #3 means. What could it be? Oh, do you want more visitors? Most of the staff wants to stop by if you just say the word. I'll come back after lunch."

"I love the way you quickly jump from things you don't want to talk about. Don't block me from #3. Tell the staff to wait until I get home. You come back. I wish you could bring my Ernie."

"I'm going to check how Ernie can get to be a comfort dog. He certainly has all the requirements. Anything else you need?"

"I'm good. Thanks. When you come back you can fill me in on what's going on with our puzzle. See you later."

"Dammit!" Everything was complicated. Nothing was simple, or obvious. Just the opposite. She needed Howie's help, but wouldn't jeopardize his health. Isaac's puzzle must have triggered his attack. A Google search on the latest research on stress and heart attacks only re-affirmed what Jan already knew. With her head in her hands, she couldn't escape feeling desperately alone.

59

Jan needed a workout—badly. She got the last bike in Brandy's noon spin class. A sweaty mess after almost an hour of intense cardio, her mood changed thanks to the release of endorphins. Gone was the overwhelmed feeling, replaced by the challenge few people, if any, ever faced. Her attitude shifted 180^0 from dreading the situation to eagerly anticipating solving the puzzle. The first challenge awaited as she pulled into the hospital parking lot.

"Hi Howie, thought I'd stop be on my way back to the office. How you doing?"

"Guess I'm feeling better. Not sure what they keep pouring into me but I'm ready to go home."

"Do you think our puzzle caused your heart attack or at the least was the catalyst?"

"I know where you're going. I know you too well.

You're worried if you continue to involve me I'll have another attack. Don't worry. The real crazy shit has to be behind us. Look, my friend, I'm an old man living a tranquil, often boring life. We're trying to solve what could be the biggest story in history. I haven't felt this alive, this excited about anything—ever. I know it will be difficult for you but you've got to share what's going on with me. You're doing the heavy lifting—anyway. I'm guessing you knew this is exactly what I'd say, right?"

"You know me too well. I don't want to lose you and I'm not alone. Isabella and your Ernie feel just as strongly. How should I deal with you?"

"You picked that trick of turning things around from me. If you did, you learned well, but keep me in the loop. Plus, share Isaac's emails and anything significant your research uncovers. Most importantly, massage my ego and ask for my opinion and advice."

"Howie, I love you. I figure you've got at least another 20 years if you cut out doughnuts, all those fried chicken luncheons and get some exercise. I'll go along with your suggestion if you promise to take care of yourself and clean up your life. You know the drill. Do we have a deal? Pinky swear!"

"Pinky what? Where did that...Isabella! Here's my little finger if you can work around all the tubes."

Jan walked out of the hospital with a big smile on her face and a bounce in her stride. One problem solved, one awaits. Charlie, where are you?

60

Ernie was waiting, his tail wagging in circles, as Jan opened the Star-News door. She immediately called the seven staff members still in the office into the coffee room for a Howie update and to answer questions about upcoming stories and assignments. Meeting over, she checked to see if there were any messages for Howie that couldn't wait, then said good-bye to the staff, called for Ernie and headed to pick up her daughter.

Ernie's tail signaled Isabella must be approaching even though Jan couldn't see her—yet. "Hi, Sweetie!"

"Bonjour. How's Uncle Howie?"

"He's better. Hopefully he'll go home soon, maybe even tomorrow. We'll see him tonight. I've got an idea. Are you up for a yoga class? There's one at 4:00. We've got time to stop home and change."

"Oui, I'll wear the new yoga pants Dad got me."

Jan welcomed the activity time with her daughter,

consciously trying to spend more time with her. The peaceful atmosphere, soft music and deep breathing also helped center her thoughts. Class over, she opened her purse to find her phone light flashing.

Hi Jan, miss you and can't wait to see you. I'll be home around noon tomorrow and will call as soon as I can. I love you. c

"Charlie must have called or left you a message. Your eyes came alive."

"It was Charlie. He's coming home tomorrow. What do you want for dinner? I have stuff for a salad. After we eat let's go see Uncle Howie. How does that sound?"

"Oui, easy peasy!"

61

"Montgomery, we need you at Fort Meade tomorrow 0900." Charlie was caught totally off-guard by the brief phone call. This was a first. The first time he was ordered to report to NSA Headquarters. Because his recent work was routine he hoped this wasn't about the obvious,

Leonard Rosen/Isaac Stone.

After contacting NSA Travel and arranging a flight to Baltimore-Washington International Airport, Charlie's thoughts turned to Jan. He knew disappointing her again would only reinforce her fears that it was impossible to have a relationship with him and her reaction would be totally justified. Who lives a life like his? He wasn't just an employee of a government agency. He was their soldier, their servant subject to their orders. Charlie dreaded the phone call he had to make.

"Hi Charlie, I'm so happy you called!"

" I just got a call from my Division boss. I'm so, so sorry. I've run out of excuses. There's no way to spin this. I just got an order to report to Fort Meade tomorrow at 9:00 a.m. I'm in route to the airport now. I'm so sorry. Jan, are you there?"

"Hold on, I'm here."

"Isabella, I'm going to take Ernie out before we go to the hospital."

Walking with Ernie down the hall Jan waited till they got outside before responding to Charlie. "I can't take it. I can't, Charlie. With everything that's going on I like to think I can depend on you, but I obviously can't. You've made your choice. I can't live a life of constant fear and disappointments. You can't believe all that's going on

269

with me. I really need you."

"I totally understand your frustration. I've got to quit—now. My lip service doesn't cut it. Everything you just said is totally justified. I'm terribly disappointed in myself. You're more important to me than any job, or career. You are. I've got to act on what is right for my boys and us and quit the NSA—now!"

"Charlie, I've got to go. I can't live this fantasy. Good-bye."

Jan couldn't hold back the tears and disappointment. She stood motionless, shaking, next to Ernie's tree. Fuck being strong! Her life was disintegrating. She felt alone and overwhelmed. She didn't even get to tell him about Howie or the latest about Isaac. As she led the always affectionate Ernie up the stairs she couldn't hold back her tears."

"No, not again! Let me guess. It's Charlie. It's not fair. He must know that." Isabella wrapped her arms around her trembling tearful mother and hugged her tightly.

"Oh Bella. I tried! I tried to make it work with Charlie. I tried. Enough, I've had enough. I'm going to rinse my face off and then let's go to the hospital. Uncle Howie will be glad to see you."

Jan visited with the now familiar hospital staff as Isabella ran ahead to her Uncle's hospital room. A visibly subdued Jan followed but let her daughter carry the conversation. Ever perceptive, Howie quickly noticed and assumed it had to be either Isaac or Charlie. Isabella narrowed the choice to Charlie when she commented about his surprise call. Howie, thankfully, didn't bring out the "I told you so card" and luckily his Jeopardy on TV deflected further comment. After hearing the good news Howie should be going home in the morning, Isabella and Jan said their good-byes and headed home.

The air was gone from the Cooper apartment this Thursday night. With Howie at 50% and Charlie not available, Jan was alone as she literally confronted the weight of the world. There was little hope she'd sleep. Only Ernie by her side brought her any comfort and kept her in bed—crying.

62

Not sure if she slept at all but wide awake at 5:30, Jan started a pot of coffee. Although getting Howie home and settled was her immediate concern she couldn't stop thinking about Charlie and the "what if questions". Turning on her computer there were no emails from Charlie or Isaac, only seven emails from the Star-News staff. Ten minutes later, emails answered, she read the entire Star-News. Pouring a third cup of coffee she welcomed her daughter into the kitchen. "Good morning. I hope you slept better than me."

"Bonjour. I slept good. I mean well."

"There's juice and the cinnamon raisin bread you like for toast."

"Is Uncle Howie coming home today?"

"I think so, but I'm not sure what time. Hopefully he'll be home by the time you get out of school and we can visit him. I know he wants to see Ernie, too."

"Everybody always wants to see Ernie. He's been spending more time with you lately. That's good, you need him. He knows Charlie and you are having problems."

"I don't doubt that and please change problems to issues. I'm going to shower. You better get your butt in gear, too."

After dropping Isabella off at school, she called Howie. "Good morning. Any idea when you can go home?"

"Good morning. Doc Kumar is supposed to come by around nine. I'll call you as soon as I hear. And when you do come make sure you bring my boy with you."

"He'll be happy to see you. Just this morning he told

me how he misses you and those huge power biscuits."

Half the staff was in the office. Jan gathered them into the coffee room and gave them a Howie update. Then she sent out an email to the rest of the staff. Anticipating Howie would be able to go home she finished everything necessary for Monday's paper.

"Pick me up at 11:30. They'll wheel me out to the curb. Some sort of liability issue."

"Fantastic! See you with your friend at 11:30."

Since it only 10:15, she had an hour to start Howie's lifestyle turnaround. With Ernie sitting in the front passenger seat she drove to the market. Shopping for Howie turned into a real food adventure. Focused on healthy alternatives she was amazed at all the options. Quickly tired of reading labels, calorie counts and ingredients she threw brands she knew were healthy into the cart. Howie's diet was about to change.

63

Eight hundred miles from Raleigh, Charlie walked out from his meeting with a big smile on his face. He was surprised, excited and anxious to make one call. "I can't believe what just happened. Can you talk?"

"I've got about 20 minutes until I've got to pick-up Howie from the hospital. What now?"

"Howie from the hospital! What happened?"

"He had a heart attack around 2:30, Wednesday morning. He called 911, was picked up by ambulance and taken to the ER. Luckily he's going to be okay but he needs to clean up his life. It was one of the two huge events I couldn't wait to tell you, but you haven't been available."

"I'm so, so sorry. I had no idea. I need to see you. I've got a flight back to Chicago in two hours. I've got to tell you about my meeting and I want to hear everything that's been going on. I'm guessing there's more about Isaac. I can drive down later this afternoon. I can't wait to tell you about my meeting with my Division Chief at NSA Headquarters. Will you at least see me?"

"Oh, Charlie. I feel like a rubber band and I can only stretch so far for so long. Because of all that's been going on I was devastated by your last call. You snapped that rubber band into pieces. I needed you more than I've ever needed anyone in my life and I can't live like that. I won't live like that."

"You won't have to. I thought my meeting was going to be about Isaac, but it wasn't. I was surprised. I want to tell you what happened in person. I love you. I can be there by five."

"Listen Charlie. If you're going to sing me a different version of the same old song don't waste your time. I'm not going through that same dance again. Do you have any idea what the last few days have been like for me? Howie can't help me like he did before the attack. The stress from what I shared with him about Isaac's puzzle was, at the very least, the catalyst for his attack. He can't handle that much stress and I won't expose him to what could kill him. Charlie, what I've figured out from Isaac's clue could be the biggest discovery in history. That's why I needed you. I was devastated by your last call. I'm tied up in emotional knots. I'm being pulled, pushed, squeezed and hammered. You don't know the latest revelation from Isaac because you were too busy doing what you do for whoever you work for. And, I've been all alone. First Howie, then you."

"Oh my God, I must be the world's biggest asshole! I don't deserve you but I'm not coming down to tell you, yet again, that I'm thinking of quitting the NSA. Things are different. I want to share what happened at my meeting with you. I've got to come down. I wish I could hold you—now. I can't let you go. I love you and it kills me to hurt you the way I have. I hear it in your voice. Please see me and hear me out. We do have a future. I know we can work things out and I hope we will."

"Charlie, I want to love you. That's why it's so damn painful when I can't. Can you understand? Your priority is your job. Not your sons, not me. Don't come down unless that's going to change. If you drive down, we'll talk but I'm not giving you any promises. I can't just paste my heart back together. Sorry, but I've got to pick up Howie from the hospital. Charlie, I'm running out of hope. Bye."

She made it just in time. Howie was being wheeled out of the hospital by a slender male nurse. Ernie's tail did rapid circles once he spotted his friend. Jan stopped directly in front of the concrete walkway, opened the back door and let Ernie run to greet his buddy. The broad smile on Howie's face was better than any medicine. "Thanks Reuben. I appreciate all your help. Nurse Davidson was right. You do a great job."

"God, it feels good to get out of there. I'm going crazy being in the dark, not knowing what's going on. You've got to bring me up to speed. Are you expecting company? That's a lot of food for you and Isabella."

"Say hello to your new diet. I'm going through your refrigerator and pantry. Out with the old crap and in with healthy alternatives. You're going to be the healthiest you've been in years. I'm doing this for my own selfish reasons. I need you around."

"January, you continue to amaze me. Isaac's right, you are extraordinary."

64

Howie's two-bedroom brick house was on a quiet cul-de-sac in the nicer part of Raleigh. The interior's what you'd expect, worn out leather furniture, a 56" flat screen TV in the living room and an old Sony Trinitron in his bedroom. However, that's not what overwhelmed the eye when you walk into the house. That would be the thousands of books, large stacks of newspapers and piles of magazines, none arranged in any discernible order.

While Howie got settled Jan began tossing food culprits from the refrigerator and pantry into two large Hefty bags. Replaced by heart friendly options Jan hoped Howie would adjust. Then she hit the medicine cabinet tossing everything that had expired. "Really Howie, even your Viagra expired eight years ago."

"Someone gave me the bottle for a gag gift. Luckily, I don't need it. Please don't touch the alcohol. I need it for company. Now tell me what's going on?"

Luckily, Howie was up to date on Isaac's puzzle and Jan didn't have to face censorship decisions. "My research has convinced me no one in history has ever listened to more than Isaac and no one has been better equipped to evaluate what they heard. That's a unique combination. I've been waiting for his next email that should tell us more about #3. Ernie, how did you find those biscuits?"

Howie rather enjoyed the long needed house cleaning even suggesting he might get rid of the loose unbound newspapers. "Have I thanked you for taking care of the office. I assume everything's okay and hope the staff hasn't realized I'm really unnecessary."

"Stop! You're necessary. I couldn't and wouldn't want your job which reminds me you should send out a staff email. It makes sense for you to ease back to work. You should work from home next week then go to half-days."

Howie nodded as he sat down on his recliner, Ernie at his side. "How's your spy? What does he think of Isaac and his radio bursts?"

"Charlie's been unavailable. I haven't shared my email with him that I sent you. While you were in the hospital I needed him but he wasn't around. That hit me hard, and it reinforced why a relationship is impossible if he remains a spy. He called me a couple hours ago and told me he just got out of a meeting at NSA Headquarters. Apparently, there's a big surprise he can't wait to tell me. Since I unloaded on him I don't think he'd drive down if he didn't have good news. We'll see! He'll be here later this afternoon. What about you. What can I do before I leave?"

"Thanks, but I'm fine. You've got a good handle on what needs to happen with your spy. Now come here and give me a big hug. You too, Ernie."

With Howie settled Jan's attention turned to Charlie. She had no idea what to expect or how to prepare, but that could wait. Ernie's wagging tail meant the one constant in her life, her beautiful daughter, was walking towards the car.

"Bonjour!"

"Hi Sweetie. I just left Uncle Howie's. He's settled back home. I bought him lots of healthy food and threw away all the junk he had in his refrigerator and pantry. That's a start. Now we need to get him to the gym or at least walking regularly. He should rest today but we can visit him over the weekend. I got a call from Charlie earlier. He says he's got important news to share with me and he's driving down later this afternoon."

"Mom, I don't want him to hurt you and I don't want

you to be alone but Sandy's having girls over for a slumber party tonight. If you're going to be okay, I'll go to Sandy's."

"Isabella, you're so thoughtful. Thanks for always looking out for me. Call Sandy and find out what time."

"Way ahead of you. I just texted her and she says anytime. I'll pack some stuff and you can take me to Sandy's if you promise to call me if you need me. Pinky swear!"

"That's the second pinky swear I've done this week. Thank you, Isabella. I love you more than you'll ever know."

65

Back home after dropping Isabella off Jan uncharacteristically sipped on a glass of afternoon wine. Tonight, promised to be very different. No sexy outfit, no candles, no romantic music, not even a special dinner to leave uncooked. There's only one thing she wants. Their only chance is if he quits being a spy. It wasn't complicated and she intended to make it very clear.

Unsure exactly when he would arrive, Jan didn't want to talk to him until she could see him. She passed time sitting and thinking about the past month. Ernie was the only alarm she needed. He had no issues with Charlie and was excited to hear him walk up the stairs and down the hall. Never underestimate what's behind the door. There stood Charlie wearing a 3' tall dunce cap with the word "Asshole" printed across the front. The crazy, hilarious sight perfectly broke up what could have been a very awkward hello.

So much for good intentions. She did a jump hug wrapping her legs around his waist. "Oh Charlie, sometimes you are just irresistible. You just changed everything I was going to say or do. I hope what you're going to tell me translates to a lifetime of these hugs. You'd better come in and properly say hello to Ernie, and you might want to take your hat off. We've got a lot to talk about. Tell me about your meeting. Let's sit on the couch."

"First, I apologize—again. I had no idea what you were going through. Your plate was more than full with just Isaac's puzzle, but then add in Howie's heart attack and my bullshit. It had to be overwhelming. Let me see if I can get off that list. I got a call on Thursday to report to NSA Headquarters at Fort Meade. I thought it had to be about Isaac Stone. I had no idea what they knew but I guessed it had to be pretty significant to order me to Fort Meade on such short notice."

"Who was at the meeting?"

"Just me and Division Chief Simpson. Without any small-talk he asked me if I was happy with my job. I told him, very directly, it was placing an unbearable burden on my relationship with my two young sons and with the woman I hoped to marry. He nodded his head and said he could relate. That's why he wanted to talk with me about an opportunity to head a new group based out of the Chicago office. I was exactly what they were looking for, an attorney with considerable field experience. There will be six in the unit and I'd be in charge. It's basically oversight over what the NSA can and can't legally do. The job comes with a substantial raise and pretty-much a forty-hour work week. The Chicago NSA office is also less than 15 minutes from my apartment. That's my news. What do you think."

"I'd be screaming YES if I didn't have Isaac's puzzle hanging over my head."

"Of course, I understand. This new position could be the ideal transition into the private sector. It doesn't have to be permanent and might even help, in some way, with the Isaac equation. Also, if the position doesn't fit it will be much easier to leave the NSA. No more middle of the night assignments or extended jobs across the country. What do you think?"

"I think everything you said makes sense. It's certainly a big step in the right direction. You've pulled a rabbit out of that dunce cap—Cowboy. Charlie, kiss me then please rip my clothes off! I love you!"

"Wait, where's Isabella?"

"She conveniently went to a friend's slumber party. Bless her beautiful heart."

Nothing compares to make-up sex. The living room looked like it was hit by a tornado. Clothes were scattered amongst couch pillows and a jealous Ernie was resting his nose on Jan's pink panties. Both stark naked, Charlie grabbed Jan's hand as they got into the shower for round two.

After they ran out of hot water, Charlie carried Jan to bed. Knowing full well where it would lead, she rested her head-on Charlie's flat stomach. He was a happy man. An hour later, entwined together, Ernie's wet nose diverted their attention.

Retreating to the kitchen in just a t-shirt, Jan opened her laptop to show Charlie the email that precipitated Howie's heart attack. As he read, she fed Ernie and started their dinner—pancakes.

"Unbelievable! I can't imagine where this is going. Now I see what affected Howie. What's to come? Proof there's life outside earth is the biggest story ever! You've had time to digest this. Where's it going?"

"I have absolutely no idea. I've been waiting anxiously for the next clue. It's mind boggling. I keep reminding myself Isaac had a reason for everything. Nothing he's done has been by accident. There must be more. Hope you're hungry. Pancakes have become a staple around here. Ernie cleans up what we don't eat."

While Charlie took Ernie for a walk Jan quickly cleaned up the kitchen, living room and her bedroom. Wearing a robe over a naked body wasn't only sexy but also made picking out what to wear superfluous. She pondered Charlie's job offer trying to think of relevant questions. She thought of two.

The boys could be heard running down the hall. "I just love this dog. There's never been a sweeter face. I like that robe on you but I feel compelled to see what's underneath."

"Before you go searching I've got two questions about your new job offer. First, and I know this speaks to my paranoia, but do you think the NSA knows about Isaac's puzzle and wants to keep you close to me for surveillance purposes? Secondly, what does the job change entail and when would you start?"

"Your first question is valid but very unlikely. If the NSA wanted to spy on you there's better ways. This is where we need to rely on Isaac. He took the necessary steps to insure secrecy and the execution of his plan. Regarding the new job, I'd start a week from Monday once I give them my okay. If I do it will probably take me a week to get up to speed on legal issues, review case files and get to know the staff."

"Did you give them an okay?"

"No, first I had to discuss it with you and then with my boys. I'm sure they'll love the idea but I need to involve them in these decisions."

"I love that answer and I love you. Have you reloaded, Cowboy?"

Sexually reignited Charlie had fun playing inside Jan's robe and for the second time in the last three hours she ripped off his clothes.

66

Waking up next to Charlie's naked body was the perfect way to start her day. Fearing dreaded morning breath, she tip toed to the bathroom and her toothbrush. Charlie nakedly popped out of bed when she returned.

"I can't believe I forgot a change of clothes. I hope

my pants are still in one piece without your teeth marks."

"Very funny, Cowboy. I'd better call Isabella. She'll set my schedule."

"Good morning, Bella. How was your slumber party?"

"So much fun. We played with Sandy's karaoke. How was your night? Tell me what happened."

"Everything went great, much better than expected. Before you ask, Charlie's still here and says hello. What time should I pick you up?"

"Later this afternoon. Sandy's Mom's taking us to lunch and shopping. I'll call you when I'm ready to come home. Say hi to Charlie and give him a high five from me."

High five executed Charlie dressed in his wrinkled clothes as Jan started a fresh pot of coffee and pulled out bacon and eggs from the fridge. Charlie was on his phone, and judging by the conversation, talking to his boys as he walked into the kitchen.

"I was talking to my sons. They've got games this afternoon. I better leave after breakfast. Even though it's Kathy's weekend I want to see their games plus it will give me a chance to talk to them about my job offer. That way I'll be able to give my boss an answer on Monday."

"Sounds like a plan. We'll have to figure out our

schedule."

"We will. I'll call you later. Give Howie my best and tell him lots of fiber. Thank you for being so understanding. It was a fantastic night and I'm excited about our future. I love you."

"I love you, too. Drive safely, Cowboy!"

Occasionally reality surpasses expectations. This was one of those times. Jan smiled as she cleaned up the kitchen. Then her thoughts turned to Howie and she picked up her phone. "How you feeling? Did you sleep?"

"It feels great to get back in my own bed. How's your spy? How did it go?"

"It went better than I could have expected. I'll tell you more when I come over. Assume you'd like a visitor."

"I'd actually like two visitors. Bring my boy. I'd also love a glazed doughnut or two. Just kidding. I'm sure I'll get used to that plant based cereal prune mash in a year or two."

"You'll learn to love it. See you in a half hour."

As Jan ended her conversation she noticed her email light flashing on her phone. CLICK!

Jan
EEG
Neurons

Waves 5+1
Isaac

There it was. The email she's been waiting for. Isaac's timing was good; yesterday would have left her in total panic. There was no way Jan could wait. She Googled EEG and discovered the first twenty letter word she'd ever seen: electroencephalogram. Conveniently the description of neurons was in the next paragraph.

The brain consists of billions of neurons that use electricity to communicate with each other. Joined combinations of millions of neurons moving together form a neural network that can be linked to a state of consciousness.

Jan was relieved it was a clue she could share with Howie. She grabbed her computer and headed out the door with Ernie at her side.

67

Ernie ran to the door that quickly opened. "Hi Howie,

it's great to see you up and about. I've got lots of news."

"I'll bet you do. You can't hide that big smile or the glow on your face. Shove those magazines away, sit down and start talking. Wait a second, I'd better get Ernie a biscuit. He looks hungry."

The description of Charlie's job offer was brightly colored by Jan's enthusiasm over how it would positively impact their relationship.

"If he's smart he'll give up this spy crap, take the new job and hold onto you. Of course, I could raise the how long have you two known each other card. What, three or four weeks."

"You're right, I ask myself the same question. We're not rushing into anything. Seeing him last night was about whether we could have a future, not whether we would. Certainly, the intensity of all we've been through has affected our relationship. I still need to see how our compatibility plays out. Then there's Isabella and his boys to consider. Time will tell. We'll see. We're not flying to Vegas tomorrow."

"Well, with all you've been trying to figure out, Charlie shouldn't be too difficult."

"Something else happened. I'm telling you because I think you can handle it."

Slowly and very calmly, she showed Howie the latest

clue on her laptop screen along with the research she uncovered leading her to believe the fast radio bursts that key life elsewhere in the universe must somehow connect to brain waves.

"You're on to something. Not only does Isaac know how you think but you know how his mind works. I've got lots of time. I'll research EEG's and neurons and brain waves. Excuse me for not offering sooner but would you like some granola with soy milk or a dark berry fruit smoothie?"

"Sounds great but I had a big breakfast. Let me know what you find online. I'll keep searching, too. Is there anything you need before I go?"

"How about a pepperoni pizza? Just kidding! I'm good. Thanks for stopping by and bringing my boy. You're always welcome to leave him here if you need a dog sitter."

"I'll come by tomorrow with your boy and Isabella. Call me if you need anything."

Just past noon, Jan had time to go home, change and go for a run. Ernie got excited when he saw her put on her running shoes. Before they left, she texted Isabella telling her they were going out for a run and would be back home in about an hour.

The beautiful fall day was the perfect backdrop for

Jan and Ernie's five miles. Running back to the apartment, Ernie got to his water bowl before she could open a bottled water. The text from her daughter was brief.

Call U later.

Getting out of the shower and putting on her bathrobe immediately triggered flashbacks to Charlie. Assuming he was at his son's game she decided to wait and call him later to share the latest Isaac clue.

Sipping on her second bottled water Jan got back to Google and her search for more relevant information about brain waves. She was fascinated by a subject she knew little about. An EEG was described as a tool that reveals brain wave patterns and our thoughts, emotions and behaviors triggered by communication between neurons within the brain.

Her ringing phone had to be Isabella.

"Bonjour, can Sandy come home with me and sleep over?"

"Sure. When do you want me to pick you girls up?"

"Anytime. We'll be ready."

"I'll be by in a half-hour."

"Cool."

After bookmarking several articles and quickly

changing into shorts, t-shirt and flip flops, Jan and Ernie were out the door to pick up the girls.

Not surprisingly, their clocks were in sync. Isabella and Sandy came walking out the door as Jan pulled up to the curb. She was ready with answers to what promised to be probing questions about her night with Charlie.

"Girls, how was your slumber party?"

"So fun. We tried some new make-up. I loved the eye lashes and pink lip gloss best. Tell me everything about last night. Are you and Charlie back together? And how's Uncle Howie?"

"Uncle Howie's seems to be doing fine except it will take him some time to get used to his new diet. I'm sure Sandy's not interested in details about Charlie. We'll talk about it later."

"Sandy's interested, aren't you?"

"Pretend I'm not here. I don't know Charlie but he sounds cool."

"Isabella, I'll fill you in later. Do we need to stop at the market? Girls, what do you want to eat? Sandy, what do you feel like for dinner?"

"I can eat pizza every night with mushrooms and olives."

"Bella, you okay with that? There's still ice cream for dessert. I'll call Katie's when we get home."

"Perfect! I know it's Saturday night but I don't think we can do a movie tonight. We've got some other stuff. You can tell us about Charlie at dinner."

"Thanks for that suggestion, I can't wait."

68

"Pizza's here. Where do you girls want to eat?"

"We'll be in the kitchen in a minute."

Knowing her daughter's perseverance, Jan was ready with a condensed, PG version of her evening with Charlie. Isabella was right on cue. As soon as they sat down at the kitchen table she asked for a Charlie rundown.

"Charlie has an opportunity for a new job based in Chicago with much less travel. That'll make it much easier for us to see each other. We'll have to see how things go. Before you dig deeper, we talked a lot. It was a fun night. Charlie loves playing with Ernie."

"I know when you say 'it was a fun night' it's just code for sex. I want you to be happy. Mom, you're blushing."

"Sandy, do you have fun quizzing your mother the way Isabella does with me?"

"My parents live sort of a boring life except for my brother and me although they started doing this date night thing about six months ago. They get nervous talking about sex with me. All the girls think you're so cool, Ms. Cooper."

"Thanks Sandy for the complement. Isabella and I have some great books that trace everything that happens to girls as they grow up. I wish my mother had read them with me."

Finished with dinner and the Charlie conversation, the girls took big bowls of ice cream back to the bedroom with Ernie. For once, Jan was happy Isabella closed her bedroom door. She called Charlie and turned on her computer as she waited for his return call.

"Hi Jan, I missed you today. How's Howie?"

"He's seems to be doing fine. It's going to be difficult for him to change his diet and start exercising but he's got no choice. He doesn't have options. I did share Isaac's latest clue with him. It's tame since the 'we're not alone' that set off his heart attack. I just emailed you the clue. Before we talk about it tell me how things went with your boys."

"Of course they're happy. I knew they would be, but I'm glad I talked to them before I decided. The same as I was with you. Wow, this clue's different. I know a little about EEGs and neurons, but have no idea what Waves 5+1 means."

"We're thinking alike. This clue seemed different to me, too. It seems like we're getting closer to whatever it is Isaac wants us to know. Aha, I just think I figured something out. Howie mentioned it this afternoon."

"You mean like an 'aha moment'?"

"Exactly. Howie's always told me Isaac knew how I think. That's why he can predict how I'm going to react and what I'm going to do. Howie also thinks I've got a good handle on what Isaac's going to do and how his mind works. I'm thinking all the clues have been Isaac's way of showing me or teaching me something. Everything's leading to what he's about to tell us. I know I'm rambling, but does it make sense?"

"Absolutely! I've just had a little 'aha moment' of my own."

"If you're kidding me, it's not funny."

"No, no kidding. I know what Waves 5 refers to."

"Really. Shoot, Cowboy!"

"First back up a little and let me give you a little background on the NSA. They've been experimenting with brain waves and how to influence human behavior for a long time. Were you in a sorority in college?"

"Where the hell did that come from?"

"Brain waves, it's how I remember the five types of brain waves: Gamma, Beta, Alpha, Theta and Delta. That explains Isaac's clue except for the +1."

"Charlie, we're really figuring out Isaac's puzzle. Aren't we? What do you think?"

"It sure seems like it. Here's more perspective. Isaac knew how the NSA works. Hell, he built most of their technology. He knew he had to disguise what he wanted to tell you. That explains the cryptic messages only you would understand or figure out. But, what he did also taught you how his mind worked. Now, he wants you to execute what he knew he couldn't. Does that make sense."

"I've got goosebumps! Have we figured things out except for +1? All that remains is +1. That's got to be the key. Charlie, I've never felt the sense of accomplishment I feel now. Never in my life. Never! What are you thinking?"

"You're remarkable. Isaac knew it. That's why he chose you. I want to hold you. I can be there in two hours."

"Oh Charlie. I want you, too, but Sandy, Isabella's bestie is spending the night. It might be a little awkward. How about tomorrow. Drive down tomorrow and we can visit Howie together. Can you? Will you?"

"Yes, absolutely. I'll be there by 10:00. How does that sound?"

"Perfect. It sounds…Isabella, Charlie says hello. He's driving down tomorrow morning around 10:00."

"So cool! Tell Charlie I can't wait to hear about his new job in Chicago."

"Well, you heard my daughter. She came out to get some popcorn but she's back in her room with Sandy. I can't wait to see you, Cowboy. Thanks for all your help and your patience. Guess we make a pretty good team."

"I sure think so. I love you. See you in the morning."

"I love you, too."

69

Jan knocked on Isabella's door before opening it slightly. "Rise and shine girls, it's almost 8:00. Charlie's going to be here around 10:00. Come on Ernie, I'll take you out."

After showering and checking on the girls, Jan turned on her computer. The absence of email except for a few from Star-News staff was a welcome reprieve. After making a fresh pot of coffee, Jan thought back to her conversation with Charlie and brainwaves. She was excited to do more research.

"Good morning Sandy, how about some of my famous pancakes? Where's your friend?"

"Oui, merci. She's getting dressed."

"Do you speak French, too?"

"Isabella's teaching me. We're going to France together when we get older."

"That's great. I went to France during a trip to Europe after college. What time did you girls get to sleep? Either you were very quiet or I was very tired because I didn't hear you."

"We were pretty quiet except for Ernie's snoring."

"He must have been sleeping on his back with his legs in the air."

"Exactement!"

"Here's my daughter. Can I get you girls some juice?"

"Juice is great, Ms. Cooper. I can't wait for your blog. Are you going to call it Ask Jan?"

"My blog. Interesting. I'm sure Isabella will tell you all about it when we finalize everything. I don't think I could do it without her. In fact, I'm sure I couldn't. Right, Isabella."

"Mom, be nice, we have company and I like 'Ask January' better!"

"Bella, what are your plans for today?"

"We have a school project we're going to work on."

"When Charlie gets here we're going to Uncle Howie's. I've got to talk to Howie about Star-News stuff and Charlie wants to talk to him about working in Chicago. Can you and Sandy work from here?"

"Sandy, you can stay, can't you?"

"Sure, I think. I'll call my mom."

"Good. Now let's have pancakes."

Charlie, as usual, arrived right on time. Even with the girls in Isabella's bedroom Jan resisted her usual run-up hug in favor of a regular embrace, with a hidden hand squeeze of his butt. Ernie led the girls out to greet Charlie.

"Hi Charlie, this is Sandy, my best friend."

"Hi Sandy, that introduction is high praise coming from Isabella."

"Charlie, Mom says you might have a new job in Chicago."

"I think so, Isabella. My present job requires way too much travel on the spur of the moment. Makes it hard to make plans. I'll be working for the same people, just a different division. The new job will let me spend more time with my sons and your mom."

"Cool."

Uncomfortable where the conversation might lead, Jan interrupted, "Girls, we've got to go. Howie's expecting the two of us with Ernie, his new best friend. Isabella, I'll call you later and let you know when I'll be home. Call me if you need anything."

Walking out of her apartment Jan chuckled, "I love to watch you and Isabella interact. She likes you a lot. She's the best judge of how happy I am. I can't wait to meet your boys."

"You will, soon."

Ernie ran ahead to greet his friend as soon as Charlie opened the back door. Jan was thankful the anticipated meeting to discuss Isaac's puzzle was finally going to happen.

"Hi Howie, great to see you. You certainly don't look like someone who's just had a heart attack."

"Charlie, I'm glad you're here. Jan told me about your new job. I sure hope it works out."

"Thanks, so do I."

"In between eating gluten free all natural plant food cereal I've been playing in Jan's world and using Google to research all sorts of info on EEG's, neurons and brainwaves. Let's talk. Jan, you lead."

For the next two-hours they compared what they knew, what they had yet to discover and where they thought

Isaac was taking them. The timing for their meeting couldn't have been better. Howie's research confirmed much of what Charlie told Jan and there was agreement they were closing in on Isaac's objective.

"Guys, I've had an epiphany just listening to you two. I think the 'one' in the '5+1' is a new brainwave Isaac discovered that connects to fast radio bursts. Isaac may have invented a paradigm shift, of sorts. What he discovered could change how we think. Does any of that make sense?"

"Holy shit, that could be it. A new brainwave, the sixth. Why didn't I think of that? You're thinking like Isaac. He's succeeded. He knew you would get to this point. Unbelievable! I'm still digesting how one person can have an 'aha moment', an 'epiphany' and predict a possible 'paradigm shift' within fourteen hours."

"Thanks Charlie. Maybe I should try to use all three in a sentence. Howie, what do you think?"

"I think I might have hired the smartest, most over qualified reporter in the world. We're close to learning something monumental that can't be overstated. Think back to how far we've come in the last month. I can only repeat Charlie's word—unbelievable! It's all unbelievable! And Charlie, I'm thrilled you're going to be nearby."

"Howie, how do you feel. What's your heart monitor read. You can't get too excited. I don't want you back in the hospital."

"I'm okay, only 110. The excitement I'm feeling is more about the satisfaction over what we've accomplished. Charlie, I hope you realize what a special person you've grown attached to. She not only saved my life but has given me life."

"Believe me, I know. That's why I fell in love so quickly."

"I hate to interrupt all the sweet compliments but I've got a question for you both while we're together. Do we just wait for Isaac now or try to figure out what this brainwave is or does?"

"It's not our call. Isaac chose you for a reason. Your question must be, what should I do—now? Let it percolate in that head of yours. You'll figure it out."

"I totally agree with Howie. I'd only add I think we'll hear from Isaac—soon, very soon."

"Well, I feel good about how far we've come and I agree with you, Charlie. I think we'll hear from Isaac very soon. Howie, what's your pulse?"

"Down to 99, Doc Cooper."

"That's fantastic! Charlie, I think our work's done here. Take me home and then you better get back to Chicago. Tomorrow's going to be a big day for you."

Howie got hugs from Jan, Charlie and of course Ernie. On the drive home Jan called her daughter, "Hi Sweetie, have you girls had lunch?"

"Not yet."

"Charlie's got to get back to Chicago but I'll take you girls out to lunch. Think about where you want to go. See you in a few minutes."

"Charlie, I hope we've figured things out. I love you."

"Thanks for helping me make a decision that's long overdue. I can't wait to live our future. Call you tomorrow after I talk to my boss. I love you."

70

A good sleep and Jan was up with her alarm for a change. She threw on her sweats and flip flops, stopped to wake-up Isabella, and took Ernie out to visit his tree.

Returning to her apartment she started her coffee and turned on her computer. Six of her eight emails were from Star-News staff. One of the two left was from Charlie but that had to wait because the other email got her immediate attention. She CLICKED and for the next six minutes sat with her mouth open and goosebumps up and down her arms.

My Dearest Jan

1 of 5

Surprise, this is not a cryptic email. You've had enough of those. Instead, this is the first in a series of five emails that will explain how, with your tremendous help, we can make unprecedented positive change throughout the world. The United States and the world face a catastrophic tipping point. Our global threat is ideology based, poisoned by extreme religious beliefs. Conventional wars fought by outdated military strategy relying on obsolete weaponry limited by scope and scale, is rapidly being replaced by technology ignited without limitations. Digital wars will shut down and destroy civilizations with the push of a button on a smart phone.

Before I go further, there are two words I must tell you that seem woefully inadequate considering all you've done: THANK YOU! Not only for your friendship and love, but also for your tireless, extraordinary efforts solving a puzzle riddled with necessary challenges. I'm certain you can and will succeed. Also, a big thank you to Howie, who I know has given you help, support and opened his rolodex for you. Please accept my belief ev-

erything you're about to act upon will be well worth your incredible efforts.

One more thing before I explain how I found you. Matchmaking was new to me, but I did think you and Clifton, Cliff, Charles or perhaps you call him Charlie, would connect. Your profiles certainly match. He's a good man and hopefully you two can resolve his career choice, which must be causing consternation, and develop the serious relationship you so deserve.

Contemplating retirement, the NSA firmly requested I change my identity and relocate. Since they knew they'd always have me under 24/7/365 electronic surveillance they agreed to let me choose my new identity and where I wanted to live. My new alias, Leonard Rosen, as I'm sure you've discovered, was a nostalgic choice. How I ended up your neighbor in Raleigh requires a further explanation.

Faced with rapidly failing health, much worse then you knew, and constant surveillance from the NSA, I realized I'd never be able to execute my intricate plan. Having failed twice in my lifetime, with consequences and personal guilt beyond belief, I couldn't risk a third failure, especially since so much depends on my plans success. I had to find that person best qualified to carry out, quite possibly, the most important mission in history.

Fortuitously, I helped pioneer, build and perfect search engines over the last forty years. I found you after building a singular purpose search engine that analyzed and weighed eighty-six different human characteristics. That search scraped every bit of information in our digital world and chose you from a pre-qualified group of 6.2 million people. The fact you had a vacant apartment next door was an incredible stroke of luck that set my plan into motion. Please understand my death was a conscious, calculated and necessary choice. My only regret is that I subjected you and Isabella to discover my collapsed aging body. However, I assure you it was an absolutely necessity before I could start my plan.

This concludes my first letter, but stay tuned for the second to follow shortly. It will give you a historical perspective of Isaac Stone. Keep doing exactly what you've been doing and please give your wondrous daughter a big hug from her Papa Lenny.

Much love,

Leonard/Isaac

After reading Isaac's letter for the third time, Jan was lost in her own whirling head. There was a sense of relief, confusion, intimidation, accomplishment and sadness. She desperately needed to share the letter with

Howie and Charlie, but Charlie's availability was questionable. Informing Howie was a different issue. How could she show him this letter without provoking another incident? Searching for anything, she took her own heart rate. 122 was twice her normal rate but still far less than the 150 she often reaches during spin. Taking a cautious approach, she decided to hold off telling Howie until she discussed the letter with Charlie.

Isabella interrupted her train of thought. "Aren't you going to the office?"

Closing her laptop she rushed to the shower while all her thoughts stayed focused on Isaac's letter. Reality hit when she walked into the Star-News office and was peppered with questions about Howie. Setting a 10:00 staff meeting gave her a little breathing room, but running the Star-News was not her priority.

Turning on her computer she found five emails from the staff and one other she had forgotten from Charlie. CLICK!

Jan, it's a big day for us and our life together. Loved yesterday and I love you. Call you later to let you know how things went. C

"Hi Howie, how you feeling?"

"Okay, but I'd be lying if I said getting use to this new food is easy. How do people eat this crap? It tastes like wet cardboard."

"Isn't that how most people feel about Scotch or vodka when they first taste it. You'll learn to like it. I'm forwarding the staff emails to you. It will give you something to do. If you haven't already, I'd suggest you let them know about visiting hours. We're having a staff meeting at 10:00. I'll answer the questions I can then suggest they email you with any other questions. I've been sending you copies of everything I email to the staff."

"Sounds good. Are you coming by today?"

"Yes, thought I'd stop by after I pick Isabella up from school."

"Good. Call me if anything comes up. I'll be here. You can drop Ernie off if you go to the gym. What else? I'll bet you're going to get something from Isaac very soon."

"Can't disagree. See you later."

Jan was relieved this would be her last staff meeting. Howie could handle them over the phone and respond to questions and assignments via email or text.

The fifteen-minute meeting over, she grabbed a cup of coffee, smiled at the new assortment of healthy snacks and withdrew to her office. Almost lunchtime, Ernie stayed with the food.

Another reading of Isaac's letter gave Jan an interesting perspective she didn't have before. His plan was about redemption for the perceived failure and guilt of not being able to stop the Kennedy assassination and 9/11. She was in disbelief and humbled by how he chose her from millions of other people and amused by his reference to what she might call Charlie and his luck at finding a vacant apartment next door.

His letter also answered the question why he didn't execute his plan. His health was failing much more than Jan or even his doctor realized and he knew the constant monitoring by the NSA precluded him from carrying out his own mission.

The way she presented the email to Howie would be critical and certainly accompanied by Isabella wasn't the appropriate time. Waiting until tomorrow would also allow Jan to get Charlie's opinion on how he thought Howie would react. Now it was time to pick-up Isabella and visit her Uncle Howie.

71

The visit to Howie's was pleasantly uneventful. Not surprisingly, his bitching about his new healthy diet persisted. Ironically, despite her own eating habits, Howie listened to Isabella's opinions on food.

Back home Isabella retreated to her bedroom while Jan called Charlie's number and waited for his return call.

"Well, congratulate me, I've got a new job!"

"That's fantastic! I'm so excited for you!"

"For us. My schedule should be light this week. All I've got is to summarize the activity on my old files, review new files and meet with the woman who's taking my place. I'd love to see you."

"A woman replacing you. I like that. Cowboy, check your email. I just sent you something you might want to read—right now."

For the next few minutes all Jan heard were short gasps, intermittent swearing in disbelief and the repetition of a few of Isaac's words. Not surprisingly, reading the letter once wasn't enough.

"I'm extremely flattered over how he chose me, but terrified of the enormous responsibility it brings. It feels like the weight of the world has landed on my shoulders. How about the reference to you and what I call you? How insightful is that? Somehow he knew, or somehow planned, you'd be picking up his things. It's all so un-believable. I can't get a handle on his mission but we'll find out soon enough. Four more letters. Only four more. I can't even imagine where this is going!"

"If you can't, no one can."

"I need your opinion on whether I can share this with Howie. I held off because I wanted to talk it over with you. My thinking is that I must do it in person. What do you think?"

"Couldn't agree more. You being with him is a neces-sity. You can tweak your presentation by how he reacts. It will give you options plus you can keep monitoring his heart rate."

"I know him better than anyone. It's not just the most consequential event of my life, it is for him, too. I can't shut him out, but I need to monitor him closely. I'm glad you agree. Now when am I going to see you?"

"Maybe Wednesday or Thursday. I'll know more to-morrow."

"Let me know when you've got your schedule figured

out. I'm going to do more research on brain waves to-night. I think Isaac expects me to."

"I love you. Call me if you need anything. I'm on my way to pick up Max and Harry. We're going to din-ner and then I've got to take them shopping for winter clothes. They're growing so fast, it's one year and done."

"Bye, Cowboy. I love you, and congratulations on your new job!"

With Isabella consumed doing whatever it is she does with her girlfriends on their phones, Jan opened her lap-top and searched the five types of brainwaves. Call them parts of the Greek alphabet or a sorority row: Beta, Al-pha, Theta, Delta and Gamma. Not only do they vary in frequency but also in amplitude, which is the depth and height of each wave. When she searched for the "sixth brain wave" she found a wide range of speculation that appeared to be from a sci-fi movie. Of course, she could argue the entire Isaac puzzle was the ultimate sci-fi mov-ie. Only, it's a true story.

Tired of searching, she pulled out her journal. Both Isaac and Charlie needed to be brought up to speed. There promised to be lots of additions in the very near future.

"Isabella, what do you want for dinner?"

"Don't laugh but how does popcorn sound?"

"Sounds perfect! How did you know that's what I was thinking? Guess you really are my daughter."

"I can always tell when you've talked to Charlie!"

72

Jan fell asleep dreaming about her future honeymoon then woke in the morning not sure where she left off other than they were on a beautiful beach in Maui. Back to reality, her morning routine in motion, she sipped her coffee as she checked her email. CLICK!

My Dearest Jan,

2 of 5

Your tireless, extensive research has discovered much of my background. My parents were not only brilliant but also very forward thinking about how best to educate their son. Thank my mother, a high school French teacher, for my love of the French language I was teaching your amazing Isabella. My father, a brilliant mathematics professor, gave me the foundation and freedom to always ask beyond why and not fear the challenges caused by disrupting existing thought.

Each of us is born with unique talents. My mental capability has been a wonderful gift that I harnessed to a tech explosion. Recognizing my innate intelligence my father introduced me to a host of scientists and mathematicians before my tenth birthday. As you've discovered, this led to my collaboration with Professor Richard Schneider who became a dear friend and my traveling companion for yearly Grateful Dead concerts.

My year at MIT was devoted to perfecting an algorithmic information intelligence gathering and analytic program with Richard that became the foundation for the collection and analysis of information from multiple sources. As a byproduct of this research I was contacted by several NSA officials doing research at MIT. This led to my interview and job offer from the NSA. At the height of the Cold War, 1963, a naive seventeen-year-old was both flattered and proud to begin work at the NSA.

Soon after my start with the NSA I deployed our algorithmic program to analyze disparate bits of information that when connected led me to believe an assassination attempt on President Kennedy would occur during his trip to Dallas. This appeared a likely event, meaning greater than 80%. Following NSA protocol, I filed my report on Tuesday, October 15, 1963. With no response from my superiors I re-filed my report on Wednesday,

October 30, 1963. This time I received an abrupt phone call reply, "Mr. Stone, we have received and reviewed your report and are taking the appropriate action. You file is now closed. Nothing more is required of you."

On Friday, November 22, 1963, I was devastated and never escaped the guilt of not being able to stop the assassination of President Kennedy. I unsuccessfully rationalized it was my age, inexperience and lack of relationships at the Agency that precluded others from taking my findings seriously. Hours after the assassination, I was visited by a Secretary of something at the NSA who told me all Kennedy intel was on lock-down and he demanded all my work on Kennedy. This sticks out in my memory because the officer just stood in front of my desk and waited until I gave him what he thought was all my paperwork. However, it was NOT my only copy. Included with this correspondence is Exhibit A, my complete Kennedy file.

The Kennedy Assassination was obviously a defining moment in my life. With many opportunities in the private sector I seriously contemplated leaving the NSA. Then in 1965, everything changed. I was assigned to oversee a new Top Secret surveillance mission directly the result of the exploding Space Age. The goal was to collect and analyze the noise (radio waves) from outer space as detect-

ed by high powered radio telescopes around the world.

At first, this seemed like boring research with no specific objective, but after several months it not only became fascinating, but also the only reason I remained with the NSA for almost fifty years. I was the only person in the world with total access to all the noise from the universe. Listening became my job and my passion. More importantly, it became the basis for my third major discovery. Much more of this later but I thought I'd better answer the obvious question of why I stayed at the NSA.

There's always been inherent problems in a secretive agency with an agenda that includes internally spying on their own citizens. When you add in almost no transparency and little accountability accentuated by changing administrations one finds the perfect mechanism for uncontrolled, abusive power. This continually frustrated me and forced me to build a wall around my work, first paper than digital, that existed until the day I left. The threat of what I knew was offset by my superiors having no clue exactly what I did. Whoever was in charge left me alone in my own little world. And, from 1965 till the day I left the NSA I listened and recorded everything.

By the summer of 2001, eight different administrations had been in power during my tenure at the NSA.

The ability to collect intelligence information increased by a factor of 50 thousand from 1963 to 2001. The advent of the computer age, the Internet and cell phones greatly increased the enormity of information collected. Specialized search engines, most that I built, targeted and profiled whoever and whatever I chose.

In 2000, I started to hear an increasing frequency of communications describing a planned terrorist attack against the U.S. It was not until June of 2001 that I connected the dots. My prediction was an attack on the United States by commercial airliners deployed as missiles targeting landmark buildings in NYC and Washington DC was imminent. My first report was sent to the reigning powers at the NSA on June 7th. With no response, on June 9th, I submitted my report for the second time. Copies of both reports are included as Exhibit B. On June 10th, I received an email from the Deputy Director marked Top Secret. (Also included in Exhibit B) I was told my findings were being investigated by a Special Unit at the Agency directly charged with addressing potential terrorist attacks. September 11th was the worst day of my life. I was so thoroughly frustrated, make that devastated, by my inability to stop the attack I seriously considered contacting the New York Times or 60 Minutes.

Allow me to lighten the tone of this email. I know how relieved you were I always wore my headphones because of your distaste for the lengthy songs from my favorite band, The Grateful Dead. However, the Dead were my accomplice, not because they recorded so many fantastic songs, but because they gave me the ideal cover to listen to what I needed to hear.

Before I left the NSA, I went through a two-week debriefing, at least that's what they call it. It was their attempt to insure I took absolutely nothing with me, and therefore could never support or document what I knew. Ironically, I took everything, and have been challenged more by video games than their exit interview. It wasn't difficult since I built most of the technology that recorded what they were trying to stop me from taking. When you'd see me in my apartment working at my little desk you were walking into a field office of the NSA.

Hopefully, this email has shed light on how we arrived here. Up next, #3, a description of my plan and why it's so important.

Much love,

Leonard/Isaac

Jan was numb, nothing moved except her wildly spinning mind. Isaac revealed much, answered questions, filled in some gaps and even included funny antidotes. As much as she wanted to call Charlie and dissect the letter she had to get ready for work and drop Isabella off at school.

"Let's go, school's waiting."

"I'm coming. Do you have Ernie's leash?"

"Way ahead of you, come on."

Ernie instinctively still ran to Howie's office when she opened the Star-News front door. Jan followed, pulled out a chicken flavored biscuit that Ernie devoured in two gulps and headed to her office. After turning on her computer, she called Charlie. Seconds later her phone rang. "Good morning, how are things in Raleigh?"

"You'll see, check your email. I'll hold until you finish reading."

A hundred miles apart, Jan re-read Isaac's letter waiting for a response from Charlie. "Wow, I don't know what to say. He's answered questions we've had then created a bigger question about what's next. What's your take?"

"I'm with you and wondering how I just assumed he was listening to the Grateful Dead for all those years."

"You weren't naïve. It gave him cover with the NSA for almost a half century. I'm heading to the office but let's talk later. Have you told Howie—yet?"

"Not yet. I'm going to his house after I finish some Star-News stories. Wish me luck!"

"You make your own luck. I love you."

"Wait. I've got to tell you about the dream I had last night. I dreamt we were walking on the beach in Maui."

"I like that dream and I'm making a mental note about Maui."

"You'd better make it more than just a mental note. We were in Maui for our honeymoon, Cowboy!"

73

Ernie couldn't wait. As soon as Jan opened her car door he ran ahead to Howie's front door, somehow pushing the doorbell with his nose. The smile on Howie's face when he saw his Ernie was a positive sign for a nervous Jan. After small talk about the paper, she matter-of-factly revealed she got an email from Isaac that wasn't cryptic, but rather, explanatory. With her laptop open to the first letter Jan started her discussion with Howie. The format worked. Two parts of the letter stuck out for him: the mission to positively change the world and the way he located Jan.

"Holy shit, that explains a lot. Great summary. I know you're concerned about me but my heart rate's only 96. I'm well within my safe range. What's your take on his letter?"

"First, the format. Thank God, no more of those cryptic clues. I'm flabbergasted over how he chose me out of six million people. Obviously, I'm terribly troubled and extremely sad he felt compelled to take his own life, regardless of how sick he might have been."

"What did Charlie have to say?"

"Pretty much the same as us. Oh, guess what? Charlie took the new job. I'm not sure where that's going, either. Howie, what's happened to my life? It's all so beyond bizarre. I don't know how to feel?"

"I'll string along with Isaac. There's a good reason he chose you. I still remember our first meeting. You impressed me as soon as you spoke. My only trepidation was you were way too smart for the job which you obviously are. By the way, how's that journal coming?"

"Thanks for reminding me. I'll work on it this afternoon."

"After you go over tomorrow's paper, of course."

"Of course! Call me if you need anything. I'll call if anything comes up. I must confess I wasn't sure how our new discussion procedure was going to work, but it does.

Come on Ernie."

"Thanks Jan!"

Too late for Tony's noon spin class, she stopped to pick up a sandwich and yoghurt on her way back to the office. As she ate she reread Isaac's #2 of 5.

After finishing her Star-News stories she opened her journal only to be interrupted by her phone before she started to write. "Good afternoon you beautiful, brilliant woman who dreams of Maui. How did it go with How-ie?"

"Much better than I expected. His heart rate only got to 96, but I still decided to hold off with Isaac's second letter until tomorrow. His take is the same as ours. When am I going to see you? Isabella's with her dad tomorrow night. Can you drive down?"

"To see you, I'd drive anywhere. What time?"

"Any time after 5:00. Is this a booty call?"

"Booty call. It's not a booty call when you're in love, is it? I thought that was the rule."

"You're funny. Do you have Max and Harry tonight?"

"I do. Pick them up from school in an hour, then shopping and out to dinner. Of course, they'll both tell me they don't have any homework and I'll play along with them. I did the same thing with my dad."

"Girls are different. I believe Isabella when she tells

me she doesn't have homework. Speaking of my daughter, I've got to pick her up. Send me one of your romantic emails before you go to bed, Cowboy."

"You got it. I love you."

With her life in chaos, Jan appreciated a routine, quiet late afternoon and evening and a chance to catch up on her journal. Not just to write but to analyze her behavioral patterns. After observing her for years, Isaac must have known how she'd react to every situation. Was she that predictable or was he that smart? It was easier to just accept that he was that smart. She was more concerned with Charlie's predictability as she opened his email.

I graciously accept your sexual invitation to rendezvous tomorrow night at 6:00. I love you more. c

74

"You're washing clothes before work. Let me guess. Charlie's coming tonight."

"Very funny but you're right, Charlie's driving down tonight. Your dad's picking you up from school and I'm sure you can twist his arm to take you shopping."

"When are you going to introduce them?"

"Hadn't thought of it. I only met Charlie a little more than a month ago. Isn't that kind of soon? We'll see. Eventually, if everything goes well. Are you packed for your soiree with your dad? Get your stuff and let's get you to school."

It was Jan's day to pick-up snacks for the office. Instead of the doughnut shop she stopped at the market for apples, bananas, granola and non-fat milk. Let's see how the "I'll eat anything staff" reacts. On the drive to the office she called Howie. "Good morning, how you feeling?"

"Better, a bunch of my loyal employees came by last night."

"Good, I knew they would. I'll be over in about an hour. Can I leave Ernie with you while a take a noon spin class."

"Absolutely, I'm not going anywhere."

No sooner did she hang up with Howie then she got another email, CLICK!

My Dearest Jan,

3 of 5

Although the word fortuitous has always been a favorite, I never thought it would lead to the most significant discovery of my life. By now I'm sure you've researched fast radio bursts and discovered the monumental importance of what they reveal. What you don't know, until now, is how these fast radio bursts lasting only a few milliseconds will dictate the fate of civilization.

You now know my headphone history but what you don't know is what I'm about to tell you that, rather unbelievable, happened years ago. First, I built a unique technology platform that magnified the length of fast radio bursts from milliseconds to actual seconds. This began my study of these, first thought to be, random radio waves. Then one night, everything, including the future of the world, changed.

With headphones on, I was experimenting with fast radio bursts. It was very late and I had probably been working for at least 18 hours straight. Exhausted, I fell asleep with the headphones on listening to the repetition of FRB 121102, over-and over-and-over again. When I woke the next morning, I felt something I'd never felt before in my life. I was totally dumbfounded and whatever it was had changed me in some unexplained way.

This began my targeted experimentation to analyze fast radio bursts and their impact on the human brain, my brain. I would stay up beyond exhaustion until I would fall asleep with headphones on. When I woke, I'd measure a broad series of questions to help define what I was feeling. The years of strain this sleep pattern took on my body obviously accelerated my existing health problems. However, it was a risk well justified by my ultimate findings.

Eventually I connected fast radio bursts with my brain waves to alter my behavior. Please read this last sentence again and again and again. I cannot overstate its importance.

When I retired from the NSA and my search found you, my goal was to affect positive change to the world and implement a platform that would eliminate the threat of all wars, including cyber wars and bring peace to the world.

Fast radio bursts, as you have deduced by now are my +1. The sixth type of brain wave. For years, we've known brain waves could alter human behavior when imposed during stages of sleep. My discovery took a giant leap forward. Now brain waves could change human behavior towards a specified goal based on frequency, much like many machines that are connected to the body with different electrical frequencies to produce or affect a desired goal.

I can only imagine what you're thinking. Let me take a giant step backwards in the study of human behav-

ior, more specifically "change". We know how difficult conscious change can be. It's a flaw in human behavior. However, I discovered a way to change human behavior unconsciously by programming frequencies to the brain during sleep. The fail-safe component is that my program has been written to only create positive change. Going one step further, and this is an area of my discovery I'm particularly proud, I discovered these frequencies to the brain can be connected to a targeted person through a device most people in the world now have: a smart phone. This function doesn't even require a call between two phones. The frequency can be sent to any phone, at any time, when the power is on. We can positively change human behavior and you are going to be the person who implements this change.

I know this plan is difficult to digest but understand the ramifications on a global basis. The behavior of global leaders can now be changed 180^0. Fear can become hope. Lies can become truth. Hate can become forgiveness. Acts of war can be eliminated through peaceful solutions. Conflicts can become resolutions. And, most importantly today, terrorism can be eliminated and cyber wars blocked.

I wish I was now there with you to respond to your many questions. Hopefully, I will answer those ques-

tions in #4 and #5, to follow. Please, please, my brilliant friend, try not to let what you've just read overwhelm or intimidate you. Instead, think of the ramifications of what you'll be doing. You, my dear friend, with a little help from me will change the civilized world.

Much love,

Leonard/Isaac

She couldn't breathe. She couldn't move. What did she just read? What does she have to do? Unbelievable! It was all so unbelievable! Her heart raced. She started to shake. She needed fresh air. With Ernie at her side she walked around the block, once, twice and a third time, oblivious to everything except the enormity of what Isaac was proposing.

Back in her office she tried to organize the thoughts in her spinning head. Howie, what could she tell Howie? Not what she just read. It could kill him. If these questions were troubling what was it going to be like when Isaac revealed his plan of action—her action? She headed to Howie's.

As Ernie ran ahead to Howie's front door, Jan took a series of deep breathes hoping her boss would just assume her flustered appearance or behavior was the result of Isaac's second letter—not what followed in his third.

"Good morning. Your buddy can't wait to see you. How's your rehab going?"

"Rehab! Is that what it's called? I'm sleeping better. Notice anything different?"

"I do. I can see light coming in from the windows. You got rid of all that crap, the old papers and magazines."

"Most of them. Kept a few, stored in a box in the garage. Actually, I recruited help from a few of my employees to move all that so-called crap."

"I'm sure they were glad to help. I've got another letter from Isaac to discuss with you. Do you want to stay out here or sit at the kitchen table?"

"Let's sit at the kitchen table. I need to get Ernie a biscuit. He's lucky, his diet hasn't changed."

Opening her laptop to Isaac's #2 she started with the obvious question to Howie. "Before I start, what's your heart rate monitor read?"

"81, let's go."

"This letter follows his history with some interesting tidbits and foreshadows what's to come. We know all about Richard Schneider and their work together and that his mom was a French teacher and his father, a math professor. They recognized his brilliance, early on."

"You're right, we know all that, don't we?"

"Yes, I think so. He does write about how the algorithmic platform he built with Schneider led to his Kennedy prediction and how he made the same report twice but was ignored both times. He never escaped the guilt of not being able to stop the Kennedy assassination and contemplated offers from the private sector. Then in 1965, everything changed. He was assigned to collect and analyze the noise collected by telescopes around the world from outer space. The new division he led was the direct result of the space boom. Significantly, he was the only person in the world with total access to all this noise."

"So that's why he stayed with the NSA? I wondered since he must have had all sorts of offers from universities and the tech industry. This stuff is tame. My heart rate's only 86."

"You'll get a kick out of this. It was no secret he was a Deadhead and everyone at the NSA assumed he was listening to their music because he always wore headphones. He kept wearing them even after he left the NSA, as we know. All the while he was listening to the sounds of the universe. Meanwhile, no one at the NSA had any idea what he did. He built a wall around his work that the NSA never was able to penetrate."

"The headphone story is brilliant. The perfect cover.

Hell, it fooled us."

"In June of 2001, he discovered bits of communications that led him to predict 9/11. For the second time, the NSA chose to ignore him. 9/11 was the worst day of his life."

"I can't imagine what he felt. Twice in a lifetime. It's unbelievable."

"Finally, he remarks about his exit interview with the NSA. They tried to debrief him over two weeks to insure he didn't take anything. Quite the opposite, he took everything. He sent me the files for Kennedy and 9/11 but I haven't had time to read them, yet. Finally, he closes this letter by indicating his next letter will include a description of his plan and why it's so important."

"This letter lays the foundation for what's to come. My heart rate's only 93. Thanks for keeping me in the loop. This format's working well."

Ernie and Howie said their goodbyes as Jan left for her much-needed noon spin class. Amazing how an hour surrounded by other sweaty bodies keeping beat to pulsating music cleared her mind. The clutter had been attacked and replaced by endorphins. She felt back to normal when she stopped at Howie's to get Ernie.

"Everything okay here? Do you need anything besides a double bacon cheeseburger and fries?"

"I guess that spin stuff really does work. You seemed pre-occupied before, but back to normal—now. Maybe I'll get well enough to take spin. I haven't ridden a bike in 50 years. Which instructor do you recommend?"

"That's easy. Either Brandy or Tony. They're both great, for different reasons. Regardless of class you'll be surrounded by hot, sweaty, fit women."

"Perfect! Now get back to your day job!"

With free time before Charlie's arrival Jan thought of shopping for dinner but realized they rarely get to dinner. She still had enough candles to light up an airport runway and a playlist full of Al Green and Marvin Gaye songs. Other than throwing her wet clothes in the dryer the rest of her afternoon was delightfully free. A rare afternoon nap even sounded appealing.

With Ernie on the couch next to her she turned on Ellen thinking that would put her to sleep. Forty minutes later, still wide awake, she pulled out her journal and entered the origin of Isaac's unbelievable plan.

75

She loved Charlie's punctuality even if the excited

Ernie blocked the front door. "Flowers, you're so sweet! I love them and you! Should I just rip your clothes off before you sit down or do you have a better idea?"

"If you think I'm going to say anything except please, we're both crazy. Let me start unbuttoning you."

"That should be easy, Cowboy. There's only one button and one snap. Are you going to do it with your teeth?"

Quickly naked, Charlie carried Jan over his shoulder to bed. If their passion was being tested they passed with flying colors in ten minutes. But, just to be sure they continued to work on their timing for an additional hour.

"I'm glad you don't have one of those belly button rings. It would scrape my face or get caught in my hair."

"That's a compliment I've never heard before. If I had one, I'd be afraid you might chip a tooth or cut your tongue."

As they playfully tried to guess the words they were writing with their fingers on each other's body, Jan had to tell Charlie, "I got another letter from Isaac, but it's not just another letter. I've got to show it to you—now. Stay here, I'll get my laptop."

Sitting up in bed, Charlie read Isaac's #3 of 5 as she watched his eyes and facial expressions. She had never seen him move his lips as he read.

"Unbelievable! It's unbelievable!"

"That's what I said!"

"I'm trying to grasp the scope of what he's written. Are we starring in the best sci-fi movie of all time? To connect radio waves from God knows where to the brain, and then figure out how they can be used to alter human behavior via a cell phone. You kidding me! Isaac had to be the smartest man who ever lived or perhaps an alien from wherever those radio bursts came from!"

"Wait, you're kidding, right? I hadn't thought of that. You've got to be kidding! He couldn't, could he? That's impossible, isn't it?"

"At this point I'm not ruling out anything. He's dropping the world upon your shoulders. How do you feel about that?"

"I had a panic attack when I first read it. Now I'm not sure how I feel, although I'd rather not have it described as dropping the world on my shoulders."

"You haven't told Howie yet, have you?"

"No, I couldn't. It could kill him. I don't know what to do. I was going to ask for your opinion. The stuff I've told him from the first two letters has been tame. This letter is different."

"I don't have any answers on how to handle Howie. That's your department. You'll figure something out. Hell, if Isaac believes you can implement his plan I've

got confidence you'll figure out how to deal with Howie."

"I appreciate your confidence. I'm just not sure I share
the confidence in myself that Isaac does."

"It's unbelievable falling asleep with the headphones
on triggered his plan. You can't write this. No one could
come up with this scenario. Isaac planned everything,
step by step. Each step was designed to lead to the next
step. There's been a reason for everything. I can't imagine you reading this alone. I need to get up. Let's get
dressed and go for a walk."

"We are compatible. That's what I did after I read it."

For fifteen minutes, they walked holding hands, with
barely a word spoken. They only stopped when Ernie
had to mark a tree or smell something. There were no
five-minute kisses, only contemplation. When they returned to the apartment, Jan made their dinner of choice:
pancakes with a side of bacon for Charlie and Ernie.

"I think I know how I'm going to deal with Howie.
I've got to temper my narrative. I can't get too excited or
let him know how this shook me up. I'll keep one eye on
his heart monitor to make sure it's not jumping too high.
How does that sound?"

"It sounds a lot better than anything I can come up
with. Knowing your relationship with him it would be

impossible to keep this from him and who knows what will follow. What about your daughter?"

"God, I haven't even thought how this is going to affect her. Whenever I bring her into the equation I lose it. How can I do whatever it is Isaac's going to suggest and keep it from her. Howie's hard enough but Isabella, too! This is overwhelming, it's driving me crazy. Charlie, hold me!"

And, Charlie didn't let go, carrying her to bed. After she fell asleep, he quietly took Ernie out. As he crawled back into bed next to the woman he wanted to spend the rest of his life with, he carefully wrapped his arm over her shoulder and gently kissed the back of her neck goodnight.

76

Charlie was up at 4:00. He had to get back to Chicago for an early meeting. Realizing she was alone in bed and hearing him in the kitchen, Jan threw on a robe and joined him.

"I'm sorry. With all that was happening last night I didn't get a chance to tell you I need to get back home for a meeting this morning."

"I'm so glad you drove down last night. I would have gone crazy without you. I feel like I'm constantly walking up a hill that keeps getting steeper. I need you."

"You've got me. I can't imagine all you're going through. I'll do whatever I can to support you. Do you think I should rent Isaac's old apartment?"

"What? Where did that come from? That's either an interesting possibility or an awkward suggestion. I hadn't thought of it. Logistically it might work for us but I don't know how I explain it to my daughter. Wouldn't it complicate things, even more?"

"You think about it, the plusses and minuses, then we'll talk, okay? The last thing you need is something else to worry about. Let me think more about it, too. I'm glad I drove down. Oh, there is some good news. I'm getting a new phone. We'll be able to talk like normal people"

"Thank God. Charlie, I love you. Drive safely."

"I will. I love you, too."

Come on Ernie, let's go back to bed. Hoping she was going to fall back to sleep was wishful thinking. It didn't happen. Lying in bed, her head spinning she wondered how many different things a person can worry about simultaneously? She had Isaac, Howie, Isabella and

Charlie and they were all connected. Drawing from yesterday's stressful craziness she knew getting away for strenuous exercise every day was a must. She had to make the time to keep her sanity.

Motivated by her own pep talk she put on yoga pants, a sports bra, t-shirt and her running shoes. With Ernie leading the way she headed out for a morning run. The FOR RENT sign on the front lawn always seemed to catch her attention and different scenarios dominated her thoughts for the first three miles of her five miler.

With Rick dropping Isabella off at school, Jan had a little extra time before she needed to be at the office. Besides continuing to marvel at Isaac's genius she pondered Charlie's comment about where Isaac was from. Was it possible, even in the realm of possibility? Could Isaac somehow be connected to the life force that sent the fast radio bursts? How crazy is that! Thankfully her phone interrupted a conversation she was having with herself that was going nowhere.

"Bonjour! How's Charlie?"

"Good morning Isabella. Charlie's fine, he left a little bit ago. How was your time with your dad?

"You were right. We went shopping. Wait till you see what I got! I'm walking into school but wanted to say good morning."

"Thanks for calling, Bella. See you after school."

After finishing a few stories for tomorrow's paper Jan decided to repeat yesterday's routine. Visit Howie, discuss Isaac's latest email, leave Ernie with him and take the noon spin class. "Come on Ernie. Let's go visit your buddy."

One routine didn't need any tweaking as Ernie ran to Howie's door that quickly opened. "Good morning. It's great to see you up and about. How you feeling?"

"Better every day. How you doing?"

"Charlie drove down last night. Isabella was with Rick."

"Sounds like a booty call to me."

"Funny you'd say that. Let's sit down. We've got another letter to discuss."

"Isaac built a technology that magnified the length of fast radio bursts from milliseconds to actual seconds. Then one night a very fortuitous event occurred. Thoroughly exhausted, he fell asleep with his headphones on replaying repetitive fast radio bursts. He woke in the morning feeling very, very different. Fascinated by what happened, he replicated the process over, and over again. He'd stay awake until utterly exhausted listening to magnified fast radio bursts through his headphones. Eventually, he'd fall asleep and when he woke he'd answer a series of questions he created to analyze his feelings.

After years of experimentation he connected fast radio bursts with brain waves to create a blueprint to alter behavior, but he didn't stop there. He built a fail-safe switch that insured the programmed behavioral changes would be positive. This was all done by experimenting with different frequencies."

"That's incredible, absolutely incredible. That's the most unbelievable thing I've ever heard in my life."

"What's your heart rate?"

"114, still safe but my brain's having a hard time believing that's possible."

"There's more. Isaac's able to connect his behavioral frequency program to a targeted person through their cell phone."

"Wait, stop! You're telling me he can transmit this through a cell phone. Holy fuckin shit!"

"What's your heart rate now. Whenever you use that phrase you're amped up."

"123. It's gone up but I'm still in the safe zone based on what Doc Kumar told me. 125 is his red line."

"Let's slow down. You've got the major points. Here, here's a glass of water. Ernie, do your best impression of a 'comfort dog'."

"He's the poster child for 'comfort dogs' with his innate ability to search out people who need him. I've seen him in the office and at church. Look at him. He knows we're talking about him. I'm down to 121. Thanks, Ernie!"

"Let me know when you get below 120 and we can wrap this letter up. Meanwhile, I need your advice on how to handle Isabella."

"Good luck. She's so perceptive. Plus, she can hear everything in your apartment. I know you've told her you're working with Charlie and me on this Isaac puzzle. I'd suggest you hold off telling her anymore at this point. Does that make sense?"

"Yes, perfect sense." Howie's rush was over, his heart rate dropped to 114. Several minutes later, when it dropped below 110, Jan grabbed her laptop, gave big hugs to Howie and Ernie and headed out the door for her noon spin class, thankful another potential incident had been avoided.

77

A blueberry, banana smoothie hit the spot after spin. Stopped for a red light on the way back to the office her phone signaled a new email. The traffic light turning green took precedent over opening the email, but once back in her office, CLICK!

My Dearest Jan,

4 of 5

Let's start with a cool surprise. You might want to stop by the FedEx around the corner from your office tomorrow. You're finally getting a new phone, a very special iPhone. I've totally reengineered their supposedly impenetrable platform. This unique iPhone will enable you to connect to each target. On your iPhone, this appears as the HOPE button that can only be opened by pressing your right thumb on the green fingerprint recognition circle. Don't worry, it still functions as a normal iPhone.

Let's talk about targets. HOPE has a program that summarizes data on over 12,000 potential targets including: heads of state, elected officials, military leaders, religious leaders, celebrities, media personalities and a special section devoted to terrorists. Your new phone is connected to global databases and the rare factual news source to insure the target list is always up-to-date as are the phone numbers provided for each target. The list is fluid with real time updates of individual traits and numbers.

The positive behavioral changes have been broken out into 38 virtue, They can be combined to the inclusion of six virtues for any one target. Examples of these virtues include: acceptance, compassion, cooperation, courage, ethics, generosity, harmony, honesty, integrity, kindness, love, peace, respect, self-discipline, truthfulness, trust, and wisdom.

Let me stress that armed with up-to-the-minute data, you will always choose the target with one possible exception. I've taken the liberty to choose the first target, if he's still in office, for HOPE. My obvious choice: The President of the United States. But anticipating his very precarious situation should he not still be our President the first choice is all yours.

HOPE automatically receives technical feedback during deployment and there is one "red phone feature" built into the system. Should a conflict of major global consequences occur you will be able to target multiple individuals involved in that specific conflict much like a conference call.

Because of the challenges of rapid, almost overnight, technological change, I've incorporated an automatic update feature in HOPE that insures timely relevance. Also, any language issues have been resolved and encoded into HOPE.

I can imagine all you've just read has been intimidating, but let me ease some of your fears. The technology in HOPE has been totally programmed and automated except for the two decisions you will make. The first is the choice of target(s). The continually updated data base of 12,000 people will provide you with all the appropriate information necessary to choose each target. A specific search engine embedded in HOPE matches targets with the most applicable cause, incident or purpose. Your second decision will be the choice of virtues you believe are necessary to positively impact each target and affect change.

When you hold your new phone, you are holding the most powerful instrument of technology ever built. However, that technology cannot reach its full potential and ultimate success until you've designated your choices. How fitting the two of us can shine HOPE on the world.

Much love,

Leonard/Isaac

Jan wanted to scream! Isaac's plan was rolling out with 12,000 potential targets, but it was the first target, Isaac's choice, that grabbed her attention and wouldn't let go: The President of the United States. The future of the world in her hands! The flood of thoughts running through her mind were quickly brought back to earth. It was time to pick up her daughter and head over to Howie's. She was sure about one thing. Now wasn't the time to discuss this email with Howie, certainly not with Isabella in the house.

"Bonjour, where's Ernie?"

"Hi Sweetie, Ernie spent the afternoon giving therapy to your Uncle Howie. How was your time with your dad?"

"So fun. I got me some yoga pants."

"Interesting grammatical context. We need to take more yoga classes."

"I want to hear everything about your date with Charlie."

"We're at Uncle Howie's, we'll talk later. Let's go see how they're doing."

Howie and Ernie were a team. After acknowledging Jan, then Isabella, Ernie walked back to Howie and sat down alongside his recliner with his head resting on Howie's leg.

"Doc Kumar wants me to get a stress test next week. Think they put me on a treadmill. If everything checks out I can go back to the office and start exercising. I think I'll start by walking to the office."

"That's a great idea. Must be a couple of miles. I'll

go shopping with you to pick up a good pair of walking shoes. Those wingtips and penny loafers won't cut it."

"Uncle Howie, you need a dog like Ernie. Then you could walk together."

"That's a great idea, Isabella. Howie, why don't you get a dog?"

"If I could find a dog like Ernie, I'd get one in a heartbeat, no pun intended."

"Labs are the most popular breed. You'll find one you like. You know they come in colors."

"Uncle Howie, Ernie needs another friend. I can't wait!"

They hadn't pulled away from the curb when Isabella asked again for details about Charlie's visit. When Jan answered with her familiar words to describe their evening: fun, good time, and I like him, Isabella dug deeper, "Where did he sleep and did you shoot another video?"

"Isabella, do you enjoy embarrassing me? I promise to tell you when things get really serious, okay?"

Getting nowhere Isabella changed topics, "Can I wear my new yoga pants to school?"

"Show me the pants when we get home. Sometimes they can be sort of like a sheer dress and you need to wear panties underneath them."

"But you never do."

"Why do I feel like my car seat is heated and turned to high. Thank God we're home."

Isabella's questioning served one purpose. It took her mind off Isaac's latest letter. Then, just before they walked into their building Jan stopped suddenly. The sign was gone. The FOR RENT sign was gone. She was livid. How could he?

"Why are you stopping. What's wrong?"

"I just noticed the FOR RENT sign's gone. Have you seen anyone looking at Papa Lenny's old apartment?"

"I've seen a few people write the phone number down. You seem shocked."

"Interesting, that's all. Do you need help carrying your stuff upstairs?"

"Easy peasy!"

Jan now had two topics to discuss with Charlie. She decided to hold off on the apartment conversation until after they talked about Isaac's #4. Who knows, he might even say something—first. She emailed Charlie Isaac's incredible letter.

Wanting privacy for her conversation with Charlie and anticipating her daughter's response, she asked a rhetorical question."

"I'm going to change and then take Ernie for a walk. Want to come?"

"No, you go. I'm going to unpack."

78

Jan called Charlie and waited for his return call, wondering when he was going to get a phone he'd answer? "Hi, just saw you called and got your email."

"It's letter #4. Call me back after you've read it. We need to discuss it."

Several minutes later Charlie called back, out of breath as if he just finished running a 400-meter dash. "Amazing, just amazing! 12,000 potential targets, 38 virtues and he chose the President of the United States for the first target although he realized he might not be President when you implement HOPE. Ironic he calls his tech platform HOPE. Love that, it's the perfect word to describe so much of his goal. That's going to be some FedEx package you're getting tomorrow. The future of the world in your hands! I'd call that beyond anything I could ever imagine. How do you feel?"

"Totally amazed and intimidated. It's all so unbelievable! He lived next door to me for years. I can't imagine anyone has ever had a higher IQ than Isaac. Can you

drive down tomorrow morning and go with me to FedEx? I need you, Cowboy."

"Hmmmm, I'd like to be with you, but I've got a
meeting at 10:00. Let me see if I can change it. Call you
right back. We need to talk more about Isaac, too."

"Wait, is there anything else you want to tell me?"

"There certainly is, I love you."

Jan was bewildered. Not over Charlie's interpretation
of Isaac's letter but over how he reacted to her baited
question about the apartment. Glad she didn't get the
chance to be accusatory, it didn't appear he rented the
apartment. She rationalized, with good reason, that her
attitude was the result of his previous behavior, the damn
trust issue. She decided to just tell him the FOR RENT
sign was taken down.

"Okay, we're on. I moved my meeting to 1:00. What
time does FedEx open? "Early, 7:00 or 7:30. I've got to
drop Isabella off at school a little before 8:00. Can you
meet me at the Star-News at 8:15?"

"Yes, but I'll need to leave Raleigh by 10:30 to get
back for my meeting."

"Guess what?"

"There's more! Now what?"

"The FOR RENT sign is down."

"Wow, I guess that makes any future conversation unnecessary. Wait, wait a minute. You didn't think I rented it, did you? Is that why you asked me that question about anything else I wanted to tell you? Come on, you can't think I'd do something like that behind your back. I know I've said some things that made you, rightfully, question me, but that was work stuff. You can't think I'm so stupid I'd rent that apartment without discussing it with you first."

"You're right on all counts. I was wrong, I apologize. I have this little trust red flag still in my head. I'm sorry."

"Apology excepted. I wonder who rented the apartment? Guess we'll find out soon enough. Let's get back to Isaac's letter. How about the HOPE platform, and the 'red phone feature'? That's some iPhone you're going to get. Isaac creates technology that's not just state-of-the-art, it's state-of-the-future that no one else in the world could build. You're right, it's unbelievably amazing!"

"I can't wait to see you tomorrow. I'm glad you'll be there with me. I love you."

"I love you, too. See you in the morning."

Jan was relieved the apartment discussion had been diffused before she blew it totally out of proportion. It reminded her why she liked to have either Howie or Charlie's opinion. Walking into her apartment, Isabella was waiting for an opinion as she modeled her new yoga pants.

"I like those pants on you. They're fine for school."

`"They're so comfy."

While Jan searched Google for anything even remotely related to Isaac's HOPE and iPhone modifications, surprise, surprise, Isabella made a big salad for dinner and Jan got exactly what she needed, dinner and a quiet evening at home with her daughter.

79

What she was about to pick up from FedEx kept Jan tossing and turning all night. She was on auto-pilot as her morning ritual began. Get Isabella moving, start her coffee, take Ernie out, check her emails and review the Star-News. Unable to settle her nervous stomach she turned to her safety food. "Bella, are you hungry? I'm going to make pancakes."

"No, merci."

"Ernie, I don't have to ask you. Come on Isabella. I need to be at the office a little early."

"Now you tell me. Deux minutes."

Her mind was so preoccupied with FedEx and the iPhone she hadn't thought about Charlie coming to town. She rushed to put on a sexier top, then to the bathroom for a little dash of perfume. "Let's go, Bella."

"You changed tops."

"Very observant. I spilt some pancake batter on the other one."

Five minutes earlier than usual there was no line of cars at Isabella's school. A nervous wreck, Jan drove by the FedEx office to make sure it was open. Walking into the Star-News, the five staff members in the office all appeared to be working. As Ernie made his rounds, Jan visited the bathroom trying to quell her upset stomach. Unsuccessful, she sat down at her desk, turned on her computer and Googled a random question about iPhones she thought of somewhere between pancakes and Isabella's school. How many iPhones have been sold? Wow, she's literally going to pick up one in a billion.

"Hi Bert, this is Jan Cooper."

"You must have read my mind. I've was just going to call you. We've got a package for you."

"Great, I'll be by in a few minutes to pick it up."

"Bring Ernie."

"Will do."

Ernie's bark signaled Charlie had arrived. Screw the office gossip. She gave him a big hug and pushed him into her office. "I'm so glad you're here. I'm a nervous wreck. My stomach's doing jumping jacks. I just called FedEx and Bert told me he has a package for me. I've never been more nervous in my life. Charlie, hold me for a minute—please."

Charlie held her tightly whispering in her ear, "I'm so glad I'm here. You are extraordinary. I love you."

Ernie ran around the counter to say hello to his friend, Bert. After introducing Charlie, Jan quickly signed the paperwork forgetting to ask questions that might help explain the logistics of how Isaac got the package to this FedEx office on this particular day.

"Charlie, you hold it. Should we open it in the office or take it back to my apartment?"

"Wherever you feel most comfortable."

"Let's go back to my apartment. I'll grab my stuff from the office and meet you and Ernie at my apartment. I'm so nervous. I've got to pee, again. You hold onto the package. No one has been following us, have they?"

"We're clear. I'm making sure were not being followed. It's a habit."

Jan parked behind Charlie. "Can you even imagine what we're about to open and discover? Everything's happened so quickly. Isaac's plan is beyond brilliant. How can one person be so much smarter than anyone else! And then choose me to help execute his plan to save the world. Am I acting crazy? I don't know what normal means anymore."

"No one—ever—has been asked to do what you're doing. You never cease to amaze me. You don't realize how remarkable you are, but Isaac knew and I know."

The three of them ran up the stairs, down the hall and into the apartment. They settled on sitting at the kitchen table. It was 9:10. Charlie had an hour and twenty minutes. Within seconds the package was open. It looked like a normal iPhone box. As Jan opened it Charlie checked out the two other items in the package: a silver colored case and wireless headphones.

"Well, here goes. My hands are shaking. It's a 7 Plus or at least that's what it says. It's a lot bigger than my phone. Do you think it's charged or do we need to connect the charger?"

"Most phones are bigger than yours. I've probably had a half dozen iPhones and they normally come partially charged. I'm going to take a photo of you turning on the phone for the first time. It'll be a cool memento. Just press the power button on the top right."

"Here goes! Oh, my God, that's Isaac. He made a video."

For the next eighteen minutes Jan and Charlie sat

mesmerized. Isaac, seated at his desk in Apartment #11 created a detailed tutorial video, a how-to for this very special iPhone, but more importantly his HOPE platform.

"Charlie, tell me what we just watched? I can't believe it."

"I'm as awestruck as you. We need to watch it again and take notes."

"Good idea. I'll probably watch it twenty times before I figure out everything he says. Let's take our own notes. You'll probably see things I miss."

For another eighteen minutes, they watched intently making numbered notes and starred comments. Then they exchanged their sheets.

"Charlie, your list has lots of stuff I missed. It's obvious I've got a lot of homework to familiarize myself with HOPE and the iPhone."

"Do you realize what we just watched. Isaac replaced the Set-Up Assistant installed in every iPhone with his own video. How about him importing all your contacts from your old phone. Figure that out. He's also activated the iPhone and you now have a second phone number. Don't give out the new number to anyone. Before I leave let me show you the basic functionality of the phone. It's very intuitive. Wait until you start going over the target list and familiarize yourself with the search engine Isaac built for it. Don't forget the virtues! Everything's going to take time, don't get discouraged."

For the next ten minutes Charlie went over the basics, a few nuances of the iPhone and then mounted the silver protective case. Time to leave, he gave Jan a big hug and a long kiss.

"Jan, we both need to take a step back and digest Isaac's incredible work. It's got to be the most brilliant plan in history deploying technology that's beyond cutting edge since Isaac built it and now we're the only people who know about it. We've been so preoccupied lately we haven't even talked about this weekend. I'm going to call Kathy and see if she'll take the boys, at least for one day. I need to be with you. Let's talk later. I love you."

"Oh Charlie, I love you, too. Thanks for driving down. I need you now, more than ever."

80

Jan sat motionless, stunned by information overload and unable to focus on anything. Howie, she forgot about Howie. What should she tell him—now. She still had

Isaac's #4 and now the iPhone. She called him.

"Hi Jan, good job with today's paper."

"Thanks, how you feeling?"

"Think I'm getting a little stronger every day. Been looking at dogs online. Maybe I need a dog."

"It's a great idea. I was going to stop by after my noon spin class."

"I'm not going anywhere. Drop Ernie off on your way to the gym."

"Sure, I know he loves to visit you."

Jan had a new problem. What does she do with her new iPhone? Leave it where? Take it with her? She called Charlie and anxiously waited for his return call. "Charlie, what do I do with the iPhone. I'm taking a noon spin class."

"Either hide it in your apartment or lock it in the trunk of your car. The problem is iPhones are the most stolen product in the world. I'll come up with a better solution."

"Wish me luck. I'm going to talk to Howie after spin. I still need to tell him about #4. Telling him about picking up the iPhone can wait. Once again, Cowboy, you've bailed me out. I love you more than ever."

"Hang in there and say hello to Howie. I love you."

Before she left her apartment, she pulled up her skin-tight yoga pants and using two mirrors made sure they weren't see through. Thanks, Isabella.

Following Charlie's advice, she pulled out a small brown bag, wrapped the iPhone in a towel at the bottom of the bag then filled the bag with folded dish towels before she put the bag in the trunk of her car.

"Howie, Ernie gets excited when I turn onto your street. He recognizes your house. He's all yours. See you in a couple hours. We've got another letter to discuss."

"Good, I can't wait to hear."

Jan double checked her trunk was locked before she went into the gym. Seated on her favorite bike she quickly tried to lose herself into the fervent beat of the Foo Fighters. Fifty minutes later she was a sweaty mess, finished her second bottled water and upon seeing her car thought, thank God it's still here. In ten minutes, she was back home in the shower. In twenty minutes, she grabbed a yoghurt, another bottled water and headed back to Howie's.

"I'm back. Hi Ernie, how many biscuits did he give you?"

"Can I fix you a green salad or a yoghurt smoothie?"

"No thanks, my stomach's been a little upset. Let's talk about Isaac. What's your heart rate monitor read?"

"85, let's go!"

Parts of the letters were beginning to overlap and allowed Jan to speak with broad strokes assuming Howie would remember the talking points but not necessarily what letter they came from. She opened her laptop and Isaac's #4.

"Isaac started #4 with a surprise, telling me he sent me a FedEx with a very special iPhone. Rather than a meaningless acronym or a code he named his program for what he wants it to bring: HOPE. He built HOPE to open when I apply my thumb to the screen. Another part of HOPE identifies 12,000 potential targets that includes: heads of state, politicians, military leaders, religious leaders and a special section devoted to terrorists."

"That's some iPhone. HOPE is more than brilliant. I'm fascinated by him naming the platform HOPE. Is what he's proposing possible? It's seems very idealistic and futuristic. Can you change a person's behavior or attitude with an iPhone? I'm trying to play it out in my head. I don't know! What do you think?"

"I think Isaac knows what he's doing. We're not capable of evaluating what he's built. We don't have to. He's done that for us. Remember, he's the same person who predicted the Kennedy Assassination and 9/11 and has the most brilliant mind—ever. Yes, I think it will work. Where's your heart?"

"105. I'm good."

The 38 virtues, HOPE updates, and the "red phone feature" were compelling and kept Howie's heart rate at 105. Then she dropped Isaac's choice for the first target."

Howie yelled, "You fuckin kidding me, the POTUS and he realized given the fractional state of our country POTUS #45 might not be our President when you implement HOPE. Unfuckinbelievable!"

"Heart rate, please."

"128. How could I not react to that! What if the government finds out what you're doing and who knows what the President might do if he's still in office? Is there any chance they can trace this back to you?"

"Thanks, just what I need, more to worry about. I'll ask Charlie. That pretty much covers #4. Now I know what's going to elevate your heart rate. Howie, everything's moving so fast, it's so consequential. It's up to me. The pressure keeps caving in on me. I hope I don't have a nervous breakdown."

"Isaac knew what he was doing by choosing you. I wish I had something to say that would lessen your fears but I don't."

"Now where's your heart?"

"123, it's coming down."

"Good, I'd better pick-up my daughter. Come on Ernie. Thanks for dog sitting."

"He's always welcome. Keep me posted, and call me if you need me."

Waiting behind three cars Jan thought of another problem. She decided to wait until later to call Charlie and ask him what she should tell her daughter about her new iPhone. Ernie's tail brushing the back of her head could only mean one thing. "Hi girls. Sandy, are you coming over or am I dropping you off at your house?"

"Sandy's coming home with us. Her mom will pick her up later."

"Easy peasy, do you girls want to stop for a smoothie or ice cream."

"A smoothie sounds yummy, Ms. Cooper."

"Mom, easy peasy is so yesterday. No one says it anymore."

"Really, and I've sort of grown fond of it."

Back in the apartment, the girls retreated to Isabella's room while Jan took Ernie for a walk that camouflaged her call to Charlie. "Hi Jan, I'm at the Apple store with my boys."

"Are you getting them both iPhones?"

"Yes, but nothing like what you got today."

"I need your help. What do I tell Isabella about my iPhone? How do I explain why I need two phones and what do I do when she asks to see it?

"Good questions. I'm still thinking about where to keep the iPhone. Here come the boys. I'll call you tonight. Bye."

Back in her apartment, she pulled out her journal. There was much to add.

Filling in Charlie's side was easy; Isaac's was much more challenging. A half hour and three pages later Jan reflected on what she had written. It was a thriller novel or sci-fi movie except no one would believe it—would they?

81

Loose ends kept resurfacing and Jan totally forgot about the Exhibits. The more pressing question is whether she should leave the iPhone in the trunk of her car or bring it upstairs?

"Sandy, I think your mom's here."

"Bye Ms. Cooper."

"Isabella, how about pasta for dinner?"

"Oui, but that smoothie filled me up."

"We can eat later; I've got work I can do."

While checking the stories for Monday's paper her

email notification came on. CLICK!

My Dearest Jan,

5 of 5

You've absorbed an amazing amount of information in a very short period. My emails have been designed to serve multiple functions: 1) Increase your knowledge base; 2) Help you develop a specific problem solving process; 3) Pique your inquisitive nature fueling your research habit; and 4) Enable you to implement HOPE.

Fortunately, over the last 50 years, the world has enjoyed mostly the positive effects of technology. Tragically, that trend has reversed. Globally, we now face potentially catastrophic damage from technological terrorism. Because it doesn't require a military presence and can be deployed by techies, not troops, it's become the weapon of choice. Cyber wars are not bloody conflicts, but rather computer vs. computer attacks that can shut down a country and its population through the touch of a screen. Extreme religious zealots with access to the latest technology represent a destructive force unlike anything the world has ever seen. The goal of HOPE is twofold: 1) stop any immediate threat; and 2) reverse the spiraling downward trend that will ultimately destroy humanity.

Recognizing the importance of being able to evalu-

ate the success of HOPE, once it has been connected to a target, the HOPE platform automatically evaluates success based on nine criteria. And, because success is not indefinite, the program continually updates based on behavioral changes.

Aware of your additional time requirements to implement HOPE, the last thing you need to worry about are financial constraints. Although, I declined direct remuneration or royalties for my technology platforms, programs and inventions, I did realize rather substantial gains from early investments in what I considered to be tech game changers including: Microsoft, Intel, Apple, Google, Amazon, Priceline, Facebook and Netflix.

Attached to this email are documents for two accounts, both in your name. The first insures your total financial freedom and security. The second names you as the Trustee for the account set up for Isabella. It makes me smile to think of you two visiting Paris.

I would be remiss not to discuss security. Please don't share any of my emails, disclosures or the product of your research with anyone other than Howie or Clifton-Cliff-Chuck-Charlie-or whatever you call him. Once the seal of secrecy has been broken the chances for leaks or discovery increases exponentially. You, and only you, has total control of HOPE.

The NSA was certainly a major part of my life. Permit me to elaborate and provide perspective on the Agency.

1)Other than six countries, the NSA is the most powerful entity in the world.

2)At 17, I was the youngest person ever employed by the NSA, and worked there the longest, 48 years.

3)I built more than half the technology still used today by the NSA.

4)The NSA deploys more cyber-attacks than the rest of the world combined.

5)The NSA has collected more data, listened to noise, more phone calls and intercepted more communications than the rest of the world combined and I had access to everything.

6)99.9% of everything online can be hacked.

7)There is absolutely no transparency in the NSA.

8)There is absolutely no congressional oversight of consequence to the NSA.

9)Never assume the rare public statements from the NSA are true.

10)The NSA will deny my conclusions about fast radio bursts just as they ignored my predictions of the Kennedy assassination and 9/11.

11)The interests of the NSA do NOT always coincide with other U.S. intelligence agencies.

12)Snowden, or someone like him was inevitable. Years ago, I thought it might be me until I realized I'd be labeled a traitor and become the victim of the NSA for the third time.

One final warning about the NSA. The power struggles exacerbated by special interests are relentless and internal squabbling yields highly questionable, often illegal actions. The NSA remain the biggest threat to the successful implementation of HOPE. I know this creates a thin line between paranoia and legitimate pre-cautions, but it's a line you have balanced thus far and I'm confident you'll avoid their threat. But, beware they are always out there listening to everything, and everyone and that's why your iPhone has a 25-digit encryption firewall that I'm confident will keep HOPE secure.

I leave positive I've left HOPE in the hands of the person best suited to effectively administer the program. There is no better gift than helping others and you are about to embark on a journey that will prove to be the greatest gift—ever. I am eternally grateful to have found you.

Godspeed,
Leonard/Isaac

Isaac's fifth email wrapped everything together. The inheritance was a total surprise. Jan had never inherited anything and before the Isaac puzzle began her reaction would have been to yell and jump with joy! She was shocked as she looked at the two accounts. A million dollars for her and $500,000 for Isabella was a lot of money but what mattered most was Isabella's future was now secure.

Jan couldn't fool herself about what Isaac chose her to do. She realized, even with Charlie's presence, there was a huge element of danger in executing Isaac's plan and his description of the NSA only reinforced that fear.

She needed Charlie's analysis and help, but resisted calling him knowing he was spending time with his sons. Then unexpectedly a feeling of sadness overcame her. Although Isaac passed more than a month ago she still felt very close to him because of the email attachment. Now, it appeared that lifeline was gone—forever.

The five letters were full of important details and because they arrived in such a short timeline Jan decided to read them all again to insure she didn't skip anything. She pulled up all five emails and started to read. There were two Exhibits attached to the email for #2. Exhibit A was Isaac's file on the Kennedy assassination and Exhibit B was his file on 9/11. She had to be the only person in the world who knew these files existed. Then she was quickly brought back to reality.

"Mom, are we going to eat?"

"I'm sorry, Bella. I started to read and lost track of time. I'll boil water for the pasta now. I have some Bolognese sauce. Will that work for you? Would you like a glass of wine, too?"

"What. You'd better repeat that. You didn't just ask me if I wanted a glass of wine, did you?"

"I was checking to see if you were listening to me or so engrossed on your iPhone that you didn't hear me. You passed my little test but the wine can wait a few years. I do have a favor to ask. I'm thinking of getting an iPhone. Will you give me a little tutorial with yours? Show me how it works and what features you like best. You can leave out all your social media stuff."

"Oui, after we eat."

Jan couldn't help but smile. She wanted to pat herself on the back for not only discovering she needed to review Exhibits A and B but also figuring out a way to explain her new iPhone to Isabella. She just had to buy an identical 7 Plus and case.

Dinner and dishes done Isabella gave her mother an iPhone lesson worthy of YouTube. After her daughter retreated to her room Jan sent Charlie an email with Isaac's

#5. Almost 8:30, she hoped he'd call. Ernie's evening walk included a stop at the trunk of her car to pick up the paper bag with the most valuable iPhone in the world after deciding the inside of her apartment was safer than the trunk of her car.

As she was starting up the stairs her phone rang, "God, I'm so glad you called. So much has happened. I need you to stop me from running in circles."

"It was great to spend the day with my boys but I kept wondering how you were doing. I got your email and read #5. It must be a relief to have the financial freedom to pursue Isaac's plan and now you don't have to worry about Isabella's financial future. Only had time to glance at Exhibits A and B, but they validate the historical issues with the NSA that continue, as Isaac indicated in the list of the NSA characteristics. I've never seen the NSA described the way he did, but I certainly can't argue with his assumptions."

"You're almost up to speed. Guess what, I solved the iPhone issue with Isabella. I told her I'm buying an iPhone. Of course, it will be identical in appearance to the phone from Isaac. She already gave me a tutorial on her iPhone. She won't be able to differentiate between the two phones."

"Great idea! Solves lots of problems."

"I've been keeping the iPhone in a paper bag in the trunk of my car but I decided it's safer in my apartment. I'm holding it in my free hand with Ernie at my feet just outside the door to my building. Any ideas how to keep the phone secure?"

"I need to check out your apartment. I want to put in a hidden safe. Keep doing what you're doing until then. Do you really think we've heard all we're going to from Isaac?"

"It seems that way but I gave up trying to predict his moves weeks ago. The tone of #5 seems different, doesn't it?"

"Agree, #5 does seem like a wrap-up except for your inheritance and the vivid description of the NSA."

"Charlie, what are the personal risks to me in carrying out Isaac's plan. Can anyone trace things back to me? What about the NSA? Can I be arrested for treason or something else? I should know exactly what the risks are? I need to know? I know you have your boys but will you have time to talk over the weekend? What's your schedule at work going to be like next week?"

"I've got good news. Kathy's going to take the boys on Sunday morning. I'll drive down to see you, probably around 11:00 but I'll have to drive home later in the afternoon. I'll call you from their games tomorrow."

"Great! I love you Cowboy. Email me if you think of anything."

"I'll stay in contact. Even though I have my boys tomorrow, I'll call you back if you call. I finally get my new phone on Monday. I love you more every day."

Walking upstairs Jan realized the three things she needed every day to keep her sanity: time with her daughter, time with Charlie and exercise. She promised herself to make all three a daily priority. Everything else would follow. Before she crawled into bed she hid the most valuable lunch bag in the world in a shoe box in her closet.

82

Surprisingly, Jan slept well but her memory was still overloaded and she couldn't remember if this was Isabella's weekend with Rick or not.

It was the picture Jan needed to see. Peeking into her daughter's bedroom, Isabella and Ernie were peacefully spooning with Ernie somehow hogging two thirds of the bed. Slowly, Mom walked next to her daughter's side of the bed, kneeled and just sat quietly for a moment until

Ernie slowly opened one eye and started to wag his tail.

Walking out the apartment building's front door created a flashback scene. In front of her building at 7:00 was a moving truck. It wasn't Sunday morning and there was no hot guy supervising but there were two movers with red shirts. There was also a middle-aged woman carrying a pet carrier.

After Ernie paid tribute to his tree Jan approached the woman. "Good morning, are you moving into this building?"

"Yes, do you live here?"

"We do, #12."

"We're neighbors; I'm moving into #11. I'm Carol Vincent. I hope your beautiful lab likes cats?"

"Welcome Carol, I'm Jan Cooper and this is Ernie. He likes everyone, including cats. My daughter, Isabella, is still sleeping upstairs. Are you from Raleigh?"

"No, Chicago. I outgrew Chicago or vice versa. It's just me and my little Pearl. She's an indoor cat."

"Is there a Mr. Vincent or any children moving in with you?"

"No, my husband passed away three years ago. My son, Bruce, lives in Miami. I keep waiting for him to get married so I can visit him in the winter. What about you?"

"My ex lives in Chicago but keeps an apartment in Raleigh because we share custody of Isabella."

"I'm glad we're neighbors. I'd better go upstairs and let the movers in."

"I'll walk up with you. Stop by if you need anything or for a cup of coffee."

Walking into her apartment, Jan couldn't help but reflect on her first meeting with Leonard Rosen. There was only a hello and an exchange of names. To think what grew from that initial meeting was beyond mind boggling.

"Isabella, are you up?"

"Way ahead of you."

"We've got a new neighbor. Her name's Carol and she seems very nice. Guessing late 40s and you'll like her. She's got a cute cat named Pearl."

"Nobody can replace Papa Lenny. I still miss him."

Jan swallowed hard thinking, if you only knew! "I miss him—too. Is your dad picking you up?"

"No, why would you think that? You're taking me to Sandy's. You didn't forget?"

"Right, why would I forget?"

"Mom, we'd better go."

"Let me grab my laptop. Come on Ernie."

Not wanting her visit to conflict with any staff members, she called Howie. "I'm coming over if you don't already have a house full of guests."

"Come over. I could use some mental stimulation."

Howie looked healthier, likely the effects of time, rest and his new diet. Hopefully his Monday stress test would free him to get back to the office and start his exercise program. Their discussion of Isaac's #5 was anti-climactic except for the inheritance and NSA description.

"I've got a new neighbor, Carol, another refugee from Chicago. She's moving in today. You might like her. She's attractive, a widow, guessing late 40s. Seems like your type."

"Thanks for thinking of me but worry about your own relationship. How's Charlie and his new job?"

"So far so good. He's driving down tomorrow to help me figure out where to hide the iPhone. I'm getting the same phone, a 7 Plus with the same case for my personal use. That should eliminate Isabella's curiosity."

"Good idea and God knows you've needed a new phone for a long time."

"What time's your stress test on Monday. I'll go with you."

"11:30. Probably should leave here by 11:15."

"I'll pick you up. Come on Ernie, let's go."

A free Saturday afternoon was a rare luxury. As much

as she wanted to take a run on this cool October Saturday, it looked like rain so she stopped at the market instead hoping it would clear up later.

The moving van gone, Jan stopped by Carol's on the way to her apartment. "Hi Carol, how's your move going?"

"It's going to take me a few days to get settled. Luckily most of my furniture fits."

"I've got to put groceries away but why don't you come over in say ten minutes for a cup of coffee or tea?"

"I'd love to. Thanks!"

As she was putting her groceries away Jan heard her phone email notification. CLICK!

My Dearest January,

Think of this as a P.S. It would be terribly irresponsible of me to leave you with just that single iPhone considering all the potential unforeseen hazards that might arise. Always best to take precautions and that's why you should be receiving another FedEx package with an identical iPhone and case. Once our plan has started, turn this phone on every couple of days and it will update automatically.

Also, your iPhone will update automatically when Apple invariably releases new models.

There is a quote I'm fond of attributed to Albert Einstein. "It has become appallingly obvious that our technology has exceeded our humanity." Unfortunately, the intersection of optimism and reality has no signals. I try to be optimistic especially considering the designation of HOPE. Although, the Internet offers terrorists simple access to a global stage without boundaries exponentially propelled by social media, I'm confident HOPE will remain relevant for years to come.

Three other matters. First, the intention of my letters was not to put the fear of God in you. I have full faith in your capabilities. Secondly, I have a somewhat frivolous request. I ask that on your trip to Paris with Isabella you take the elevator to the top of the Eiffel Tower and remember your old, nerd-like neighbor who loved you both so dearly.

Finally, I must address what now must be your amazing journal. You often kidded about never winning a Pulitzer at the Star-News. Don't be so sure. The world and your iPhone are full of surprises!

With all my love,
Papa Lenny

Jan was a sobbing mess. This final email is how she

wants to always remember Leonard Rosen. It was fitting he signed Papa Lenny because that's the person she knew all those years. Isaac Stone came after he was gone. This genius with the incredible mind was haunted by totally unfounded, yet relentless guilt that motivated him to create a tech platform for HOPE. Pulitzer, surprise, what...?

The knock on the door brought her back to reality. "Come in, Carol."

"Jan, are you okay. You look like you've been crying."

"I just read something very sentimental that brought me to tears. I'm okay. What can I fix you? Coffee or tea?"

"Coffee would be great. What do you do here in Raleigh?"

"I'm a reporter for the local paper, the Star-News. It's not the Tribune but it has other benefits. What about you, do you work?"

"I taught second grade for years. After my husband passed away I decided to follow my passion and write children's books. It's a hard way to make a living but I manage with the life insurance benefits. How did you settle on Raleigh?"

"I met my ex-husband Rick at Northwestern. After we married I stayed home to raise my daughter. Rick and I grew apart or, as I like to say, we grew up, and realized we married too young and divorced. He's a great dad, and now happily married. We're good friends which is great for our daughter's sake. After our divorce, I wanted to get away from Chicago but not too far because Isabella needs to be close to her dad. Raleigh fit what I was looking for."

"How about you. How did you end up here?"

"A little like you except no divorce. My husband, Andy, was killed by a drunk driver while driving home during a bad storm. He was the only man I ever loved. I was and still am devastated. My escape is writing. I know the psyche of children and can relate to their humor, insecurities, innocence and challenges. I never wanted to do anything but teach and write. Most of my family lives in Pittsburgh but I have no desire to move back there. My 24 year old son got a job last year in Miami and when he moved I started looking for another place to live. Miami is a different world so I drove down here one day about six months ago and then decided to move here last month. It seems like a nice, friendly small town close enough to Chicago."

"That's exactly what Raleigh is. I'm glad we're neighbors. You'll have to meet my daughter."

"I look forward to it. I better get back to emptying

boxes. Thanks so much for your hospitality. It means a lot."

"My pleasure, Carol."

Jan welcomed the diversion from the sadness brought about by Isaac's email. Ironically, the diversion was from her new neighbor, who replaced Isaac.

83

Jan peered out the kitchen window to see partly cloudy blue skies, perfect for a run. After changing, she followed Ernie out the door and started her five miles. She couldn't help but be pleased by Isaac's email. He was her neighbor and friend first and she relished how he closed with such a personal touch.

Invigorated by her run, she called her daughter. "Hi Bella, what are you girls doing."

"We're making dance videos. They're so cool. We want to use Ernie in a video. Everyone loves Ernie. Can we?"

"You'll have to ask him. What time are you coming home? It's 3:30 now."

"Can you pick me up in an hour?"

"I can. I'll bring your potential star. You can pitch your idea directly to him. Bye."

As soon as Jan said goodbye to her daughter she remembered a call she had to make. "Hi Bert, this is Jan Cooper. Did you get another package for me?"

"Hi Jan, I don't think so but let me check. No, nothing here. I'll call you if I anything comes in."

"Thanks Bert. Let me ask you something. Is there a return address on all FedEx packages showing the sender?"

"Most of the time."

"Do you keep a record of all the packages you receive with the sender's listed."

"We've got a master list of all packages we service. Anything particular you're looking for?"

"I'll talk to you when the other package arrives. Thanks, Bert." Glancing at her computer screen she sent Charlie an email.

Hi Charlie, attached is an email I received from Isaac today. It seems like a great idea to have a duplicate phone considering everything that might happen. I loved the way he closed the email and it left me in tears. Not sure what to make of Pulitzer reference and surprises. I love you!

Isabella was excited to tell her mom about the videos they shot with their iPhones. Naturally, she wasn't hungry but they still stopped at Pizza Katie's for a pie to go.

"Our new neighbor, Carol stopped by for coffee today. She's a widow and taught 2nd grade in Chicago. Now she's writing children's books."

"Cool, but it's weird to have anyone besides Papa Lenny next door."

"I know, but it had to happen. Oh, Charlie's driving down tomorrow around 11:00, but he has to get go home later in the afternoon."

"Booty call! I'll make plans with Sandy. You don't need me hanging around here."

"I don't know where to start with your response except to say you don't have to disappear, he's not coming down for a booty call and you're the only one in this apartment shooting videos. I'm hungry. I'm going to have pizza. You can eat when you're hungry."

"I've got to play around with Ernie's best angles."

"You do that."

With a slice of pizza in one hand and a glass of wine in the other Jan thought of what she needed to discuss with Charlie. The safe and where he wants to put it was first on her list. Then, would he help her work through HOPE and get the exact same iPhone and case? Finally, what's her legal exposure, if she's discovered implementing Isaac's plan and what can she do to protect herself?

Munching on her second slice Jan skimmed through the Isaac side of her journal. So much had happened, so quickly, she felt overwhelmed and retreated to her happy place, her dream of the beach in Maui. Utterly exhausted, she moved to the couch, turned on the TV without bothering to look at the screen and dozed off.

84

It had been too long since they had been to church, but this Sunday Jan felt the need to be grounded, more than ever.

Leaving church Isabella's attention turned to her iPhone and setting up her day to give her mom alone time with Charlie. Back in their apartment, her day successfully planned, Isabella had time for a pancake before Sandy and her mom picked her up.

Jan knew if Charlie said 11:00, he'd be at her door by 11:00. At 10:50 she began watching from her kitchen window. Her anticipation increased further upon his arrival when he slowly pulled a large carton out of his back seat. Obviously, very heavy, she ran down the stairs to open the door to her apartment building. "Let me get the door for you, Cowboy."

After Charlie gently placed her new safe on the living room floor Jan jumped into his arms. "I'm so glad you're here."

"Me too. I liked Isaac's last email. I've never seen that Einstein quote but it certainly rings true today."

"Where are you going to put that safe? How heavy is it?"

"It's 64 pounds. We'll put it on the bottom of one of your closets. It attaches easily to the floor with just two bolts. Is someone at your door? Don't open the door until I get the safe into your bedroom."

"Be right there. Hi Carol, come on in. Charlie, this is Carol, my new neighbor. She moved here from Chicago."

"Nice to meet you, Carol. I live in Chicago. Drove down this morning. You've got a great neighbor."

"I know. Jan, do you have one of those funny screwdrivers with the different top I could borrow?"

"You mean a Phillips. Let me get it. It's in my 'Girls Tool Kit'. Here you go."

"Thank you. Charlie, great to meet you. Enjoy your

Sunday."

As soon as Charlie heard Carol's door close his comment shocked Jan, "I've seen her somewhere and I never forget a face."

"What does that mean? What are you saying?"

"I'm not sure but be careful what you discuss with her until I can check her out. What did you say her last name is?"

"Vincent, Carol Vincent. You're scaring me."

"Just being cautious. What else do you know about her?"

"She was a 2nd grade teacher, now she writes children's books. She has one son, Bruce, who lives in Miami. I think she said he's 24. Her husband, Andy was killed by a drunk driver. Her family lives in Pittsburgh and she has a cat named Pearl. She's from Chicago. You probably saw her there."

"Maybe, we'll see. That should be enough info. Before I leave I'll get a photo of her."

"How you going to do that?"

"I'll put my spy hat on. Where's Isabella?"

"She decided I needed alone time with you. Don't worry, she'll want a full report."

"As much as I'd like to do other things to you, I'd better install that safe first."

"You'd better hurry."

Twenty minutes later the safe was securely fastened to the floor, hidden behind shoe boxes in Jan's closet. Two minutes later they were naked in bed. An hour later they were seated at the kitchen table having pancakes, bacon and coffee. Charlie had a one-word response to her suggestion he accompany her to buy her new iPhone 7 Plus, "When?"

"As soon as possible. I need the camouflage to limit my daughter's curiosity. I also need to practice with Isaac's iPhone. Will you help me with it before you leave?"

"Sure, let's do it. Do you remember the combination to your new safe?"

"My memory's not that bad. I'm going to get the phone, right now."

"Wait, I added a little something to the lock on your safe. After you've entered the combination place your thumb onto the #2. Just a little added safety precaution. Only you and I will be able to open the safe."

"Charlie, I love you!"

For the next hour they intently scrutinized Isaac's iPhone and HOPE. She took detailed notes. Charlie kept shaking his head in disbelief over how much Isaac had built into HOPE. "This has to be the most amazing technology ever conceived. Think about it. It's unbelievable! Put the phone back in your new safe place and let's take a walk. We need to digest the HOPE platform and one more important consideration."

"What's that? Carol, the safe, the iPhone, HOPE. Now what?"

"I love you."

And with those three words her smile was covered with the tears streaming down her face.

85

Hand in hand they walked quietly trying to digest the events of their morning. Jan flipped through her mental list of all the issues she needed to discuss with Charlie, and asked the question bothering her most—first. "How would you evaluate my exposure to either physical harm or legal retaliation?"

"You sure ask difficult questions and you might not like my answer but it's the only one I have. I don't know. This is un-chartered territory. Theoretically, any target you choose could potentially target you back and we know who Isaac wants to be the first target, assuming he's still President. Now that I've probably left you terrified let me tell you what mitigates all the potential dangers including the NSA. That's one word—Isaac. He had to anticipate potential danger and as I've said many times, you're the last person in the world he'd want to jeopardize."

"Thanks for being honest with me. I understand everything you said, but what bothers me is Isaac failed twice. I don't want to be a casualty of the third time."

"I don't think he failed twice. He was right, both times. The NSA failed twice. I'll do everything I can to make sure the third time is an incredible success. You, January Cooper are going to save and change the world!"

"Oh Charlie, I hope so. Thanks for your perspective. You're right, he didn't fail."

On the walk back to her apartment Jan called Isabella. She was shopping with Sandy and Sandy's mom, but guessed she'd be home by 4:30. It was almost 3:00 when Jan and Charlie got back to the apartment.

Relaxing on the couch together, and to lighten the mood, Charlie wrote sweet notes on Jan's back. When she figured out, "One day Maui" her tears returned.

"Stay and say hello to Isabella. She'd love to see you."

"Sure. Drive up and visit me and we can get your new iPhone.

"Rick has Isabella Wednesday night. Will that work?

"Perfect. Walk me to my car when I leave. We can stop at Carol's. I'll be discreet."

"Sure, Mr. Bond."

Ernie heard Isabella's happy footsteps first. "Bonjour, Charlie. It's cool you drove down."

"Bonjour Isabella. I'm glad I got a chance to see you before I leave. How about your mother getting a new iPhone?"

"She's been talking about it for a long time. I gave her a lesson. She's a little slow but she'll learn. Mom says you have a new job with lot less travel."

"Yes. It's about time I spend more time with my boys and your mother. Now I'm afraid I need to get back to Chicago. Isabella, I can't wait to see your videos."

"Au revoir Charlie."

"Au revoir Isabella."

Charlie got his surreptitious photo of Carol on the way out and a big kiss from Jan behind a tree that obstructed Isabella's view from the kitchen window. Walking back to her apartment she reflected on how destiny works in such strange ways.

"How was your day?"

"We made another video and then Sandy's mom took us shopping. It's cool because I can try on clothes for

Dad to buy me. You know how bored he gets shopping."

"I know. You figured that out sooner than I did."

"How was your afternoon with Charlie?"

"Fantastic but too short. He gave me a lesson on his iPhone. I've got two good teachers. I think I'm going to drive to Chicago on Wednesday and get an iPhone at the Apple store with Charlie. Your dad picks you up Wednesday after school. A word of advice. I wouldn't mention you're going to wear your yoga pants to school. Sometimes men, especially Father's, have a different perception of the world than we do."

"I know, you're right."

"I'm taking your Uncle Howie to get a stress test tomorrow. They'll wire him up and have him walk on a treadmill. If the results are okay he can go back to the office and start his exercise program. If you can believe it, he even wants to try a spin class. Keep telling him he needs a dog. He'll listen to you. There's pizza left. Are you hungry."

"No, but don't worry, I ate. I'm working on our next video."

"I guess that's good. Listen, my beautiful daughter. I know what you did today and I appreciate you giving Charlie and me some space. I love you Isabella."

86

Jan woke wondering how to handle her inheritance and how to explain it to her daughter. Monday morning was routine until she called Bert. "Good morning, this is Jan Cooper, anything for me—yet?"

"Just got it, come by anytime."

"Thanks, be right over."

Bert had her package ready and an answer to her sender question. "There are services that will deliver packages to FedEx with a specific delivery date. This is most common when the sender is going to be out of town and a package needs to be delivered for a birthday, anniversary or graduation."

After hearing Bert's explanation Jan realized it didn't matter. Before going back to the office, she drove home and placed her second iPhone in her new safe. There was one other item in this package, a commemorative gold coin with the Eiffel Tower on one side and the Arc de Triomphe on the other. She decided to save the coin for Isabella's trip to Paris.

Rather than return to the office she drove directly to

Howie's. "Good morning, I thought I'd come over early. I've got two emails from Isaac to share with you. The first is his #5 email and the other is a P.S. Let me pull #5 up on my laptop. There's nothing in either email that should set off your heart rate. You can read it."

"You're right, #5 is more like a summary with added details. He does clarify HOPE and how to evaluate its success. The inheritance is remarkable, you're a millionaire. I hope that doesn't mean you'll quit the Star-News. His NSA description shows his disdain in very graphic terms."

"That's exactly the way I read it. Getting back to the inheritance, how do you think I should handle it with Isabella? I haven't told her about it—yet? I know she's going to ask me how Isaac got all that money."

"Tell her he was able to save the money because he lived so frugally, which he did. You don't need to mention your million if you don't want to. You can tell her later."

"Good idea. Heart rate, please."

"101, just fine."

"It's only 10:45. Let me show you his P.S. It's only a couple of paragraphs."

"That really was a P.S. I'm glad he's sending a duplicate iPhone. Can you imagine if that phone was stolen or dropped in the toilet like I did to one of my phones! I do love that Einstein quote, quite prophetic. His last paragraph is very sentimental and seems to be his way of telling you how much he loved you and Isabella. It's the most emotion he's shown except for his self-acknowledged guilt. Of course, I love the reference to the Pulitzer and your journal. Surprises is a fascinating word to leave you with especially coming from him."

"Your interpretation is identical to Charlie's and mine except I was in tears after reading the last paragraph and seeing the way he signed goodbye. Did you notice."

"I noticed he signed it Papa Lenny which is the only person you knew when he was alive. It was the man you cared for and gave life. I totally understand your tears and would be more surprised if you didn't have them."

"We should go. I'll tell you about Charlie's visit on the way to the doctor's office. Let's go Ernie."

The five-minute drive to Doc Kumar's office was still plenty of time to give the highlights of Charlie's visit. Not surprisingly, Howie thought the safe was not only a great idea but also a necessity.

The nurse attached electrodes to Howie's chest that connected to an EKG machine and put a cuff on his arm to measure his blood pressure as he walked. After he was wired up Doctor Kumar came in.

"Mr. Nafzinger, it's good to see you. Hi Ms. Cooper. How you feeling Mr. Nafzinger?"

"I keep feeling better. Jan's trying to change my diet. She threw out just about all the food I had in the house and dumped the outdated prescriptions. She's also convinced me to get a dog I can walk with."

"Great idea! We're going to ask you to walk for about 15 minutes. We'll increase the speed and incline and monitor your heart rate and blood pressure. Even though we'll be monitoring, please tell me if you have any discomfort of any kind."

"Gotcha!"

The test went without a hitch and Howie was given an okay to go back to the office and start his walking program. He also got a prescription for Lipitor to control his cholesterol.

"Thanks Doc for all your help. How's your beautiful fiancé, Nurse Davidson."

"She's fantastic. I'll tell her you said hello. She still gets a kick out of the way you first met."

"I apologize Doc, to you and her. Had to be the effects of all the medication I was taking."

"Apology accepted but unwarranted. See you in 60 days but call me if you have any problems."

"Will do."

On the drive to Howie's they stopped to get his prescription filled, buy a pair of Rockport walking shoes and have salads for lunch.

"Thanks for coming with me and for all your help. Isaac's not the only old man who loves you. I'll see you in the office tomorrow morning and tell Isabella I'll call her when I'm ready for my dog."

87

Ernie's tail signaled the girls were coming. "Hi Isabella, hi Sandy. Are you coming home with us or do you want me to drop you off at your house?"

"She's coming with us. We're taking Ernie to the park to shoot videos. Hope Katie's there. We want to shoot a doggie romance and get 100,000 views on YouTube."

After the girls left for the park Jan checked the safe was still there, then sat on the couch with her journal. Just as she started to write on Charlie's side he called. "Don't jump to any conclusions but we might have a situation."

"What does that mean? That's spy talk. Don't scare me, Charlie!"

"Sorry, I don't want to alarm you. I'm just trying to confirm Carol's identity. If you can, try to drive here tomorrow and bring the screwdriver you lent her."

"What does that mean, trying to confirm her identity?'

"I'm not sure. There might be a connection between Carol and the NSA. I'm not certain— yet."

"No, no, she can't be! I can't take anymore! I'm already a nervous wreck! I'm shaking!"

"Forget tomorrow. I'm driving down right now. Try to get the screwdriver back or have her over for a cup of coffee, just don't wash the cup. I'll be there in a couple hours, after I make one stop."

"Hurry Charlie. Please hurry."

Jan felt like she was struck by lightning, again, as she placed a cold washcloth over her face. Her sweet new neighbor couldn't be involved with the NSA, could she? Terrified, she had to visit her neighbor. "Hi Carol, how you doing?"

"Hi Jan, I'm glad you stopped by. Can you hold my little stool while I hammer in the picture hook? I can't reach it without the stool."

"Let me see if I can. I'm a few inches taller. There, how's that?"

"Perfect. The other picture goes right alongside. Can you see my pencil mark."

"Got it. Moving is a pain in the ass."

"Oh, here's your screwdriver."

Awkwardly Jan cautiously took it by the metal shaft rather than the plastic handle. "There's Pearl. How's she adjusting?"

"She'll be fine as soon as she gets acclimated."

"If there's anything else you need, just holler."

"Thanks Jan, I will."

Still holding the shaft of the screwdriver Jan carefully placed it on top of a dish towel as she tried to think of an excuse Isabella would believe for Charlie driving back tonight. Then, on cue, he called. "I got you an iPhone 7 Plus with the same case and it will automatically sync everything from your old phone. Apple got that right. I'm on the road and will be there in less than two hours."

"Great! I got the screwdriver and didn't touch the plastic handle. I assume you want fingerprints."

"Just want to be sure, one way or the other. How did it go with Howie?"

"He passed his stress test, the Doc put him on Lipitor and he can go back to the office and start exercising. I showed him Isaac's #5 and the P.S. He suggested I tell Isabella about her inheritance but not necessarily mine. He thought she'd believe Isaac saved that much money because he was so frugal, which he was. Does that make sense?"

"Perfect sense."

"You know Isaac's loaded up a series of practice runs that takes you through each step of HOPE. Another example of his genius. I'll show you tonight."

"Do you think I need to rent an office or can I work from home or the Star-News?"

"Let's talk about it once you figure out exactly what kind of space and privacy you need to execute HOPE."

"My daughter's running up the stairs. I'll see you in a little bit. I can't even begin to tell you how much I love you."

"How was your video shoot?"

"Ernie's a natural but Katie wasn't there. We need a co-star."

"It's tough dealing with canine actors. Isabella, Charlie surprised me and got me a new iPhone. He's driving down with it right now. Before you ask, he's not staying the night. Sandy, do you want to stay for dinner?"

"No thanks, my mom's picking me up."

With the girls working on their video Jan checked out instructional videos for her new iPhone on YouTube.

As Sandy left, Charlie arrived and the two converged on the apartment stairs. "Bonjour Charlie."

"That's me. Great to see you Sandy."

Jan and Isabella couldn't help but smile as they heard the interaction. Charlie greeted Isabella with a gentle high five and her mom with a roving one armed hug. "Jan, look what I've got."

"My new iPhone. I'm so excited! Look Isabella!"

"Isabella, if we both help your mother with her new phone she should have it figured out in no time."

"If you say so, Charlie."

"Is anyone else hungry, besides me, Isabella?"

"You guys go eat. Ernie and I will hang here."

"Do you want us to bring you back anything?"

"Ice cream, bring some ice cream back."

"Let's take my new phone to dinner. You can show me your moves, Charlie." Jan winked at her daughter as she walked into the kitchen to get her purse and conceal the screwdriver in it as best she could. She was glad to give it to Charlie but nervous about what the fingerprints might reveal.

88

It seems ages since they ate at Mario's. What a difference five weeks makes. Ever romantic, Charlie asked for the same booth. "Here's your new phone. Be fitting if you make Isabella your first call. See if you can."

"Isabella, how does my new iPhone sound? You're my first call."

"So proud of you."

"Guess where we're having dinner?"

"That's easy, Mario's."

Charlie continued his iPhone tutorial as they waited for their salads. Jan confidently realized her learning curve was rising rapidly and she felt much, much better about implementing HOPE knowing Isaac had automated all the tech issues. She only had to make two choices, target and virtues. "Charlie, everything's happening so quickly. I've been terribly nervous about whether I'd be able to execute Isaac's grand plan, but not anymore. Knowing my interface with HOPE is limited to making two choices then monitoring results, I feel confident I'll be okay."

"That's what I've been waiting to hear. You've always acted the same way when you've been confronted with a problem. First you're overwhelmed. Then you break out what you need to do and conduct extensive research. You ask questions and find the best possible solutions. As your process moves forward so does your confidence. Isaac obviously knew this. His search engine recognized this ability within you. Isaac was brilliant, an absolute genius, but you January Cooper are his remarkable partner. Just as you could never do what he's done, Isaac could never do what you've done and what you will do. I'm in awe of both of you."

"Charlie, you make my heart blush. I can't believe how lucky I am to have you in my life. I love you."

So much for dinner. As with their first visit to Mario's, they took home a bag full of containers with their untouched food. After picking up ice cream they headed back to apt. #12. Along the way, Charlie brought up Carol. "I'm not sure where I've seen her. We just need to be sure she's not a threat. That's why I needed her fingerprints. Just to be careful. I'll know for sure in a couple of days."

"God, I hope you never saw her or maybe she works at your cleaners. Just when I'm starting to feel more secure this pops up. Is there always going to be something else? Is that part of the process? Is that my new norm?"

"Another question for which I have no answer. I'll come up with you and have some ice cream but then I've got to get back home. Want to jump in the backseat for a little fun?"

"First a booty call, now a quickie. It sounds inviting but I'll let your enthusiasm keep growing. It's my fault.

I'd better pull my hand out of your pants before you explode. I didn't mean to frustrate you, well, maybe just a little."

Sitting around the kitchen table with Isabella they quickly finished off both pints of ice cream. As Ernie licked what was left in the bowls they all got out their iPhones. As Isabella and Charlie compared their favorite apps and shortcuts, Jan took mental notes. "Ladies as much as I'd like to stay I've got to get home. Isabella, it's always great to see you."

Standing up from the table, Jan walked Charlie to the door and gave him a big hug."

"You guys are so cute together."

"Thanks, Bella. I'm beginning to think so, too. Sit down, we've got something to talk about."

"I get nervous when you say that."

"Don't be, it's nothing bad. It's about something your Papa Lenny has done. Something wonderful."

"What?"

"He left you a little inheritance. Actually, it's a lot more than a little. Isabella, Papa Lenny left you five hundred thousand dollars. I'm the trustee on the account until you're 18."

"Oh my God, I can't believe it. Really? Five hundred thousand? I never thought Papa had much money. He didn't live like he had lots of money. Was he really rich?"

"I think he was able to save so much because he lived so frugally and invested wisely. You know what he always wanted you to do, where he wanted you to go?"

"Oui, oui. Paris, must be Paris. Does trustee mean you help me watch the money?"

"You've got it right."

"Wait, Stop, I want to do something right now before I even think of Paris. I want to split the money with you."

"Tears welled up in her mothers' eyes."

"Don't cry Mom."

"I can't help it. I can't begin to tell you how proud I am of what you've offered to do. Thanks for looking out for your mother but Isaac left me money, too. You need to know if anything should ever happen to me, that money will be yours. We'll discuss what we want to do with the money later. I know you're probably curious but reluctant to ask so I'll tell you. Papa Lenny left me a million dollars."

Starting to jump up and down and clapping her hands together Isabella let out with a big, "Whoopee! Oh my God. I can't believe it. I'm so excited. I can't wait to go to Paris."

"I know, Isabella. I didn't believe it at first, either. Do me a favor. Please let's keep this to ourselves for now, and let me tell your dad."

"I understand. I won't tell anyone, not even Dad or Sandy."

"There is a little something we're going to do very soon. It's not Paris but we're going to take a shopping trip to Chicago. How does that sound?"

"So excited, I can't wait."

"You better get ready for bed. I'll take Ernie out."

Walking down the stairs Jan was emotionally spent. Her life was like a runaway train with speed bumps, sink holes, suspicious looking passengers and occasionally a wonderful surprise.

89

Considering her new norm Jan slept soundly. Her mind jumped around as she made her coffee. In celebration of Howie's return to the office, balloons seemed a better idea than a cake. What about Charlie? How were they going to have any time alone? She didn't want to displace Isabella, but wanted to spend more time with Charlie.

Sipping her coffee, she opened her laptop and pulled

up tomorrow's Star-News. "Isabella, come quick, you've got to see this. Look, look you've got to see this photo. This could be Howie's new dog!"

"She's the cutest. Molly, I love that name. I wish Ernie could see her."

"She's a chocolate lab, our Pet of the Week in the Star News. That's a feature in tomorrow's paper. We've got a day's head start. We found Molly because of you, Bella. See you this afternoon."

As soon as Jan opened the Star-News door Ernie ran to Howie's office, jumped into Howie's lap and licked his face.

"Welcome back, boss. Instead of a cake I got you a couple of balloons. Boy, do I have a beautiful girl you've got to see, her name's Molly. Pull up tomorrow's paper to page eleven."

"Holly shit! You kidding me! I can't believe it. She's our Pet of the Week. This is meant to be, destiny! Let's go get her."

"Slow down. Let me call and see when we can go by."

"I can't risk waiting. We need to go this morning. Set it up. God, my hearts up to 120."

"Settle down, a dog is supposed to reduce your stress not increase it. I'll call."

Back in her office Jan called Charlie first. He called

back in seconds.

"Charlie, are you still coming today."

"I'm planning on leaving here around 3:00. I'm driving home later tonight. What's up?"

"I was thinking about what I was going to tell Isabella about you driving down again but I think I just figured that out. I'm excited to see you. After you left last night I talked to Isabella about her inheritance. She was so sweet and wanted to give me half. I had to tell her Isaac left me money, too. More good news, I think we might have found a dog for Howie. I'll tell you about Molly later. Bye Cowboy."

"Hello, I'm Jan Cooper from the Star-News calling about Molly."

"Thanks for featuring her in the paper. She's an absolute sweetheart and been spade, had all her shots and her microchip. She's two, but I guess you have all that info in your story. Do you have someone who might be interested already?"

"I do. Howie, he's the publisher of the Star-News. He's looking for a dog to exercise with and he loves labs. I've got a white lab, Ernie, who he just adores. When can we come see her."

"Anytime, we'll be here."

"Expect us this morning, I'm sorry but I didn't get

your name."

"Mary Mahoney."

"Thank you Mary."

Back in Howie's office, she tried to tone down her enthusiasm as she gave him the rundown on Molly. "When do you want to go?"

"Right now!"

As they looked for the address, Ernie seemed to sense what was about to happen. They were barely into the fenced yard when the front door opened and out ran Molly. Howie was immediately smitten and Jan was ready with her iPhone to capture her first video, sorry Isabella, of Ernie and Molly playing together. They ran, rolled about and licked each other's face while Howie talked with Mary Mahoney. Molly's previous owner, Mary's neighbor, moved to Australia for a new job and was unable to take her. His request was not for expenses but that the new owner give a donation to the local chapter of the SPCA under the name, Molly.

The office could wait, the two happy labs needed their first play date at the park. "It's a good thing you've got a big, fenced backyard. We need to stop at the pet store. You need a leash, bowls, toys, a brush and food. You can wait on clothes. Keep whatever Mary gave you as a backup."

"Did you see the way she was licking my head from the backseat. I love her already. Did you say clothes?"

"She's going to bring you so much joy. Let's go to the pet store now and then I'll drop you two off at your house. I want to take another video and get a photo of the two of you."

After Howie spent $100 at the pet store Jan drove Molly to her new home.

"I can't wait for Isabella to see her. You don't need to go back to the office, do you."

"No, they can get along without me. I'll see you and Isabella and Ernie a little later. Thank you."

90

Too late to make the noon spin class Jan decided on a run. Oops, the first problem with her new iPhone surfaced. It was too big to put into any of the usual places while she ran. Running phoneless she felt partially naked but it was such a beautiful afternoon her run took priority, phone or no phone. Back home, showered and changed, she headed out the door, past #11 to pick-up her daughter.

"Hi Sweetie, big news!"

"What? What's the big news? Where's Uncle Howie?"

"That's the news. Howie couldn't wait to get Molly. He was afraid someone else would take her so we picked her up this morning. She's waiting at Howie's now to meet you. Wait to you see Ernie and Molly together. She's a sweetheart. Did you notice Ernie's a little tired? We stopped at the park so they could play and then I took Ernie on a five miler with me. He's a little fatigued."

We're here. Let's go see Molly. When Molly pushed the door open Ernie and Molly rolled around on the front lawn as Jan and Isabella took video's. Howie just stood, watched and smiled."

"Uncle Howie, I love her. She's the sweetest. Don't you love her?"

"She's so sweet! I loved her as soon as I saw her and I have you to thank. She could be Ernie's sister from a different Mother. She has his temperament. Where does Ernie sleep at night?"

Jan couldn't resist, "We have a strict rule at our house. Ernie sleeps wherever he wants."

"Well that makes it easy. Molly, sleep wherever you want."

Isabella, Jan and Ernie said their goodbyes and headed home. Isabella didn't seem overly concerned about Charlie's return. Trying to paint this visit routinely Jan explained he was giving her another iPhone lesson at the Star-News office. Then, she downplayed his trip even more, "He's not staying the night. He's got to be at work early in the morning. I better call him and get his ETA."

"Be there in an hour."

"What would you like for dinner?"

"How about what we ordered but didn't eat last night."

"Good idea. After we eat I've got to run to the office. You can give me another iPhone lesson."

"Very clever. I catch your drift."

Charlie arrived two minutes early to an enthusiastic welcome. Dinner was great as is often the case with Italian food the next day. All through dinner, both Isabella and Charlie kept suggesting apps and features they liked on their iPhones. Eagerly, Jan cleaned up after dinner, checked on her daughter then pulled Charlie out the door and off to the Star-News.

Not surprisingly, the office was locked, dark and empty of any staff. Locking the door from the inside, Charlie had Jan half naked before she pulled him into her office. Then her right arm wiped her desktop clean with one broad swipe. Oblivious to the hard, slippery mahogany surface it was a sex scene worthy of anything online.

Not surprisingly, their initial intensity subsided quickly after absorbing the pounding against the uncomfortable surface replete with the wetness of sex. Trying to avoid the little blotches of fluids they moved onto the swivel leather chair. Passion can overcome many obstacles but Jan felt like she was negotiating a balance beam as her nails dug into Charlie's back.

"Wow, Cowboy, that's more than just a little build-up! I just wish I had the foresight to bring a few pillows and a beach towel."

"You're going to have to pull me out of what's now become a recliner. I think I'm stuck inside you, too. God, we needed that. I love you."

"Easy peasy Cowboy. I guess it wasn't quite the same as making love in an elevator, an airplane or a library but there was a threat of someone coming into the office."

"A library? That's a new one on me."

"Gee Charlie, are you saying an elevator or an airplane aren't a new one for you?"

"We'd better clean up and fix the furniture."

"Nice juxtaposition."

On the drive home Jan told Charlie about Molly and asked if he'd go through HOPE, one more time. Isabella was sitting on the couch as they walked into the apartment. "Did you guys have fun?"

"We always have fun, don't we Charlie? Now we're going to have more fun with my new iPhone."

"Isabella, your mom's quickly getting up to speed. I'm guessing that's from all the expert help she's been getting." And with another wink and soft high five Isabella and Charlie's relationship continued to flourish.

91

Still wide awake and wishing Charlie could have spent the night, Jan pulled out her journal, not to write but to reflect. So much has happened in such a short time. Skimming the Leonard/Isaac portion was overwhelming and as she turned page after page she kept silently repeating the only appropriate word: UNBELIEVABLE!

Charlie's side of the journal was an emotional roller coaster negotiating the ups and downs of compatibility and trust. Right now, she was sure she needed him more than anyone in the world. His new job was a godsend, he perfectly complemented her skill set and his experience with the NSA was irreplaceable. Yet to be resolved were how they moved forward with living arrangements and merging their families together. And, Charlie still starred in her favorite dream.

Realizing how loose ends cause her frustration, conflict and delays, Jan reviewed her mental list of all that consumes her. Always starting with Isabella, she was happy her daughter and Charlie were developing such a strong relationship. Their inheritance is more than a pleasant surprise and provides financial security for her and her daughter. Still to be determined is how the implementation of HOPE will carry over into Isabella's everyday life. Part of that equation is whether Jan needs to work outside her apartment and the Star-News office, and if so, how she explains that scenario to her daughter.

Fortunately, Howie's on the road to recovery and avoided any heart incidents when Jan verbally reviewed Isaac's emails. However, his health is still worrisome and must continue to be monitored, especially during the implementation of HOPE. Molly is a wonderful blessing.

Carol is potentially a huge problem and will be until Charlie gets back the fingerprint results. Jan didn't want to think of the ramifications of her being connected to the NSA or another nefarious group.

"Come on Ernie, let's go visit your tree." As they passed #11, Jan reflected on her brilliant neighbor and all he had entrusted onto her shoulders. Confident and hopeful she didn't fight back the tears. Then when Ernie sniffed about, Jan pulled out a kitchen knife from her back pocket. And on this special tree she inscribed,

Coop and the Cowboy

Before she crawled into her own bed, January Cooper quietly stood outside Isabella's partially opened bedroom door and stared at the joy of her life, her beautiful sleeping daughter.

As her head met her pillow a magical feeling of satisfaction ran through her body driven by the realization she was prepared for HOPE and the first target. Now, will this President still be in office?

THE END, for now...

**Please see the next page for
an excerpt from**
Stu Schreiber's next explosive thriller!

JANUARY
CHRONICLES
COOP and THE COWBOY

1

Sheets of rain flooded the streets of Raleigh, Illinois, on an October Saturday morning perfect for binge watching a Netflix series. Jan didn't have that luxury. Not after the unusual text she received that compelled her to drive to the Star-News office. Fortunately, her daughter Isabella and best friend Sandy were pre-occupied with a 6th grade school project that somehow included the Cooper's white lab, Ernie. Gripping the steering wheel with the fear that consumed her, Jan almost hydroplaned as she accelerated trying to beat the yellow light. Not surprisingly, there were no cars parked in front of the only newspaper in town.

The locked front door and dark office at least showed the dozen other staff members had the good sense to stay home. Without taking off her wet yellow slicker or soaked running shoes, January Cooper sat down at her desk to re-read the text on her iPhone.

Coop, problems with phone. Using Max's. Rain can-

celled his game. On way to Raleigh. Meet you at your office @ 11:00. c

Confronted by one of the most ominous challenges in history, and totally frazzled, Jan nervously started a pot of coffee. Charlie's text raised all sorts of red flags. The odd context, the tone, and the fact he was driving down in torrential rain when they both had other plans for the weekend spelled only one possibility: a big problem!

Drying off, she didn't want to speculate what the problem might be but couldn't convince her mind to stop running through all the threats that emanated from the NSA. As always, Isabella was her primary concern. Did Charlie discover something that puts her in jeopardy? The mere question immediately gave Jan chills.

Charlie, there's always Charlie to consider. Even with a new job that apparently takes him out of the 007 role, he still works for the NSA. They know he's in a relationship with Jan, the former neighbor of Isaac Stone, the genius whose fingerprints are all over most of the technology deployed by the NSA for the last fifty years. In love with Charlie, Jan wouldn't allow herself to believe he was spying on her as part of his job.

Could this be about Carol, her new neighbor who rented Isaac's old apartment. She appeared to be the fifty year old widow, former second grade teacher she claimed to be, at least until Charlie was almost positive he had seen her face before. Now she was potentially a dangerous suspect. Had Charlie gotten back the finger-print results. Is Carol the big problem?

Jan's high pitched scream rifled through the porous walls of the empty office, "Shit! It's Carol! It has to be Carol! Nooooo!"

This changed everything! Jan feared the NSA would never leave her alone. Carol seems like such an unlikely spy. Her age, her story all seemed so legitimate and she played her role to perfection. Jan wondered how they dare go forward with HOPE. They had to stop, at least for now.

Speculating about Carol brought Jan back to Charlie. If she could play her part that well why couldn't Char-lie? Was it just a coincidence Carol moved next door the same time Charlie was offered a new job in Chicago? Then, as if on a director's cue, there was a knock at the front door.

"Oh Charlie, thank God you're here. I'm going crazy trying to figure out what's going on."

"I had to drive down and talk to you in person. The rain was brutal. My shoes are soaked and it was bare-ly twenty yards from where I parked. Don't I get a big hug!"

"Come here, Cowboy!"

Their chemistry was never in doubt. Physically they were a perfect match. Intellectually, they complimented each other, and even though they met less than fifty days ago, the circumstances they were thrown into made it seem much longer. Jan knew Charlie's physical presence always lessened her fears. Looking into his eyes she couldn't believe he was spying on her. This Saturday morning was no different.

2

"Coop, we've got a big problem! Carol's an NSA operative!

"I knew it! I knew it! This changes everything! They'll never leave me alone! I can't believe she's a spy. She could win an Oscar. What about Isabella? What about HOPE? How can I live in my apartment? Hold me, Charlie. I'm scared."

Faced with a daunting, almost impossible task, now made even more imposing, emotions ran through Jan's body as Charlie held her tightly. Only when he felt her trembling subside did he start to describe the changes they needed to immediately enact.

"Until I make sure everything's secure, it's not safe to talk about Isaac Stone or HOPE in your apartment. Your HOPE iPhone should be okay but I'll need to re-check your personal phone and scan your apartment, again. Obviously, this changes how we approach and execute HOPE. We need to be very, very careful. Thankfully, we discovered this now, not later. We must find a safe place to work as soon as possible. The NSA's fishing, searching for information, and Carol next door requires we're extremely careful, but we'll figure things out. We will, I promise."

"Your always so calm. I'm a nervous wreck! What about Isabella?"

"We'll have to figure out a way to tell her not to discuss Isaac's puzzle and give her a reason not to share things with Carol."

"In hindsight it might have been a good idea if you rented Isaac's old apartment. Who knows what the NSA would have done then? That brings up an obvious question. Why didn't the NSA rent the apartment sooner. Isaac's been dead more than a month. The FOR RENT sign was up for weeks. What triggered the NSA to bring in Carol? Could it have been the same event that got you called to NSA Headquarters? Was there something that happened around that time? It's hard to believe it was a coincidence."

"You're right. Check your journal and let's reconstruct the timeline. "

"What about the safe? Do we have to worry about it with Carol next door."

"I wouldn't worry about the safe or the iPhones inside but there's other things we need to consider. First, it's going to be easy for the NSA to analyze our behavior. We can't do anything suspicious. This probably includes you renting an office. Let's think about how much space we need to execute HOPE. I could rent an apartment or perhaps there's space at the Star-News. Do you think Howie will go along with that? Another option might be for you to move into a house we could share. The NSA is well aware of our relationship which means my visiting you and us needing more space shouldn't raise a red flag."

"Let's ask Howie about the Star-News. It makes sense. If we rent another office it certainly would raise suspicion. I concur 100%, we can't talk about HOPE in my apartment, especially with those thin walls. I'm certainly not going to feed the NSA anything on a platter. I hadn't thought about a house, but that might be a solution. I'll drop the hint to Carol that I need more room with Isabella soon becoming a teenager and you visiting more often now that you're back in Chicago."

"Good idea, drop that hint. Let me check on the security and layout while I'm here. Have you had any new hires at the paper since Isaac's death?"

"Nope, and if the walls in my apartment are thin, the office walls are paper thin."

"I'm glad I drove down. We needed this conversation. I hope I've relieved some of your fears."

"You always do, Cowboy. Come here!"

Their playful banter that started almost immediately upon meeting was still something they both enjoyed and often carried over to sexual pleasure. Both the banter and the sex offered a welcome relief from the serious challenges that lie ahead.

"Please, not your desk—again."

"No, I've got a better idea. Follow me!"

The lunchroom had an old couch that was a little lumpy, squeaked and was a foot too short but was still a big improvement over the mahogany desk in Jan's office. The possibility someone might walk in added a little element of danger they both found titillating. Forty minutes later, faces flush, they were dressed and ready to drive back to Jan's apartment.

3

The rain stopped and specks of blue began to overtake the dark clouds. They drove separately and Jan called Isabella to find out if the girl's were hungry. Not surprisingly, they were munching popcorn for lunch. After telling her daughter they'd be home in five minutes, Jan called Howie who welcomed their visit.

Ernie was waiting at the door to greet them. Surprisingly, he was dressed in a Grateful Dead t-shirt and one of Isaac's old Cleveland Indians baseball caps.

"Isabella, we've got company."

Isabella and Sandy came running out dressed for a "Dead" concert. After Charlie and the girls exchanged greetings, the girls proudly presented their three minute video of Raleigh's Grateful Dead experience. "Girls, that was fantastic, but be careful Ernie doesn't hog the camera. We're going to Howie's. Sandy, do you need a ride home?"

"Thanks, but my mom's going to pick me up."

Ernie was relieved Charlie removed his costume. Once outside Ernie instinctively stopped by his favorite tree. "Wow, look what someone carved on Ernie's tree. I wonder who did this?"

Coop and the Cowboy

"I wanted to put the words inside a heart but the kitchen knife wasn't the ideal tool. I love you, Cowboy, but I'm frightened beyond belief!"

"We'll figure things out. We always have."

`Ernie began to whine once he recognized Howie's street. Jan assumed he was also excited to see his new girlfriend. "Wait to you see Ernie and Molly play together. Howie's expecting us."

Before they came to a complete stop, Howie's front door opened and out ran Molly. Jan quickly opened the passenger's back door for Ernie to join his new friend.

"Hi guys. Come on in. Watch out for the tennis balls."

"She's adorable, Howie. How do you like sharing your house with such a beautiful girl?"

"It's more like she lets me live with her. She's the sweetest and walks me every day. How do you like your new job? Bet it's great to be back home and close to your boys and this girlfriend of yours."

"I'm extremely happy to be close to my boys and your star reporter. Plus, my job's much safer and with very little travel. How you feeling, Howie?"

"Better every day. I owe Molly and everything else to your girlfriend and her beautiful daughter."

"Alright guys, enough platitudes. Howie, we've got things to discuss with you."

For the next thirty minutes Jan and Charlie brought Howie up to speed. His heart rate monitor shot up to 122 when Charlie told him Carol was NSA but soon drifted back below 110. He offered the Star-News as a HOPE workplace and understood the security challenges. However, he suggested they might want to consider making Jan's office secure by encasing it with soundproofing. When HOPE's first target was brought up again, Howie couldn't stop shaking his head and repeating his self-coined word, "unfuckinbelievable, unfuckinbelievable!"

"Howie, I like your suggestion about securing Jan's office. I'll re-check the walls and ceiling and see what it will take."

When Jan brought up the idea of buying a house with part of her inheritance from Isaac, Howie not only thought it was a great idea but gave Jan the addresses of two homes for sale they could check out on the way home.

"Howie, we saved the biggest problem for last. Even if I bought a house tomorrow we'd still have a problem until we moved in. Isabella, it's Isabella. She knows we're working on solving some type of Isaac puzzle plus I've praised Carol as an ideal neighbor. Now, how do I make sure she doesn't bring up the Isaac puzzle with Carol. That would be a disaster and I'm assuming Carol is expert at leading conversations. What's your advice?"

"You'll figure it out. That's why Isaac chose you. Let's talk about the President. I can easily rattle off thirty virtues he lacks. Do you realize the change that's going to come over him, to our country and the world after HOPE is successful. We'll need a lightning bolt to explain his new found honesty, compassion and humbleness if he's still in office. I haven't checked the news in the last hour."

"Getting back to Isabella, why don't you try a strategy like you used with me after my heart attack. Be creative. Don't make it just about Carol. Ask her not to talk to anyone about Isaac or any puzzle and add that includes Sandy and your new neighbor. Create a story, not far from the truth, about how Isaac's job involved new computer programs and some of his former employers are trying to find out what he was doing so they can capitalize on his work."

"Good suggestion. I told Charlie you'd offer sound advice. "

"Thanks for keeping me updated. You need to see this. Come over to the window and take a look." Resting after their play date, Molly and Ernie, exhausted, were laying next to one another and somehow Molly had her head across Ernie's two front paws.

Ernie licked his girlfriend goodbye and jumped into the backseat. The quick drive-by of the two houses Howie mentioned were in the best part of Raleigh, two story with well manicured lawns, but Charlie liked Howie's idea of securing Jan's office as they drove back to the Star-News. Once inside, Charlie took measurements with an app on his iPhone. "I think securing your office gives us the best short term solution. I should be able to soundproof your office in 5-6 hours. What do you think?"

"Obviously, you know construction much better than me. I'm all for it if you have the time, the sooner the better."

"I'll make the time."

Standing in the middle of her small office, Charlie wrapped his arms around Jan as they both contemplated their future and the future of the world.

55800161R00242

Made in the USA
San Bernardino, CA
07 November 2017